Devdas

and other stories by
Sarat Chandra Chatterji

This volume contains translations of some of the best stories
by Sarat Chandra Chatterji, one of the greatest figures in
modern Indian literature. Apart from *Devdas* and *Srikanta*,
famous novels presented here in an abridged form, the
selection includes some deeply moving stories which have
not thus far been accessible to the English reader. In his
introductory essay, the translator, has given a brief outline
of Sarat Chandra's life and discussed the distinctive features
of his art and technique.

Vishwanath S. Naravane was born in Allahabad in 1922.
He took his doctarate from Allahabad University where he
taught Philosophy for nearly two decades. He was Professor
and Chairman of the Department of Philosophy at the
University of Pune for a few years. As Visiting Professor at
several colleges and universities in USA, and as a guest
speaker in many countries, he lectured on Indian art, history,
literature and mythology, besides philosophy and religion.
Among his publications are *Modern Indian Thought: A
Philosophical Study, The Elephant and the Lotus: Essays in
Philosophy and Culture,* and monographs on Tagore,
Coomaraswamy, Premchand and Sarojini Naidu, besides
Best Stories from the Indian Classics published by Roli Books.

Devdas and other stories

Devdas

and other stories by
Sarat Chandra Chatterji

Selected and translated by

V.S. Naravane

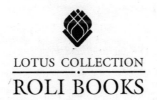

LOTUS COLLECTION
ROLI BOOKS

Lotus Collection

This edition first published 1996
The Lotus Collection
An imprint of
Roli Books Pvt Ltd
M-75, G.K. II Market
New Delhi 110 048
Phones: 6442271, 6462782, 6460886
Fax: 6467185
E-mail: roli@vsnl.com; Website: rolibooks.com
Also at
Varanasi, Agra, Jaipur and the Netherlands

ISBN: 81-7436-030-1
Rs 250

Front cover: Still from Devdas *produced by
Sanjay Leela Bhansali, 2002.*

Typeset in Galliard by Roli Books Pvt Ltd
and printed at Karan Press

To
the memory of
my beloved wife
Indumati

As I sat on that embankment I realized that the night had its own shape and form. I discovered that the beauty of the night could be observed separately from other phenomena of nature such as mountains, forests and lakes. I saw Night as a maiden sitting in meditation with eyes closed. Beauty surged all around me. How clever must be the liar, I thought, who established the notion that only light has beauty, not darkness. How did the world swallow such blatantly false propaganda? O Darkness, you who pervade heaven and earth, the sky and the nether regions, I bow to you. You are incomparable. You are a cataract of loveliness.

All that is deep, limitless and inscrutable in the universe is enveloped in darkness. The unfathomable ocean is dark. So is the impenetrable forest. Dark, too, is that Supreme Person who is the source of all movement life and beauty. And Krishna, whose adorable form flows out of Radha's eyes and inundates the world—he, too, is dark like a cloud.

Contents

A still from P.C. Barua's Devdas *(1935), in which the noted Hindi films actor of the forties, K.L. Saigal played the lead role of a romantic self-indulgent weakling.*

Preface

$\mathcal{S}$arat Chandra Chatterji (1876-1938) has been recognized by historians of modern Indian culture as one of the most important figures in 20th century Indian literature, particularly in the field of fiction. Yet, his writings remain largely inaccessible to the English reader, though they have been translated adequately into several Indian languages. Many of the stories in this volume are being presented in English for the first time.

I have selected for this volume, two novels and six stories from the collected works of Sarat Chandra in Bengali published from Calcutta by the Sarat Samiti in 1976. While remaining as close as possible to the Bengali text, I have been constantly on guard against the artificiality that can result if the translation is too literal. A detailed glossary gives the meanings of Bengali and Hindi words and also explains the myths, names of places and folk stories referred to in the text.

I cannot conclude this preface without expressing my gratitude to my English teachers at the University of Allahabad, Professor Amaranatha Jha and Professor Satish Chandra Deb. Had they been alive I would have profited immensely from their guidance and advice in preparing this volume. Through their inspiring lectures they inculcated in me an abiding love for literature. Both of them admired Sarat Chandra and encouraged me to study Bengali. Even more than their classroom lectures, I cherish memories of informal conversations with them when they made insightful comments on Indian and Western literature. It is difficult for me to convey adequately my indebtedness to those great teachers.

September 16, 1995   Vishwanath S. Naravane
(119th birth anniversary   'Shanti Nivas'
of Sarat Chandra Chatterji)   Hastings Road, Allahabad

Devdas finds solace in drink and in the arms of Chandramukhi, the golden-hearted prostitute.

Introduction

When Sarat Chandra Chatterji's first major work, *Baradidi* (The Eldest Sister), was published in the journal *Bharati* in 1907, there was a sensation in the world of Bengali literature. Readers and critics assumed that the short novel must have been published by Rabindranath Tagore under a pseudonym. It seemed inconceivable that anyone else, and particularly an unknown writer, could attain the level of literary excellence which Sarat Chandra's work revealed. Tagore's publishers, and some of his close friends, were in fact a bit hurt that he should have come out with such an important work without telling them about it.

But when the poet repeatedly disavowed authorship of the novelette, there was a scramble among editors of prestigious magazines for getting more stories by the writer who had established himself, so to say, with a single stroke of the pen. The author was, however, staying in far-off Rangoon. Novels and stories followed in quick succession. They were published from Calcutta. His popularity soared with every new publication. He was hailed as a great literary genius. There were some critics who went to the extent of saying that in the field of fiction, Sarat Chandra Chatterji had equalled Tagore and had even surpassed him in some aspects. Whether or not we accept this judgement, it cannot be denied that Sarat Chandra's writings generated a unique kind of enthusiasm, particularly among young readers.

I would like to explore in brief the reasons for this popularity. One of the first things that strikes us is that Sarat Chandra is one of those writers with whom we develop a deep sense of personal involvement. In our youth, when we are sensitive to the pathos and tragedy of human life and still have faith in humanity, characters from Sarat Chandra's stories and novels seem to speak the language of our own hearts.

His writings are not for the shallow optimist who shuts his eyes to the dark side of life. But I am equally convinced that the cynic or the nihilist will not feel comfortable with him either. He appeals to the sentimentalist who lurks within each of us. We are indignant at the tyranny of tradition, we recoil from superstition and religious bigotry, we are baffled by the strange ways of destiny, we are touched by the tenderness of love and devotion. And then we meet the women and men created by Sarat Chandra. They intensify our sense of the tragic, they enrich our appreciation of the good and the beautiful, they deepen our awareness of the mysterious and the unpredictable elements in life.

We get unexpected glimpses of wisdom and altruism even in those characters who are ostracised, ridiculed and condemned by society—the tramps, waifs, vagabonds, libertines, pimps, Jezebels and cheats. They seem to say to us: 'We are not altogether bad. We, too, can be generous, loyal and affectionate. Come, spend some time with us. We will show you many interesting things that may surprise you.'

As Sarat Chandra's appeal is so deeply personal, I would like to mention my own introduction to this great writer. In the summer of 1938, when I joined the University of Allahabad as an undergraduate student, enthusiasm for Sarat Chandra's writings had reached its zenith. The author had died a few months earlier. Shortly before his death, his short novel, *Devdas*, had been made into a movie by New Theatres of Calcutta. The author saw the Bengali version and liked it very much. He could not see the Hindi version. But he had heard and was deeply moved by the golden voice of Kundan Lal Saigal, who was to play the leading character. Brilliantly directed by Pramathesha Barua, the Hindi version of *Devdas* stirred audiences all over India and made Sarat Chandra Chatterji a household name. Saigal's fine, expressive voice and sensitive acting enabled him to communicate all the pathos of *Devdas'* unrequited love and his tragic end.

So deep was the impression made by Sarat's other stories and novels such as *Grihadaha, Kashinath* and *Charitraheen,* that there was a strong urge to learn Bengali. Very soon I became proficient in that language and, along with some friends, read Sarat Chandra's works in the original. Indirectly, it also helped us realize the richness of India's literary heritage and we turned towards other modern Indian writers in regional languages. Thus, Sarat Chandra became a catalyst for an entire generation of young readers.

To understand the value of Sarat Chandra's influence, it should be remembered that in those days students of literature in Indian universities were expected to concentrate on English writers, or European writers whose works were available in English translations. I must confess that I was more familiar with characters created by Tolstoy, Turgenev, Balzac, Hugo, Dostoevesky and Anatole France than with the men and women depicted in the works of outstanding Indian writers. In such a situation, where our educational priorities were so one-sided, the discovery of Sarat Chandra Chatterji was extremely important for us.

II

Why is it that Sarat Chandra's writings grip the reader's mind with such immediacy and power? One of the reasons is his consistent championship of the underdog. The oppressed find in him a natural ally. The peasant who has to toil from dawn to dusk so that the landlord may loll in luxury; the Hindu widow whose life is one vast desert of despair; the orphan starving for food and love—these and other victims of circumstance are portrayed in Sarat's works with a rare compassion. It is extended to those who are weak-willed, or who suffer through lack of courage, or those who are driven to their doom through inertia or inability to overcome temptation.

Sarat Chandra does not evaluate the worth of an individual in terms of categorical imperatives. He makes allowances for human frailty and fallibility. In every story we seem to hear the author plead that moral judgements should be tempered by human concern.

Sarat Chandra has been rightly praised for his realism. But true realism can never exclude ideals, nor can it underestimate the role of imagination in the creative process. I would like to emphasize a point here which has a bearing on our appreciation of Sarat Chandra's writings. The 'real' is not necessarily the ordinary or the commonplace, and the 'unreal' is not necessarily interesting simply because it does not correspond to the factual.

We often meet the author's characters in very unusual situations. And yet they appear true to life because the author has the artistic skill and the emotional sensitivity to capture the unpredictable element in life and communicate it in a vivid and convincing manner. This awareness of the unforeseeable element saves his realism from determinism. He is aware of social and economic pressures. But he does not attribute to them the causal link in explaining human relations. Characters in his work are not necessarily always manipulated by socio-economic laws.

It has been pointed out earlier that the realism and humanism reflected in Sarat Chandra's stories and novels were rooted in personal experiences and close observation of life. Some of his characters were people he knew intimately. His longest novel, *Srikanta*, has been regarded as partly autobiographical because of the close similarity of two of his leading characters with persons who influenced the author. Sarat Chandra was not one of those writers who chose to stand aloof and distant from his fictional creations. He included much of himself in his stories. I feel it is appropriate at this point to portray briefly his life and the evolution of his personality.

Sarat Chandra was born on 16 September, 1876, in village Devanandpur, not far from the Bandel railway station about eighty miles west of Calcutta. He was second of the seven children of Matilal Chatterji and Bhuvan Mohini. Matilal was a man of limited means. He had neither energy nor will to augment his income and found it extremely difficult to support his large family. He had a flair for writing and tried his hand at poetry, drama, the novel and short story. But he frittered away his talents and all his literary ventures remained incomplete. Sarat Chandra derived his inspiration, in a small measure, from his father's unfinished manuscripts.

Bhuvan Mohini was the daughter of Kedarnath Gangopadhyaya, one of the prominent citizens of Bhagalpur, a prosperous town in Bihar. She was a woman of great courage. In spite of her husband's unsteady habits, and chronic shortage of funds, she insisted on giving proper education to her children. She was gentle, generous, and cheerful in the face of adversity. Sarat Chandra loved her deeply, though some of his escapades caused her a lot of anxiety.

Two of Bhuvan Mohini's brothers were intimately associated with Sarat Chandra in his later life. The elder, Surendranath, was a teacher. He was extremely fond of his nephew and was at his bedside at the time of Sarat's death. The younger, Upendranath, was a lawyer. After retiring from legal practice, he started a literary magazine called *Vichitra*. One of Sarat Chandra's novels, *Vipradas*, was serialised in *Vichitra*.

The author's childhood years were spent in Devanandpur. Nyara, as he was known to the villagers, was a mischievous boy, though not quite a problem child, for his parents.

One of his playmates in the elementary school was a girl named Paru. He spent many idle hours with her chatting or gathering wild fruits and flowers. Paru, who was also called Dhiru, reappeared in a fictional form as Rajalakshmi in Sarat's magnum opus, *Srikanta*. The first part of *Srikanta* in which Rajalakshmi plays an important part, has been included in the present volume in an abridged form.

Having failed to support his family staying in the village, Sarat's father moved to his father-in-law's house at Bhagalpur. The atmosphere of Kedarnath Gangopadhyaya's house was marked by refinement and discipline. Sarat sobered down and became fond of reading. He continued to be a lively boy, full of fun, fond of swimming, collecting butterflies and wandering amidst mango groves and guava orchards. Sometimes for weeks he would become reflective, even meditative. He had selected a quiet spot, in a wooded area across the river Ganges, where he would spend many hours in solitude.

Sarat was thirteen when the death of Kedarnath forced his father to return to Devanandpur. The adventurous Sarat sought the company of boys who were regarded as 'rowdies'. But those years were rich in experience. He observed the life of fishermen, snake-charmers, puppeteers, impersonators, astrologers and other fascinating people. He also became a theatre enthusiast. One of his friends, a postgraduate student of Calcutta University, took him to Calcutta several times to see famous plays. He also became interested in tribal communities. He acquired first-hand knowledge of their customs, rituals, beliefs and handicrafts.

In 1894 Sarat's parents moved to Bhagalpur once again. While studying for the B. A. degree, he started writing stories. Unfortunately, these early literary efforts have not survived. He joined a dramatic club and even was in demand as an actor. Another member of the club, Rajendra Nath or Raju, became a close friend. Raju was the son of the District Engineer at Bhagalpur. Though older than Sarat, he became such a close companion that his sudden disappearance a few years later left a painful scar on Sarat.

Raju repudiated the conventions and values of respectable society. He stood up courageously in defence of victims of injustice. Sarat shared many interests with him, including fishing, football, swimming and music. Raju also initiated Sarat into forbidden pleasures such as tobacco, liquor, drugs and even visits to dancing girls. The combination of strength, sentimentality, idealism and depravity in Raju's character left a lasting impression on Sarat. The character of Indranath in the first part of *Srikanta* was clearly modelled on Raju.

Sarat Chandra suddenly left home one day and, after wandering aimlessly for a while, donned the garb of a *sanyasi*. He remained a hermit for several months, living on alms placed in his bowl. He stayed for some time at Muzaffarpur, another large town in Bihar, first as a hermit and then as an ordinary citizen devoting his time to writing. He wrote a long narrative poem and a tragic love story. Fortunately, he realized in time that poetry was not his forte. He turned to essays and stories which were published in magazines. One of his well-known novels, *Charitraheen*, was written during his stay at Muzaffarpur. In 1903 Sarat Chandra returned to Bhagalpur on hearing of the sudden death of his father. Kind and supportive relatives offered to look after his brothers and sisters. Sarat decided to go to Burma in search of a job. He was twenty-seven.

The next thirteen years of Sarat's life were spent in Burma. He found a job with Burma Railway Service on a meagre salary, barely enough for his sustenance. Sarat soon gained popularity with the Indian community at Rangoon and participated in all their cultural activities. He became a friend of Burmese writers and artists, though he never learnt their language. One of his Burmese friends, an artist by the name of Ba Thin, provided the theme for his story, *Chhabi* (The Picture), which has been included in this volume.

Several of Sarat's famous works were published in India during his stay in Burma. This was also a period of self-education for him. He spent many hours at the Bernard Library in Rangoon reading western classical literature and philosophy. His interest in music and painting deepened. He sang medieval devotional songs and, even more frequently, Tagore's songs, for appreciative audiences. He enjoyed painting portraits in oil, taking his themes from ancient myths and legends. Unfortunately, all his paintings were destroyed in a fire.

While at Rangoon, Sarat Chandra married Shanti. Her father was a drunkard who had borrowed money from an old man and, unable to repay the debt, wanted to marry off his daughter to the creditor. The girl came to Sarat Chandra for advice. He could think of no other solution than to pay her father's debt and marry her. Shanti and her infant son died of plague two years later. Before leaving Rangoon Sarat Chandra married again. His second wife, Hiranmayi, was the daughter of a poor Brahmin named Krishnadas Adhikari. Many of Sarat's relatives and friends did not know of his re-marriage for years.

Sarat's writings were in great demand. Phanindranath Pal, editor of the journal *Yamuna*, deserves a good deal of credit for his courage in publishing *Charitraheen*, a novel which was condemned by many as immoral. Another journal, *Bharatavarsha*, bagged the first part of *Srikanta*. The two journals came to be regarded as literary rivals, each staking a claim on Sarat's stories and novels. Shortly before leaving Burma, Sarat Chandra met Rabindranath Tagore for the first time. He wrote the welcome address which was presented to the great poet by the citizens of Rangoon at a memorable function. In 1916, Sarat Chandra left Burma permanently for Calcutta. Bengal's prodigal son had returned home.

The remaining three decades of Sarat Chandra's life were spent in or near Calcutta, at the very centre of the social and cultural environment which he has depicted so vividly in his writings. In spite of his great fame and popularity, he did not gain financially. He became careful negotiating royalties from his publishers, unlike in the past. He became a professional writer, perhaps the first in India, for whom creative literature was the sole source of livelihood. He lived comfortably with his wife, Hiranmayi Devi, and a devoted servant, Bhola, in a small house in Baje Shivpur in Howrah District. The house, not far from Calcutta, was in the countryside. Sarat Chandra became familiar with the life of the villagers of that region. He was pained to see the backwardness and the grinding poverty of the peasants. In many of his stories we find graphic descriptions of rural life.

During Sarat Chandra's stay at Baje Shivpur, a new force had emerged in India. Mahatma Gandhi started his struggle against foreign rule in 1921. Sarat Chandra hailed the Mahatma's arrival on the political scene with great enthusiasm. His identification with the national movement is often neglected by critics and historians of Bengali literature who focus their attention exclusively on his attainments as a literary craftsman.

Sarat Chandra was not the man to stand aside while the entire nation responded to Mahatma Gandhi's call. He worked closely with Chittaranjan Das, popularly known as Deshabandhu (Nation's Friend), one of the most prominent nationalist leaders from Bengal. The British authorities arrested and imprisoned Deshabandhu and Sarat Chandra worked for some time as the President of the District Congress Committee. He was often called upon to address public meetings. Apart from political work, Sarat Chandra was also associated with many humanitarian activities.

His days of struggle and uncertainty were finally over. His two surviving brothers and an elder sister often came to his house. The house at Baje Shivpur was too small to accommodate everybody. He built a comfortable country house in Samtabed, near village Govindpur on the outskirts of Calcutta. Some of his best-known works, including *Devdas*, were written during his stay at Samtabed.

But his health was failing. Decades of toil, struggle and privation had taken their toll. He was advised to live at a place where medical treatment was easily accessible. He moved to a house in Calcutta, at 24 Ashvini Dutt Road, where he spent the last four years of his life. His house became a meeting place of writers, scholars and people from the theatre and the cinema. From the summer of 1937 his health deteriorated. Sarat Chandra Chatterji died at the Park Nursing Home in Calcutta on 16 January, 1938.

The entire nation mourned his death. Half a million people joined the funeral procession in Calcutta. The two great leaders of modern India, Mahatma Gandhi and Rabindranath Tagore, expressed their profound grief. Tagore wrote a poem of four lines in Bengali as a tribute to the memory of his illustrious younger contemporary:

Jahar amar sthan premer asane
Kshati ta'r kshati noy mritur shasane;
Desher matir theke nilo ja're hari
Desher hriday ta'ke rakhiyechhe bari.

Here is an English translation of the poet's tribute:

Firm on the throne of love is he;
We cannot lose him by Death's decree.
Though from our country's soil he parts
He lives for ever in our people's hearts.

III

When Sarat Chandra Chatterji first came into limelight, Rabindranath Tagore dominated Indian literature. Just as small shrubs can be stunted in the shade of a giant banyan tree, so also many new writers in Bengal paled into insignificance beside Tagore's personality and his stupendous achievements in every field of literature. Sarat Chandra was one of the few modern Indian writers who established themselves in their own right and were not dwarfed by Tagore's genius. This led some critics and readers to project a comparison between the two. The comparisons were sometimes biased and unfair. Some of Tagore's blind admirers tried to belittle Sarat Chandra's work. And there were fanatics among the 'Sarat party' who hailed Sarat Chandra as a revolutionary, while Tagore was described as an 'ivory tower artist'. The differences between them were exaggerated and their affinities were ignored. The fact that the two heroes themselves had the highest esteem for each other was forgotten.

Sarat Chandra frequently described himself as the poet's disciple. In letters and conversations with friends he referred to Tagore as his guru. It was after reading Tagore's novel *Chokher Bali* (Eyesore) that Sarat Chandra felt inspired to write his first story. Later he studied Tagore's prose style carefully, taking *Gora*, one of Tagore's greatest novels, as his model. When his reputation had been established firmly, he once wrote in a letter: 'No one in Bengal today can write stories like mine except, of course, Rabindranath Tagore'. Whenever he was in a depressed mood, he found consolation in Tagore's lyrics, which he sang with deep feeling. He described Tagore as the greatest Indian poet since Vyasa. He had differences of opinion with Tagore regarding certain political issues. But throughout his life he retained his reverence and admiration for Tagore.

Tagore, in his turn, repeatedly praised Sarat Chandra who was younger to him by a quarter of a century. 'In my childhood,' Tagore once said, 'I felt the impact of Bankim Chandra. Now in my old age I see the emergence of Sarat Chandra in the same way.' Sometimes Tagore read Sarat's novels during train journeys and spoke about them in glowing terms when he met friends on reaching his destination. He dedicated one of his collections of poems to Sarat. In a message sent on Sarat Chandra's sixtieth birthday he wrote: 'His writings throb with the feelings and sentiments of Bengal. He has touched the deepest layers of the heart of Bengal. In literature the creator is greater than the preacher. I offer my garland of homage to Sarat Chandra, the creative artist.'

Sarat Chandra and Tagore were both products of a common tradition which they interpreted in the modern age in the light of their own convictions. Both of them were dedicated artists, imbued with the highest ideals of intellectual integrity. They were patriots to the core. But their love of India was untouched by chauvinism. Neither of them hesitated to bring out the dark and negative side of Indian life. While attaching great importance to the spiritual side of life, they rejected firmly the sham and superstitions that have been sustained in the name of religion.

But there were marked differences in their attitudes and lifestyles. There is a continuity and discipline in Tagore's writings because they reflect certain basic philosophical convictions. In Sarat's works such a foundation of the philosophy of life is absent. Even Srikanta, fashioned by the author in his own image, emerges as an acute and interesting commentator on human life. Sarat Chandra draws us into a world of action, of excitement, tension and conflict. Tagore leads us from excitement to serenity and points suggestively to the universal harmony subsisting behind all diversity, discord and constriction.

The work of Sarat Chandra belongs to the dimension of time. Tagore gives us glimpses of eternity.

Sarat Chandra shows a more intimate knowledge of day-to-day life as lived in middle-class families and in the homes of peasants, boatmen and other village folk. He also shows more intimate understanding of specific types—mendicants, snake-charmers, wandering actors and singers, fishermen, courtesans and impersonators. He penetrates to the core of social and economic relationships more than Tagore does. His realism is more robust and down to earth than Tagore's.

It is interesting to see differences in technique between the two writers. Tagore uses techniques of narration mainly for their suggestive, evocative value. He draws the reader to facts and actions not for their own sake but to the extent that they provide insights into human nature. For him a particular case of domestic or social conflict becomes significant because it shows the paradoxical nature of the human condition. He does not dwell upon all the details of the conflict as Sarat Chandra does. He etches it in broad strokes and then shifts his gaze to the deeper meanings underlying the conflict. Sarat's method is more analytical, Tagore's is more integral. The slower pace in Tagore's stories is seen in the leisurely, often languid conversation of his characters. In Sarat Chandra's stories the dialogues have a faster rhythm.

IV

The secret of Sarat Chandra's pre-eminence in the field of modern Indian fiction lies in his ability to combine his remarkable powers of characterization with an equally strong flair for description. This blending of the two skills raises his stories to a high level of excellence. One of the effective methods employed by him is to allow the characters to reveal themselves in stages as the story proceeds. Sarat Chandra does not portray any of his characters in a single passage or even in a single chapter. The different aspects of the character's attitudes and tendencies are brought out in diverse contexts and situations gradually until the total personality emerges. This is obviously more true of his novels than of his short stories. But even in the latter, the characters are presented as unobtrusively as the limited compass of the story permits.

Sometimes Sarat Chandra brings out the different facets of his characters indirectly. Two of his favourite devices for indirect delineation are reminiscences and letters. Reminiscences are given sometimes by the character in question and at other times by someone else who plays a minor part in the story. The story is structured in such a way that the reminiscences seem perfectly natural in the given situation and sequence of events. Introducing letters within a novel is another method of indirect portrayal of characters. Sarat Chandra handles these devices very skilfully. Effective use of reminiscences and letters can be seen in many of the stories included in this volume, and especially in *Srikanta* and *Devdas*.

In Sarat's work women are not tame or submissive, although they are portrayed within the framework of traditional Indian values, as he frequently projects their reconciliation to the inequities inherent in that tradition. Annada Didi and Rajalakshmi in *Srikanta*, Parvati and Chandramukhi in *Devdas*, Ma-Shoye in *The Picture* and Bijli Bai in *Light Out of Darkness* may be cited as examples. Sarat Chandra also shows great ingenuity in capturing the thoughts and behaviour of children. Indranath in *Srikanta* is an unforgettable character. The wayward boyhood days of *Devdas*, and the strange combination of gentleness and harshness in his relationship with Parvati, have been depicted with deep understanding, preparing us for the tragic developments in their later lives.

As for Sarat Chandra's descriptive skills, it should first be pointed out that character-creation is itself a special form of description. It is description of the inner world of thoughts, feelings, beliefs and attitudes. In depicting the objective world, Sarat shows the same acuteness of observation, the same penchant for analysis and minute attention to detail. The furniture in a room, the goods sold in a wayside shop, the costume of an actor in a folk play, the sound of a canoe

paddled in shallow water, a communal feast at a village festival—
such vignettes of life are described vividly. *Srikanta* is particularly
rich in such descriptions.

Just as his characters evolve and change in phases, Sarat
Chandra also shows an awareness of change and transformation
in his descriptions of the external world. Nature and human
life are perceived in a state of continuous flow. Through this
ability to capture the fleeting, growing, changing aspects of
the world, he imparts to his descriptions a quality of dynamism
rare in modern Indian literature. I must confess that I do not
find Sarat Chandra particularly successful in creating images of
quietude and serenity. Here and there we do get a sense of
tranquillity in his descriptive passages. But this is not one of
his strong points. No wonder in his stories there are so many
accounts of people who are always on the move. We see them
walking mile after mile, or going in a jolting bullock cart, or
travelling in barges, railway trains or steamships. In some of
his novels, railway journeys have become important parts of
the story, not just minor episodes. The train becomes a symbol
of impermanence, restlessness and the sadness of parting.

However, though human life is Sarat Chandra's main
concern, he also gives us fine descriptions of nature. Some of
these show the awesome aspects of nature—the current of a
river in flood, the scorching heat of the mid-day sun in June,
the strange sounds of the jungle at night, the vultures waiting
in eager anticipation on the trees of a cremation ground. There
are also some delicate vignettes of the beautiful and harmonious
side of nature. The river and the forest seem to have been
Sarat Chandra's favourites. Mountains do not figure
prominently in his stories. Most of the time the action takes
place in the verdant river valleys of Bengal and Bihar. The
Burmese countryside has also been described vividly.

In his descriptions of gardens, arbours, orchards and groves,
with their trees, climbers, willows, bamboos and flowering
shrubs, Sarat's style acquires a poetic quality. Nature, however,
is rarely seen in isolation from humanity. In the guava orchard
and the mango grove, in the hermitage of a teacher surrounded

by disciples, on the bank of a sacred river where pilgrims gather, and in many other places he shows us the intimate connection between human life and nature. In this respect his work is steeped in the ancient Indian tradition which regards humanity and nature as waves of the same river, as partners participating in a single universal rhythm.

V

As a creative writer who attained high levels of excellence in his own chosen field, as a patriot and a man of universal sympathies, as a rationalist and humanist, Sarat Chandra Chatterji's place in the cultural history of modern India is secure. In the early phase of his career he had to face negative and unfair criticism. The unsteady, adventurous streak in his personality was exaggerated. Even as a writer he was taken to task for his alleged lack of sophistication and occasional lapses into sentimentalism.

At the other extreme there was a tendency to make him the nucleus of a cult, a sort of anti-intellectual, non-conformist hero. Thoughtless eulogy, however, cannot serve as a corrective to prejudice or lack of appreciation. Now that his fame has been established on a firm foundation, the time has arrived to view his life and writings dispassionately. A balanced interpretation need not be cold or insensitive. In the foregoing paragraphs I have, while pointing out some of his limitations, tried to approach his work and personality with the respect and admiration that they deserve.

Sarat Chandra was a man of great courage and inward strength. He had to struggle against heavy odds. Except during the last fifteen years of his life, he had to face serious financial difficulties. His health started to fail when he was barely forty. Some of his best work was produced when he was suffering from acute exhaustion. The manuscript of a long unpublished novel and all his oil paintings were destroyed in a fire. His family life was marred by the death of his first wife and infant son hardly two years after his marriage. He did not allow these difficulties to embitter him. There was an element of the tramp in him which prevented him from evolving a harmonious pattern of life over a period. Fortunately, he enjoyed a peaceful, settled life, with reasonable material comforts, in his later years.

Although his health was delicate and he aged prematurely, he retained his youthful spirit to the end. The older he grew, the more revolutionary became his outlook on life. His later writings show his fervent patriotism and his concern for social and economic justice. He scrupulously kept away from intrigues and rivalries in the field of literature. He recognised the merit of other writers and was respectful towards his seniors. At the same time, he did not shrink from honest and frank criticism. He was extremely generous with his time and energy in helping young writers. He did not seek adulation but was genuinely happy when he was appreciated. These personal qualities were reflected in his work. 'An honest writer', he once said, 'should express himself freely and should not have any secrets from his readers.'

Sarat Chandra cannot be described as a transcendent genius. Nor was he a man with a universal vision. But he was a highly talented writer. And in the literary genre which he had selected he was undoubtedly a great master. Some of his novels and stories have an unmistakably classic quality. His love for the simple, ordinary men and women of India, his bold realism, and the skill with which he used his artistic talents in exposing hypocrisy are qualities which have exerted a significant influence on modern Indian literature. What he offered was sorely needed at a time when many writers were groping for a balance between the traditional and the modern, between realism and idealism.

Sarat Chandra's work will endure and continue to inspire writers in future generations. He has not yet received adequate recognition outside India. It is therefore important to make his works available to English readers. His works belong to India and equally have a place in world literature.

❖

Brief introductory notes on the stories selected are given below.
The Bengali titles of the original stories are given in parenthesis
where necessary.

Devdas: This is one of the most famous of Sarat Chandra's
novels. It is offered here in a slightly abridged form. Devdas,
son of a wealthy landlord, and Parvati, daughter of a neighbour
of moderate means, love each other deeply. But Devdas' father
rejects Parvati because of the difference in the status of the two
families. Parvati is married to an elderly landlord. Devdas goes
to Calcutta, falls in bad company and becomes an alcoholic.
He remains generous and affectionate till the end. But his
health is shattered. Realizing that the end is near, he sets out
for Parvati's home in a bullock cart from the nearest railway
station. Devdas dies in front of Parvati's house. She learns of
his death and is overwhelmed with grief. The pathos and tragedy
of Devdas's life is conveyed with great power.

Srikanta: This is Sarat Chandra's longest novel, largely
autobiographical. It is in four parts. A translation of the first
part is given here in an abridged form. In the first section of
Part One we see Srikanta in his boyhood, sharing many
adventures with his friend Indranath. They go to the hut of a
snake-charmer who is a drug addict and ill-treats his wife,
Annada. The two boys help her and accept her as their sister.
    In the second section we see Srikanta as a young man in the
company of a prince whom he knew in childhood. He meets
a courtesan named Peyari Bai who turns out to be Rajalakshmi,
a girl who had a crush on him when they were school children.
Srikanta shows Sarat Chandra's skill in character creation,
description and narration.

Anupama's Love (*Anupamar Prem*): This story is of a girl
whose mind is filled with romantic fantasies derived from the
novels and stories she has read avidly for years. She selects a
neighbour's son as her 'lord', her 'chosen one'. The young
man agrees to marry her but fails to show up at the wedding.

To save the prestige of his family, the girl's father marries her off to a sickly old man. The man dies a year later. The girl, Anupama, become a miserable widow. After the death of her parents, she is at mercy of her greedy, callous stepbrother and his wife. She is treated like a servant and has to put up with taunts and insults. She tries to drown herself in a lake. But a young man, whose sincere love she had spurned, saves her and takes her to his mother's home.

Mahesh: A Muslim weaver named Ghafoor is reduced to dire poverty and is unable to feed his bullock, Mahesh. Driven by hunger, Mahesh tramples upon the shrubs in the garden of the Hindu landlord. Ghafoor is punished not only for the damage that his bullock has caused but also for the sin of starving a 'cow's progeny'. Unable to bear the pangs of hunger and thirst, Mahesh knocks down Ghafoor's daughter, Ameena, and laps up the water from her pitcher. In a fit of rage, Ghafoor hits Mahesh on the head with his ploughshare. Mahesh dies, and the landlord's agents sell Ghafoor's house to meet the expenses of the ceremony to be performed as atonement for his sin.

The Devoted Wife (*Sati*): Nirmala carries her ideal of conjugal devotion to such a limit that she keeps her husband, Harish, constantly under surveillance. He cannot even look at a woman without making her suspicious. Every one admires Nirmala as the ideal Hindu wife. But for Harish the devotion and dedication of his wife are like the coils of a python around his neck from which there is no escape.

The Picture (*Chhabi*): This is a tender love story in which all the characters are Burmese. Ba Thin, an artist who is struggling to repay his father's debts through the sale of his paintings, is engaged to Ma-Shoye, the daughter of his late father's close friend. The two are deeply attached to each other since childhood. But a series of misunderstandings creates a rift between them. Ba Thin is completely engrossed in his work and Ma-Shoye feels neglected. She has inherited considerable wealth and has connections with the royal court. Ba Thin is offended by her proud and capricious behaviour. But their love is too strong to be broken by the friction. When Ba Thin is on the point of leaving the city permanently, Ma-Shoye bursts into tears and the two young people are reunited.

The Temple (*Mandir*): This is a story of religious devotion carried to excess, resulting in conflict and tragedy.

Aparna was the only daughter of Rajnarain Babu, an affluent landlord who had installed beautiful images of Radha and Krishna in a temple built in his mansion. Since her childhood she was so deeply attached to the temple that when she grew up and was married, it was a torture for her to leave the temple and go to her husband's village. The marriage was a complete failure. She recoiled from conjugal relations with her husband, Amarnath. And he tried in vain to win her love. Rebuffed and heartbroken, he went away to Calcutta where he fell ill and died a few months later. Aparna returned to her father's house and devoted herself body and soul to the maintenance and adornment of the temple.

Madhusudan Bhattacharya was an old Brahmin, in charge of the ceremonies at the temple. After his death, his son Shaktinath was appointed as the *pujari* at the temple. A sensitive and sickly young man, he was more interested in making clay images of deities than in reciting *mantras*. Aparna explained the rituals of the temple to him and trained him in his priestly duties. Their work together blossomed into a joyous partnership. Shaktinath fell in love with Aparna though he did not dare express his feelings. One day he gathered enough courage to offer her a small gift. She suspected him of making advances. Furious, she threw the gift out of the window, and turned Shaktinath out of the house. A few days later she heard of his death. It left her grief-stricken with remorse.

Light Out of Darkness (*Aandhare Aalo*): Satyendra Chaudhari, a highly educated young man of steady habits and sound character, is attracted towards an unusually beautiful woman he meets on several successive mornings on the bank of the Ganges where they both go for their bath. When her visits stop abruptly, Satyendra is miserable because by then he is totally infatuated with her. A few days later he receives a message brought by her maid asking him to visit her as she is seriously ill. When he reaches her house he discovers that she is a courtesan, a professional singer and dancer. When he enters her room he is greeted by her admirers with derisive laughter. He is insulted in various ways. The woman and her maid laugh at his discomfiture. But when he turns to go away in disgust the woman, Bijli Bai, feels ashamed of her conduct and begs his forgiveness. He refuses to believe that she is repentant and goes away. Five years later Satyendra takes his revenge. He invites her to his house along with other professional dancers to entertain his guests at a party. Bijli Bai, however, is a changed woman. She feels no bitterness at being humiliated and goes away after offering her blessings to Satyendra's wife and infant son.

Devdas

 $\mathcal{I}$ t was a hot June day. Devdas, a boy of the Mukherji family, was sitting on a torn mat in a corner of the village school. His legs were stretched out, and he held a slate in his hand. Suddenly he yawned, and decided that he could not take it any more. What was the point in staying in a classroom when he could wander in the fields and fly kites! It was break-time in school and the children were playing outside under the banyan tree. But Devdas was not allowed to go out. His teacher, Govind Pandit, knew that if Devdas went out of the class during the recess, he would not come back for the rest of the day. The teacher, after talking to Devdas' father, had decided that the boy should remain in the classroom under the supervision of an older boy, Bhola.

Parvati, a girl in the same class, was also subjected to Govind Pandit's discipline. Confined to the classroom, she was amusing herself by making a sketch of her teacher, who was fast asleep on his chair. The fact that the sketch bore little resemblance to the original did not diminish Parvati's enthusiasm. Bhola's supervisory duties consisted of glaring at Devdas and Parvati from time to time, and reminding them that they were being watched. The rest of the time, he hummed a song and cast envious glances at the children playing outside.

Devdas got up, gave his slate to Bhola, and said: 'Bhola, I can't get this sum right. You have to help me.' Bhola started calculating: 'If sixty pounds of oil cost fourteen rupees and nine annas . . . then at the rate of . . .' While Bhola was engrossed in arithmetic, Devdas sneaked from behind and tilted the bench on which he was sitting. Bhola fell into a heap of crushed lime which the teacher had stored there. The lime had been purchased at a low price, and the Pandit, who was planning

to build a house, had stored it there for future use. Bhola
started screaming. The students playing outside rushed into
the classroom. Parvati was so amused that she rolled on the
floor with laughter. The Pandit got up with a start. Shouts of
'what happened?', 'why is he screaming?' filled the room.

Pandit Govind was furious. He started shouting at Bhola.
'What were you doing there, you miscreant!' he yelled. 'You
were asked to guard that heap of lime, not jump into it.'

Bhola started crying. It was quite some time before he
could give a coherent answer. 'That ruffian, Deva,' he mumbled,
'he is responsible for all this. He pushed me.'

The teacher vowed to punish Devdas severely. The students
were asked to catch the culprit, who had bolted as soon as he
heard the teacher's voice. After a long and futile chase the
students came back. They said that Devdas had hurled stones
at them and they were too scared to go near him. Govind
Pandit's wrath was now directed against Parvati. She was
rebuked for being an accomplice in all his pranks.

The Pandit then marched to Devdas' house. Narayan
Mukherji, Devdas' father, was the most influential and wealthy
person in the village of Tal Sonapur. It was three in the
afternoon. Narayan Mukherji was sitting in the verandah. A
servant was fanning him. Govind Pandit prostrated himself
before the master of the house and told him what had happened
in the school. Bhola, who had accompanied his teacher,
corroborated the account.

Mukherji Moshay demanded angrily, 'Where is he?'

Govind Pandit said that Devdas could not be caught because
he had threatened the other students with brickbats and had
run away.

When Govind Pandit returned to the school he scared the
students out of their wits. He threatened dire punishment if
such pranks were played again. He vowed never to let Devdas
enter the school again. 'So what if his father is the landlord!'
he said, 'I don't care.'

By that time school was over and the kids started going
home. 'How strong Devdas must be,' said one. Another

expressed his admiration for the way in which Devdas had fooled Bhola. 'And did you notice his skill in hurling stones?' said another. 'His aim is wonderful.' They wondered whether Bhola would take revenge. 'But how can he,' said one child, 'if Devdas never comes back to the school?' When Parvati heard this she became very sad. She knew that she would miss Devdas.

Parvati was Nilkanth Chakravarty's daughter. He owned a few acres of land and his small brick house was adjacent to the landlord's mansion. The landlord always treated him with courtesy and generosity. Chakravarti Moshay lived with his family in reasonable comfort. They were happy and contented.

Parvati came to know Devdas through the landlord's family servant, Dharmadas. Ever since Devdas was a baby, Dharmadas had looked after him. He escorted Devdas to school, carried his tiffin for him during the recess and brought him back home. That day he was going to the school to fetch Devdas when he met Parvati on the road. 'Paro, where is your Devda?' he asked her.

'He ran away,' said Parvati.

'Ran away? What do you mean?' Dharmadas asked anxiously. Parvati recalled the comic figure of Bhola emerging from the heap of lime. She started laughing and described the entire episode. Dharmadas asked her where Devdas was. At first Parvati said she did not know. But when Dharmadas told her that he had brought food for Devdas she confessed that she knew his hiding place. 'But I won't tell anyone, otherwise I will get beaten.'

'He must be very hungry, Paro.'

'Well, then, give the food to me. I will take it to him.'

Dharmadas was pleased and returned to the mansion.

Before taking the food to Devdas, Parvati went home and told her mother everything that had happened in school. Then she went to the small, dilapidated bamboo hut, in a remote part of Mukherji Moshay's garden, which was Devdas' hiding place. He had removed the dust and cobwebs from the hut and went there whenever he wanted to smoke tobacco secretly.

When Parvati entered the hut she found Devdas smoking a hookah. His face was grim and he was imitating the movements of elders while he smoked. He was pleased to see Parvati but pretended to be indifferent, quietly took the food she had brought, and started eating. Putting the hookah aside he asked Parvati what the teacher had done. She told him that the teacher had complained to his father and that he would not be admitted to the school any longer.

'I didn't want to study, anyway,' Devdas said. After finishing the rice he asked for sweets. Parvati said she had not brought any sweets.

'All right,' he said, 'go and fetch some water.'

'Where can I find water in this remote place?'

Devdas replied irritably, 'Why did you come at all if you didn't have anything for me?'

'Why don't you go and fetch water yourself!' Parvati said.

Devdas said he had to remain in the hut for some time. When she heard this, Parvati said with tears in her eyes, 'I will remain with you, Deva, I will accompany you wherever you go.'

But Devdas persisted in his demand for water and when she refused to go, he pulled her hair and gave her a blow on her back. Parvati started crying. She went straight to Devdas' house.

Mukherji Moshay was very fond of Parvati. 'What's the matter, Paro?' he asked affectionately, 'Why are you crying?'

Parvati wiped her eyes and complained that Devdas had beaten her, and when he asked her where Devdas was, she revealed his hiding place. The teacher's complaint had already made Devdas' father angry. Now he was furious.

'It seems my son has started smoking,' Mukherji Moshay said.

'Yes, Devdas smokes tobacco,' Parvati said. 'He smokes every day. He has hidden his hookah in the bamboo hut.'

'Then why did you not tell me about this earlier, Paro?'

'I was scared. Devda would have beaten me.'

Parvati had given vent to her anger. She was, after all, still a child. But she soon realized the consequences of what she had done. She went home, refused to have her meal, and sobbed until she fell asleep.

II

Devdas was punished severely the next day. He was beaten and locked up in a room. Only when his mother interceded with tears in her eyes did Mukherji Moshay let his son free. As soon he left the house, Devdas went to see Parvati. 'Why did you report to my father about my smoking?' he asked angrily.

'Why did you beat me?'

'Why did you refuse to fetch water for me?'

Parvati kept quiet.

'You are very stupid,' Devdas said. 'Don't ever do this to me again.'

Parvati promised that she wouldn't.

'All right. Now come with me to the bamboo grove. We have to cut some bamboos and go fishing in the pond.'

There was a custard-apple tree near a cluster of bamboos. Devdas climbed that tree, reached out to the cluster and managed to clasp one end of a long bamboo. He bent it and asked Parvati to hold on to it. Parvati pulled the bamboo towards her with all her might. But it sprang back, dislodging Devdas from the custard-apple tree. The branch was not too high. He was not hurt seriously, but his body was bruised at several places. Devdas flew into a rage and picking up a small piece of bamboo, struck Parvati on her back, arms and cheeks.

'I am going to your father right now,' Parvati said, burning with shame and anger.

'Go tell him what you like, I don't care,' Devdas said.

Parvati went home weeping. Her grandmother was the first to see her. One of her cheeks was swollen and had turned blue. 'My God! Who has be   so cruelly?' her grandmother exclaimed.

Parvati said it was the teacher, Govind Pandit. The grandmother took Parvati in her arms and carried her to Mukherji Moshay's house. The landlord felt that Parvati must have done something wrong. Nevertheless, he expressed his strong disapproval of the Pandit's action. He decided that the Pandit should be summoned and reprimanded. 'We should not send our boys and girls to a such a teacher,' he said.

Parvati was happy to hear this. But when she reached home her mother was not as soft with her as her grandmother had been. 'I am sure the teacher must have had a reason,' she said. 'Paro looks innocent, but she must have done something to invite punishment.'

The grandmother said: 'Even if that were true I am not going to send Parvati to that school again.'

'Then are we to let her remain illiterate? She has to learn how to read and write.'

'A little reading and writing is all right,' the grandmother said, persisting in her opposition to further schooling. 'There is no need for higher studies. Elementary knowledge is enough. Your Paro is not going to become a lawyer or a judge. If she can learn a few stanzas from the *Ramayana* and the *Mahabharata*, we should be satisfied.'

Parvati's mother had to give in. It was decided that her daughter's school education would be terminated.

When Devdas returned home from the bamboo grove he expected the worst. He thought that Parvati must have told his father about the way he had beaten her up. He braced himself for punishment. To his surprise, his mother simply told him that Parvati would not be sent to the school any longer because Govind Pandit had inflicted corporal punishment upon her without any reason. He somehow swallowed his food and rushed to Parvati's house, laughing and panting. 'I hear that you will not be going to the school any more,' he said. 'Why? What happened?'

Parvati told him that when she was asked about the marks on her body she had said that the teacher had beaten her.

Devdas was happy and laughed heartily. He patted Parvati on the back and said: 'You are the most intelligent girl in the world.'

Devdas was really sorry. 'Paro,' he said, 'I hurt you badly, didn't I?'

'Yes you did,' Parvati said calmly.

'That is because of the way you behave. You make me angry, and then I lose my temper and beat you.'

Devdas placed his hand on her head and said, 'Paro, don't behave like that in future, please.' Parvati nodded assent, though she did not know what wrong she had done.

Patting her on the back again, Devdas said, 'All right, I will never beat you again, I promise.'

III

The two children had become very close to each other. Since both were out of school they had plenty of time to wander in the fields and groves even in the midday sun. It had become a routine matter for both of them to be rebuked, and sometimes slapped, by their parents when they returned home in the evening. But that did not prevent them from resuming their activities in the morning. They did not have any companions. Nor did they need any. The two of them were quite capable of entertaining each other and making their boisterous presence known to the whole village.

One day Devdas and Parvati had gone to the pond shortly after sunrise. They fished for a long time and then, sharing their catch, went home. Parvati's mother scolded her for being out all day and locked her in a room. What happened to Devdas is not known because he was silent about the punishment meted out to him. Next day he stood outside Parvati's window and called out to her softly. But she was sulking and did not respond. Devdas spent the whole day sitting on one of the upper branches of a *champa* tree. In the evening Dharmadas brought him down from the tree and took him home.

Parvati did not sulk for long. Soon she was as eager as ever to meet Devdas. She waited for him but he did not come. He had gone with his father to a neighbouring village for a ceremony. Disappointed, Parvati went to Manorama's house. Although Manorama was a few years older than Parvati, they had become good friends and went to the same school. When Parvati called, Manorama was not at home. Her aunt came out and said that she was at school. 'How is it that you are not at school at this hour, Paro?' Manorama's aunt asked.

'I have left school,' Parvati said, 'and so has Deva.'

'Well, that's nice,' said the aunt with a touch of irony. 'Devdas has given up his studies and you have also done the same.'

Parvati did not feel like staying at Manorama's house any longer. She was returning home when on the way she saw three wandering women minstrels of the *Vaishnava* sect. They wore sandal-paste marks on their foreheads. Playing castanets, they begged for alms. Parvati called one of them and asked whether they sang devotional songs. 'Yes, we sing *bhajans*,' she said, 'but you have to give alms to *Vaishnavis* if you expect them to sing for you.' Parvati remembered that Devdas had given her three rupees for safekeeping. She had tied up the coins in the end portion of her sari. She took out the money and showed it to the mendicants. They sang a composition by a medieval saint-poet to the accompaniment of their instruments. Parvati did not understand the words of the song. And even if she had understood the words she would not have paid any attention to the meaning because her mind was engrossed in thoughts of Devdas. At the end of the song she gave three rupees to the Vaishnavis. They did not expect so much money. 'Where did you get all this money, child?' they asked.

'My friend Devdas gave it to me. Has each one of you got your share?' The singers thanked her, gave their blessings, and prayed that she wouldn't be punished by her family for giving away so much money to wandering mendicants. Next morning, when Devdas asked for the money, Parvati confessed that she had given it away to the *Vaishnavis* who sang *bhajans* at her request. Devdas said: 'What! You gave away all the three rupees? That was stupid of you.'

'But there were three of them. Each got a rupee.'

'Had I been in your position,' Devdas said solemnly, 'I would have given only two rupees. Even then each would have got more than ten and a half *annas*.' 'But, Devda,' she said, 'those mendicants don't know how to calculate as you do.' Devdas was happy to hear this remark. He readily agreed that they were ignorant and did not do arithmetic as well as he did. Parvati held his hand and said: 'Devda, I was so scared. I thought you would beat me.'

'Why would I beat you for something like that?'

'Even the *Vaishnavis* thought that I would be punished for my extravagance.'

Devdas leaned upon her shoulder and assured her that he would never punish her unless she did something really wrong. Apparently Parvati's 'crime' did not come within the purview of the legal system he had devised for himself. Three rupees for three singers seemed to be an acceptable expense. Hand in hand, Devdas and Parvati proceeded towards the Little Market—as the village people called a cluster of small shops—where Devdas wanted to purchase kites.

IV

A year passed. Devdas and Parvati could no longer continue their carefree life. Devdas' mother was getting impatient with his wayward ways. One day she approached her husband and said, 'Devdas is growing into a worthless, ignorant rustic. We have to do something about his future.' Mukherji Moshay suggested that Devdas be sent to Calcutta for studies and that he could stay with a distant uncle.

Parvati was shocked to hear the news. She asked him whether he was really going away. Devdas said that he had no intention of going to Calcutta, and no one could force him to go against his will. Parvati was relieved. 'Remember what you have just said, Devda,' she said. 'Don't leave me.' 'Never,' said Devdas.

But Devdas could not resist his father's pressure. He had to leave. Neither the prospect of getting new experiences, nor the anticipation of sightseeing in Calcutta, could lighten his heart. Parvati wept bitterly. She found it extremely difficult to let him go. She could not reconcile herself to his absence. For some time she remained aloof and avoided speaking with him. But ultimately she revealed to him the deepest feeling of her heart. Devdas said: 'Paro, I will come back soon. And if they don't let me return I will run away.' This assurance cheered her somewhat. The baggage was placed in the carriage. Devdas touched his parents' feet and received their blessings. He moistened his forehead with his mother's tears and left.

Parvati was in agony. Tears kept streaming down her cheeks. After spending several days in this dazed condition she suddenly realized that she had nothing to do. When she used to spend a lot of time roaming and playing with Devdas, there were so many chores which she had to do for him that time flew. Now she looked for chores but found none. Sometimes she sat writing a letter to Devdas late into the night. Her mother asked her to go to bed, but her grandmother said: 'Let her write. It is better than running around aimlessly and wasting time.' Her only joy in life was to get a letter from Devdas. She would sit on the doorstep near the staircase and read his letter all day, over and over again. Two months passed. His letters became less frequent. She too became somewhat tardy.

One day Parvati told her mother that she wanted to go to the school again. Her mother agreed readily. The maidservant who escorted Parvati warned Govind Pandit not to be harsh with her. 'The girl has come back to school of her own accord,' she said. 'She will study as long as she wants and then return home.' The teacher was tempted to ask the maidservant why Parvati also had not been sent to Calcutta. But he desisted. When Parvati entered the classroom she found Bhola sitting on the same old bench, keeping an eye on the students as ordered by Govind Pandit. She was amused when she recalled how Bhola had been pushed into the lime-heap. But a moment later she felt sad at the thought that Bhola was partly responsible for Devdas' expulsion from the school.

When Devdas came home on vacation, Parvati rushed to his house to meet him. They chatted for a long time. Parvati did not have much to say. She listened while Devdas talked about his life in Calcutta. Devdas soon returned to Calcutta, leaving Parvati in tears once again. Four years passed. Devdas had changed a good deal during his period. Parvati felt extremely sad when she saw that not only his behaviour but also his feelings were different from what they used to be. Devdas was now a city lad. Life in Calcutta had altered his ways. There was no trace of his rustic simplicity, crudeness and impetuosity.

Devdas now wore shirts and jackets of the finest quality, and shoes imported from England. He carried a cane. He had cuff-links and a gold watch with a chain. He no longer derived any pleasure from fishing in the village pond or walking by the riverside. He now had a gun and enjoyed going for a hunt in the jungle nearby. Instead of village gossip he was now interested in discussing politics or cricket. Alas, how very distant he was now from Parvati and the little village of Tal Sonapur. Not that he did not have childhood memories. They meant much to him. But other interests had become so much stronger that he did not linger over these memories for long.

Devdas spent the next summer vacation somewhere else. But a year later he came back to Tal Sonapur. The morning after his arrival he went to Parvati's house. She was in a room upstairs. He spoke with her mother for a little while and then went upstairs. Parvati was lighting oil lamps for the evening worship. Devdas called her. She greeted him with folded hands and stood aside. When he saw her standing there silently, Devdas felt a strange hesitation. 'It is getting late,' he said, 'and I am not feeling too well. I will go home now.' With these few words, Devdas went out of Parvati's house.

V

Parvati's mother had been feeling for some time that the search for a groom should be started without further delay. Parvati, still in her teens, was fast growing into a woman. Although Chakravarty Moshay was not a wealthy man, he had a comfortable life. The greatest asset for the family was Parvati's beauty. Her mother had a faint hope that Devdas' parents might agree to accept Parvati as their daughter-in-law, despite the great difference in the status of the two families. She went to Mukherji Moshay's house and broached the subject.

Parvati's mother did not suggest marriage directly. She talked to Devdas' mother about the close friendship between the two youngsters. 'That is quite natural,' said Devdas' mother. 'They have grown up together since childhood like brother and sister.' When marriage was mentioned she became very guarded in her reply. She said that Devdas was still studying and there was no intention of arranging his marriage at the time. Parvati's mother returned disappointed. In the evening Mukherji Moshay was given an account of the conversation. 'You did very well in making the position clear,' he said to his wife. 'After all there is such a thing as status. How can a girl of that house become a daughter-in-law in this house? We would become the laughing stock of the entire village if we agree to this proposal. Moreover it won't be right for Devdas to have his in-laws' house in the same village as his parents'. That is simply not the convention.'

When Parvati's father, Nilkanth Chakravarty, came to know of what had happened, he felt slighted. He rebuked his wife for taking such an initiative without his consent. 'Our daughter is beautiful,' he said, 'I can get a good bridegroom for her within a week. Don't worry.' Parvati felt as though she had been struck by lightning. She had taken it for granted that she was intended for Devdas and had an exclusive right over him. She could not imagine that this right would be snatched away from her. Her heart was shaken by a storm of anguish and frustration. Devdas, however, was far less agitated by the episode. He was very fond of Parvati. But the diversions of life in Calcutta had taken the edge off his attachment to her. He failed to realise fully the intensity of Parvati's love. He could not understand that in the uneventful, repetitive life of a small village like Tal Sonapur he had become the sole focus of Parvati's thoughts and feelings.

Devdas would pass by her house when he went out for walks. Sometimes he would drop in and talk to her mother. Now and again he would exchange a few sentences with Parvati. She felt shy in his presence, now that she was on the verge of womanhood. She had her own innate pride which prevented her from seeking sympathy. Her friend Manorama came to see her sometimes. Manorama was married a year earlier but had come to the village for a few days. The two of them used to talk freely for hours about their intimate feelings. But now Parvati listened most of the time.

Meanwhile, Parvati's father had found a match for her. He was a wealthy landlord with a large property in the countryside about fifty miles from Parvati's village. He was a widower with a grown-up son and daughter. He was almost forty, but what of it? Every one said he was a fine, kind-hearted gentleman who would make Parvati happy. Devdas heard from his mother about Parvati's forthcoming marriage. She also explained to him why she could not accept the proposal which Parvati's mother had brought. Devdas heard quietly what his mother told him without expressing how he felt.

At Parvati's house a different kind of conversation took place. Manorama was trying to console Parvati. 'There is nothing that you can do about your parents' decision,' she said.

'Did you choose a husband of your own liking, Manorama?' Parvati asked.

'My situation was different. I neither liked nor disliked. And so I have no problem. But you, dear friend, have brought this pain upon yourself by getting emotionally attached to some one.' Having said this, Manorama asked Parvati to tell her more about her future husband. 'How old is he, Parvati?' she asked.

'He must be around nineteen or twenty,' Parvati said.

'What!' said Manorama, 'I have heard that he is forty.'

Parvati smiled and said: 'Manorama, there must be a very large number of people in this world who are forty years old.

What have I to do with them? I only know this much. My future husband's age is about twenty, and his name is Devdas.'

'What are you saying, Parvati!' said Manorama in a shocked tone. 'I have heard that your marriage has been arranged with some one else. Have you secretly finalized your marriage with Devdas?'

'Nothing has been finalized yet. I will ask Devdas and let you know.'

'Will you actually ask him whether he will marry you?'

'Yes, that is exactly what I will ask.'

'Will you not feel ashamed, Parvati?'

'Why should I be ashamed? I was not ashamed to tell you.'

'But I am a woman, and I'm your friend. He is a man, Paro.'

'Yes, Manorama, you are a friend. But is he not closer to me than any friend can be? Why can't I tell him freely what I have just told you? And let me also say this, Manorama. You may be wearing bangles and putting *sindoor* on your forehead, but you don't know what is meant by accepting a man as one's everything, one's lord. Had Devdas not been my lord, I would not have been prepared to die for him, as I am. When a person is willing to die, the question of whether the poison is sweet or bitter becomes irrelevant. No, I am not ashamed of saying anything to Devdas.'

These exchanges left Manorama even more bewildered and shocked. She stared at Parvati in disbelief for some time and said: 'Will you ask him to accept you and give you a place at his feet?' Parvati said that she was going to ask Devdas just that.

'And what if he turns you down?' Manorama asked.

Parvati was silent for a long time. Then she said slowly: 'Dear friend, I do not know what will happen if he rejects me.'

While returning home Manorama muttered to herself: 'What a heart! And what courage! I would never dare to utter such words till the end of my life.'

VI

It was after midnight. The stars were shining brightly. The world was enveloped in absolute silence. Parvati got up from her bed, flung a sheet about her shoulders and softly climbed down the staircase. No one was awake. She opened the door and came out on the deserted road. Very soon she was standing at the gate of the landlord's mansion. The watchman was sitting on a cot reciting verses from the *Ramayana*. 'Who is that?' he called out when he heard footsteps. 'It's I,' said Parvati. Assuming that she must be one of the maidservants the watchman continued to read without raising his eyes. Servants were sleeping in the courtyard. Parvati was familiar with the house. She easily located Devdas' room. The door was open. Devdas was sleeping. An open book lay near his pillow and an oil lamp was burning near the bed. Parvati turned up the flame of the lamp and sat near Devdas' feet. The silence was broken only by the ticking of the wall clock.

Parvati placed her hands on Devdas' feet and called him. 'Devda . . .O Devda.' He sat up, rubbing his eyes. Parvati's face was unveiled and by the light of the oil lamp he recognized her at once. 'Is it Paro?' he asked.

'Yes, Devdas, it is Paro,' she said calmly.

Devdas looked at the clock. 'So late at night . . . all alone. Did you not feel afraid?'

Parvati smiled and said, 'No, Devda, I'm not afraid of ghosts.'

'You may not be afraid of ghosts, but are you not afraid of men?' Devdas asked her whether any one had seen and recognized her. She said the watchman and some of the servants had seen her and some of them must have recognized her. 'What a shameful thing you have done, Paro,' Devdas said. 'How will you show your face tomorrow? Will you not hang your head in shame?'

'I had the courage to come, Devda,' she said, 'because I felt sure that you will protect me and cover my shame.' She started crying. Devdas held her hand in his. She clutched his feet as a drowning person clutches a branch on the bank. Devdas tried to convince her that it was impossible for him to marry her against his parents' wishes. Parvati remained at his feet. The clock struck four. As the hour of dawn approached, Devdas raised Parvati from the bed and said, 'Come, I will escort you home.' And the two stepped out of the house together, hand in hand.

VII

'You have always created problems for me,' said Devdas' father. 'It seems you are going to trouble me for the rest of my life.' Rebuked by his father, Devdas turned to his mother, hoping to get her consent for his marriage with Parvati. She was crying. 'My son,' she said, 'it is my evil destiny that makes you cause me so much suffering.' The same day Devdas packed his bags and went away to Calcutta. Parvati clung to the hope that some day he would return and accept her, even if he had to defy his parents' wishes. The prospect of being rejected by him was so terrible that it was simply beyond her imagination. She had no alternative but to go on hoping. But she could not do so for long. Within a few days she got a letter from Devdas which shattered her hopes.

This is what Devdas had written: 'Parvati, during the two days that have passed since I came to Calcutta I have been thinking of you all the time. I do not have the strength to cause my parents the kind of pain that they will feel if I try to make you happy. It is not likely that I will write to you again, so I wish to be explicit in this letter. The difference in the status of our families, and the nearness of your house to mine, are obstacles which my parents consider to be insuperable. I know the intense agony that you are enduring. You are a self-respecting girl, conscious of your dignity. You would never have done what you did three nights ago if your inner pain had not driven you to do so. I have never felt for you the complete love that you expected. But I feel extremely sorry for the suffering that is in store for you because of me. Please try to forget me. With all my heart I wish you success in this effort. I send you my blessings.'

On the way to the Post Office where he mailed this letter, Devdas had before his eyes the image of Parvati drenching his feet with her tears. He was aware that what he was doing was unfair and wrong. He also knew that his parents were treating Parvati unjustly. What if Parvati decided to plunge into the river and put out the fire that was consuming her heart? Perhaps an innocent life was about to be destroyed because of petty considerations of tradition and social status. These thoughts made Devdas restless. He had left his relative's house long ago and was staying in a hostel. He returned to his room from the Post Office and sat in an armchair. A young man named Chunnilal had been staying for many years in the room adjacent to his. The ostensible reason for his stay in Calcutta was to pass the B.A. examination. After pursuing this aim without success for four years, Chunnilal now spent his time in the pursuit of pleasure.

One evening Chunnilal returned to the hostel earlier than usual and stood outside Devdas' door. Although the door was shut, there was light in the room. Chunnilal knocked and came in. He said he wanted to smoke and asked Devdas to give him the hookah. While filling the hookah with tobacco he said: 'I thought that well-behaved boys like you are asleep long before midnight. How is it that you are still up?' Devdas remained silent. Puffing at his hookah, Chunnilal said, 'Devdas, since you returned from home you appear disturbed and agitated. There is some deep sorrow within you.'

For a while Devdas just looked at Chunnilal. Then he sat on the edge of the bed and asked, 'Tell me, Chunnilal, is there no sorrow of any kind in your heart?'

'No, absolutely none,' said Chunnilal.

'And where do you spend your nights?'

'Don't you know where I go?' Chunnilal said with a twinkle.

'I have a vague idea,' Devdas said. 'Is it true that there is a lot of fun where you go, and one can forget one's sorrow?'

'Why don't you come with me and see for yourself,' Chunnilal said. But when he came to pick up Devdas the following evening he found that his friend was packing up his belongings. Devdas told him that he was leaving Calcutta for good and returning to his village. He gave some money to Chunnilal with the request that whatever he owed to the hostel servants should be paid off. 'I am going away, Chunni Babu,' he said before leaving. 'Education, prosperity, knowledge . . . all these are merely means to happiness. If they do not lead to happiness, they are worthless.'

Chunnilal asked him whether he had decided to discontinue his studies. 'Definitely,' Devdas said. 'I came to Calcutta for education. But the personal loss that I have suffered is so great that, if I had the slightest inkling of what would happen to me, I would not have looked in the direction of Calcutta.' Every one in the hostel looked on in surprise as Devdas' baggage was being loaded into the buggy. 'What has happened to you, Devdas ?' Chunnilal asked. 'Some day, if destiny brings about another meeting between us, I will tell you everything.' With these words Devdas climbed into the carriage and set off for his village home.

VIII

Devdas reached home next morning. His mother was surprised to see him and asked whether the college was again closed for vacation. He said it was. When his father asked him, he gave an evasive reply. 'Perhaps the vacation has been extended,' his mother tried to explain, 'because it is still so hot.' For a couple of days Devdas wandered in the village restlessly. The preparations for Parvati's marriage were going on. It was difficult to talk to her privately. One day when she had gone to the river to fill her pitcher Devdas, who was waiting behind the bushes, approached her and said, 'Paro, I want to talk to you. Please sit down.' But Parvati remained standing. Both remained silent for a long time. Then Parvati turned around and started walking away.

Devdas called her again and said, 'I have come back, Paro.'

'Why?' she asked.

'Don't you remember what you said in your letters? Don't you remember what happened that night?'

Parvati's throat was dry when she said, 'I remember everything. But how does it matter now.'

'Please forgive me, Paro,' Devdas said. 'I did not realize what I am doing. I will somehow persuade my parents and obtain their consent.'

'What about my parents? Doesn't their consent count at all?'

'Of course it does, Paro. But they have never had any objection to our marriage. Now . . . if only you agree.'

'If I agree!' Parvati said sharply. 'Marriage with you is unthinkable.'

Devdas' eyes were burning like two pieces of charcoal when he said in a harsh voice, 'Parvati, have you forgotten me?'

With utmost self-control Parvati said in a calm voice, 'How can I forget you? I have known you since childhood. And I have feared you. Have you come to frighten me again? If so, you really don't know me.'

Paro's words left Devdas speechless for a while. 'So all these years it is only fear that you have felt in my presence?' he asked. 'There has not been anything else?'

'No,' she said.

'Do you really mean this?'

'Yes, I do. The person to whose house I will be going is affluent, intelligent, stable and calm-tempered. He is also religious. My parents are deeply concerned about my happiness. They will not agree to entrust me to a restless, unsteady, wayward man like you.'

'So much pride!' Devdas exclaimed.

'Why not?' Parvati retorted. 'If you can be proud, why can't I? You have good looks but no character. I have both.' Devdas looked at her in total disbelief. Parvati went on, 'You may be thinking that you can cause me harm. Very well, go ahead and harm me. But step aside and let me go.'

'In what way can I harm you, Paro?' The words barely emerged from Devdas' lips.

'You can harm me by ruining my reputation . . . by telling every one how I came to your room alone at midnight. Yes, slander me to your heart's content if that gives you satisfaction.' At this point Parvati's lips were quivering, distorted by pain and anger.

Such was Devdas' rage on hearing these words that he felt as though his entire body was on fire. 'What!' he screamed, 'I will derive satisfaction by slandering you and staining your character! Listen, Parvati. Too much vanity is not good.' He gripped his wooden flute firmly in his hand, ready to strike her. 'Look at the moon, Parvati,' he said. 'It is so beautiful that there had to be a stain on it. And the white lotus is so lovely that it has to be stained by the bee which sits at its centre. Come, Parvati, I will give you the stain you need.' He struck her hard with his flute on one side of the face. Blood flowed from her eyebrows to her cheeks.

Parvati fell to the ground and cried, 'O, Devda, what have you done!' Devdas broke his flute into little pieces and threw them into the river. 'It is not much,' he said, 'just a little cut.' He tore up a portion of his shirt, dipped it in water, and tied it round her face covering the wound. 'Don't be afraid, Paro,' he said, 'the wound will heal soon. Only the scar will remain. I leave it as a farewell gift to remember me by when you look in the mirror and see your face, beautiful like the moon.'

Devdas started going away. Parvati was weeping. 'Oh, Devda!' she moaned. Devdas turned back, came close to her and brushed her hair with his lips. 'Paro,' he said, 'don't you remember how in childhood whenever I was angry with you I cuffed your ears and slapped you?' All that Parvati could say was, 'Forgive me, Devda.' He placed his right hand upon her head, blessed her and said: 'Parvati, you know that I am not good with words. I do not think carefully before any action. I have always been impulsive. You have done well in rejecting me. Perhaps you would not have been happy with a man like me. But if you had accepted your Devda, he would have dwelt in the everlasting heaven of bliss.' And he quietly walked away.

Parvati returned home. There was great commotion when
her mother and grandmother saw the wound. She told them
that she had slipped at the river front and hit her head on a
brick. The wound healed within a week. On the day of the
marriage the bridegroom, Bhuvan Mohan Babu—the landlord
of village Hathipota—came with his party. It was a simple
ceremony. Bhuvan Mohan Babu, a middle-aged widower, had
the good sense not to appear at the ceremony dressed like a
young bridegroom. He was fair, well built, and slightly bald
with graying hair and moustaches. His expression was serious,
almost solemn, as if he were feeling guilty for what he was
about to do. Devdas' father, Mukherji Moshay, had taken charge
of all the arrangements. A box of jewellery was opened and the
bride was dressed in the traditional manner. Parvati's mother
cried when she saw her lovely daughter, resplendent in her
gold ornaments, ready to go to her husband's house.

In the evening Manorama spent some time with Parvati in
a secluded room. She blessed her friend and said, 'Whatever
has happened will turn out to be for your own good. You will
have a happy life, Parvati. I wish I could call Devdas and show
him this beautiful gold image that you have received.'

Parvati was restless. 'O my dear friend,' she said, 'if only
you could really do that! If only you could bring Devdas here
just once.'

Parvati's tone and facial expression made Manorama anxious.
'Why, Parvati ?' she said.

'I wish to take the dust of his feet and put it on my forehead,'
Parvati said. 'I would really like to do that . . . good bye,
Manorama. I am going away now.'

The two friends held each other in a tight embrace and
wept together for a long time. At night Parvati went away with
her husband to her new home.

IX

Devdas left home without even meeting his parents. On
reaching Calcutta he spent the entire night on a bench in

Eden Gardens. At dawn he got up and proceeded towards the hostel where he used to stay. On the way he staggered, bumped into people, tripped and fell a couple of times and reached the hostel with bleeding feet. Chunnilal welcomed him and asked him to bring his baggage inside the room. Devdas said he had brought nothing with him. Chunnilal invited him to stay in his room for the time being. During the next two days Devdas fell asleep from time to time from sheer exhaustion.

'Have you quarrelled with your parents . . . or with some one else?' Chunnilal asked. 'Your college examination is only a couple of months away. Are you going to resume your studies?' Devdas said that he had not quarrelled with any one, and that he had no intention of resuming his studies. 'Where do you go at night, Chunni Babu?' he said. 'Please take me with you.'

'It is not a good place, Devdas,' Chunnilal said.

But Devdas insisted on going with him and declared that 'good' and 'bad' no longer had any meaning for him. In the afternoon Dharmadas came from the village and brought many things which Devdas had left behind. His mother had sent these things, along with a considerable amount of money and a letter urging him to return. Dharmadas was in tears when he described how shocked Devdas' mother was at his sudden departure. 'Please come home with me, Devdas,' he pleaded. But Devdas refused to accompany him and asked him to go back alone.

At night Devdas went with Chunnilal to his nocturnal haunt. Their carriage stopped outside a double-storeyed house on Chitpore Road. Chunnilal led Devdas inside the house and took him upstairs. They were welcomed by Chandramukhi, the proprietress of that establishment. Devdas looked at her and knit his brows in anger and disgust. 'Why have you brought me to this filthy place, Chunni Babu?' he said. Chunnilal persuaded him to go into the inner room and made him sit on a comfortable rug on the floor. He sat there, despondent and woeful, with bent head. A maidservant brought a silver hookah filled with perfumed tobacco. Devdas did not touch it.

There was silence in the room. The only sound was that of the hookah puffed by Chunnilal and Chandramukhi. After some time Chunnilal left the room, leaving Devdas alone with Chandramukhi. He looked at her contemptuously and said, 'You take money, don't you?' Chandramukhi, who was in her twenty-fourth year, had met all kinds of men in her profession. But she had never met anyone like Devdas—so harsh, and yet so simple, direct and innocent. She said, 'Now that my house has been honoured by the dust of your feet. . . .'

Devdas cut her short. 'I am not talking about the dust of my feet,' he said. 'Just tell me whether you take money.'

Words did not come easily to her. 'If I don't take money,' she said, 'how would I meet my living expenses?'

Devdas took out a currency note from his pocket and gave it to her without even looking at the denomination. 'Are you leaving so soon?' she asked, but Devdas walked out of the room without answering her. He met Chunnilal downstairs and told him that he was returning to the hostel. When Chunnilal went back to Chandramukhi's room she showed her the currency note and said, 'Your friend has given this money. You can return it to him if you consider it proper to do so.'

'I don't see why the money should be returned. He has given it to you of his own free will.'

'No, he has given it in anger,' she said. 'Tell me, Chunni Babu, is your friend crazy?' He assured her that he was sane but was going through a period of great tension. 'I did not want to bring him here,' he said, 'but he insisted on coming.'

Chandramukhi was surprised. 'He wanted to come,' she asked, 'knowing what kind of a place this is?'

'Of course. He knows everything. I did not bring him here through deception.'

In a tone of great urgency Chandramukhi said, 'Chunni Babu, can you do me a great favour? Please bring him here again, somehow.' Chunnilal said that it might be difficult because Devdas had never visited a 'house of ill fame' before and was not likely to do so in future. But Chandramukhi persisted in her request and urged him to bring about another meeting between her and Devdas.

'What's the matter?' said Chunnilal with a wink. 'Has the insult you received from him turned into love?' Chandramukhi told him that Devdas had not even looked at the amount he had paid her. Chunnilal knew her very well. 'You are not a woman who would care so much about the denomination of a currency note,' he said. 'Tell me the truth. Why do you wish to see him again after the way he treated you?' Chandramukhi confessed that she had felt a strange attraction towards Devdas.

'What? In five minutes?'

Chandramukhi was smiling. But she was very much in earnest. 'Please, Chunni Babu,' she implored. 'When he regains his composure bring him here once again. You have to swear by my head that you will do this for me.'

X

Parvati had heard that her husband was a wealthy man. But she had no idea how large his estate was. The main building was a huge, rambling mansion built in traditional Indian style. There were separate rooms for men and women, a large reception room, an auditorium for music concerts, a pavilion for religious ceremonies and worship, a guest house, office rooms, stables and storage rooms. The number of servants, male and female, was much larger than the number of people in the family. When Parvati arrived, she was greeted by a young man of twenty. He touched her feet and said, 'Mother, I am your oldest son. This household has been in mourning since the death of my mother two years ago. We seek your blessings for happiness in the days to come.' The young man's name was Mahendra. Parvati was impressed by his modesty and his refined, respectful behaviour.

Mahendra's younger brother was in Calcutta preparing for his college examinations. His sister, Yashoda, was married. Mahendra said that he had asked Yashoda to come and greet her new mother, but she was unable to do so. Parvati's husband, Bhuvan Chaudhari, spent most of his time managing his large estate. He was a religious man, kept fasts on sacred days, never missed his prayers, and was hospitable to wandering hermits and pilgrims. He treated Parvati as a daughter rather than a wife. 'You are the mistress of this household now,' he told her on the very first night of her arrival, 'and should manage it in whatever way you please.' He praised Mahendra and assured Parvati that his daughter, Yashoda, would soon come and pay her respects.

Bhuvan Babu expressed his gratitude to his new wife with tears in his eyes. 'May God bless you,' he said, 'and may you have a long, happy life. Now that you are here, this house will see joyous days again.' He described the situation created by the death of his first wife and repeatedly referred to his advancing age. 'I have not done the right thing,' he said. 'I feel guilty. You are too young to be my wife.' And she again saw tears in his eyes as he asked for forgiveness and prayed for her happiness.

Parvati soothed her husband and beseeched him not to feel guilty. 'Please don't think about your age,' she said. 'I will also get old soon. Women age quickly.' A month later Parvati's father, Chakravarty Moshay, came to take her home. But she said it was too early for her to leave as she was still learning to manage the household. She promised to go later. After her father's departure, Parvati asked Mahendra to go to Yashoda's house and bring her. 'My daughter is angry, it seems,' she said. 'Please pacify her and tell her that I am eagerly waiting to welcome her.' Mahendra went to his sister's house and persuaded her to accompany him to Hathipota. Parvati had sensed that Yashoda was sulking because she did not want a stepmother.

When Yashoda came to see her, Parvati was decked from head to toe in the most exquisite jewellery which her husband had purchased for her in Calcutta a week earlier. Yashoda was tremendously impressed by her new mother's youth, beauty and gracious bearing. Parvati took off her ornaments, one by

one, and adorned her stepdaughter with them. When all the
jewellery had thus been transferred to Yashoda, Parvati gave
her the silk saris, embroidered shawls and other fine clothes
that she had kept beside her.

'Do not be angry with me, my daughter,' Parvati said. 'This
is your father's house. There are so many servants here. Consider
me to be one of them.' Yashoda fell at her feet and begged
forgiveness for not coming earlier to meet her. Mahendra was
happy to see how quickly his sister had been won over. Yashoda
met her father and requested him to send a message to her in-
laws informing them that she would return after two months.
When Parvati's husband came to know of the way in which she
had befriended his children, he once again expressed his
gratitude to her.

XI

For a few days after his visit to Chandramukhi's house, Devdas
was very restless. He wandered aimlessly on the streets of
Calcutta. Dharmadas, who had come to take Devdas back to
his parents' home, requested Chunnilal to help him. But
Chunnilal said that he had already tried in vain to persuade
Devdas to go home. One evening, when Chunnilal was going
out, Devdas asked him: 'I wonder with what expectation you
go to that place. What is it that you hope to find there?'

'Hope? Expectation?,' he said, 'I go there to divert myself,
to pass the time, that's all.' Devdas said that he, too, was
finding it difficult to pass the time. In that case, Chunnilal
suggested, they should visit Chandramukhi again. 'In fact, I
have given her a promise that I would take you to her house
once again.' Devdas resisted for some time but ultimately
agreed. He had already started drinking. When they reached
Chandramukhi's house it did not take long for Devdas to get
drunk. Chunnilal slipped away.

Chandramukhi had fallen in love with Devdas. She was
distressed to see him in that condition. 'Stop now, Devdas,'

she said. 'You are a beginner. You won't be able to digest so much liquor.'

'I don't drink liquor to digest it,' Devdas said, looking at her with contempt, 'I drink so that I may be able to remain in a place like this. I am here just now because I don't have the strength to get up and leave. I get drunk so that I may bear to look at you and hear you.'

He threw away the wineglass. It was smashed to pieces. Chandramukhi wiped his eyes and said, 'Devdas, there are so many people who come here but do not touch liquor.'

Devdas laughed and said, 'What! They do not drink and yet they come here? If I had a gun I would have shot them all. They are worse sinners than I am, Chandramukhi.'

Devdas remained quiet for some time. Then he said, 'If I give up drinking I will never come here again. Pain has driven me to drink. O grape, O liquor! Sole companion in my hours of misery, I will not abandon you.' Devdas sank in the bed and started rubbing his face on the pillow. Chandramukhi tried to raise him up. 'Keep away,' he said, 'don't touch me. I am conscious. I can touch you only when I become unconscious. Only I know, Chandramukhi, how deep is my loathing for women in your profession. . . . Yes, I detest you . . . and yet I will come here again and again, sit near you, talk to you . . . because I have no other alternative. Can you understand what I am saying? No, I don't think you can.' Then staring at Chandramukhi's face, he said in a sad voice, 'Oh, how much do women endure. Chandramukhi, your profession makes you the embodiment of feminine patience. You are the most glaring example of what a woman has to put up with . . . scorn, hatred, insults, abuse, violence.'

By this time Devdas had become incapable of sitting up. He stretched himself on the bed and started muttering to himself incoherently: 'Chandramukhi says she loves me. . . . I don't want it . . . no I don't. . . . People play parts. They darken their faces with charcoal . . . or whiten them with chalk . . . one becomes a beggar, another a thief . . . or a king. They talk about love . . . they weep, they laugh . . .

Chandramukhi also plays a part, yes, and I watch . . . but she
who is in my mind . . . whom I remember . . . O God, how
much I miss her . . . how much I remember . . . she went
away somewhere and I am on this path. . . . Now begins a
new play . . . lifelong performance . . . a terrible drunkard .
. . and a . . . and a   . . . but let that be . . . what's
wrong with it? . . . No hope, no joy, no faith, no search . .
. marvellous . . . wonderful   . . . bravo! . . .'

Chandramukhi was unable to make any sense of what he
was saying. Mumbling in this way, he fell asleep. She sat close
to him. Dipping the end of her sari in a bowl of water, she
wiped his forehead and face. She fanned him gently as she sat
by his side, with bent head, plunged in thought. She remained
like that for a long time. It was more than an hour after
midnight when Chandramukhi put out the lamp, closed the
door, and went into the other room.

XII

Narayan Mukherji, the landlord of Tal Sonapur, was dead. The
entire village was in mourning. His two sons—the elder, Dwijdas
and the younger, Devdas—had just returned from the cremation
ground after performing the last rites. Dwijdas was lamenting
and weeping loudly. Devdas sat in a corner, brooding. No
words came from his lips and no tears flowed from his eyes.
His widowed mother was barely conscious. She was surrounded
by women from the village. Parvati's grandmother was among
them. 'It seems Devdas has come,' she said. When Devdas
heard his name he went over to his mother and placed his
head at her feet. 'O my son!' she said and burst into tears.

After some time Devdas went to the room where his departed
father used to sleep. He sat on the floor, staring at the ceiling.
His eyes were red. The veins of his forehead and temples were
swollen. He had allowed his hair to become long, unkempt
and dry. His appearance was frightening. The excesses of his
life in Calcutta, the shock of his father's death and lack of sleep

had left their marks upon his face. It was difficult for any one who had seen Devdas a year earlier to recognize him in his present state.

Parvati's mother was looking for Devdas. When she found him, she said, 'Devdas, my son, how long can you go on like this?'

'What have I done, auntie?' he said.

She knew what he had been doing but did not say anything. She sat down, pulled Devdas to herself and placed his head in her lap. Devdas remained there for some time, sobbing in the arms of Parvati's mother.

Time heals. The sounds of weeping and moaning gradually faded and stopped. Devdas' mother resumed her household chores with a heavy heart. A few days later Devdas' elder brother, Dwijdas, brought up the subject of financial arrangements. It was decided that ten thousand rupees should be spent on religious ceremonies in honour of their late father. After that, Dwijdas said, seventy thousand rupees would come to the share of each of them.

'But what about our mother?' Devdas asked.

'Mother does not need any cash,' Dwijdas said. 'We will take care of all her requirements.'

Devdas did not like this idea at all. He said that he would take only fifty thousand from his share and the remaining twenty thousand should be deposited in his mother's name. Dwijdas accepted the offer. 'You know that many heavy expenses are ahead of me,' he said. 'My daughter's marriage and my son's thread-ceremony are going to cost a lot of money.' The elder brother was too shrewd and wordly-wise to accept Devdas' generosity without having something in writing. Devdas saw no necessity of any legal documents. But when his brother insisted, he said, 'Very well, I will sign whatever agreement you draw up.'

Having heard about the death of Devdas' father, Parvati had come to stay with her parents. One afternoon when Devdas was coming down the stairs he saw Parvati. She looked at his face for a long time, trying to conceal the pain she felt to see

him in that condition. He made enquiries about the welfare of
her husband and stepchildren. 'Will you be staying for a few
days?' he asked. She simply said 'yes' though she wanted to ask
about his life in Calcutta. 'Very good, then,' Devdas said and
went out. After he had gone out, Parvati called Dharmadas
and gave him a gold necklace for his daughter. 'I hope all is
well with you, Dharmadas,' she said.

'No, Parvati,' he said with a deep sigh. 'Everything is going
wrong. I don't wish to live any more. The master is gone. I
wish I could follow him.'

'If you go away, who will look after Devdas,' Parvati said.

'I have looked after him since he was a baby. Now he no
longer listens to me. It would be better if I don't have to look
after him any more.'

Parvati came close to him and said, 'Tell me truthfully,
Dharmadas. What does Devda do these days?'

Dharmadas struck his forehead with the palm of his hand
and said: 'What does he do? I don't think it would be proper
to mention it in your presence. Now the master is no more
and Devdas has inherited a lot of money. Things are going to
get even worse from now on.'

Parvati had heard rumours about Devdas' dissolute life.
Her friend Manorama had also written to her about these
rumours. When Dharmadas confirmed what she had heard,
Parvati's heart was filled with sorrow.

'No regular meals, hardly any sleep,' Dharmadas continued,
'and God knows where he spends his nights. Sometimes he
does not return to his room for five or six days. He is spending
money like water. I have heard that he has purchased jewellery
worth several thousand rupees for some woman.'

Parvati shivered all over when she heard this. 'Is all this
true?' she asked.

But Dharmadas went on talking without hearing her. 'Please
talk to him, Parvati. Perhaps he will listen to you. How long
can he survive if he continues to treat his body like this? I
cannot tell all these things to any one else. Sometimes I feel
like putting an end to my life.'

Parvati thought about the carefree years she had spent with Devdas. A thousand memories came back to her. She repented having treated Devdas harshly. She cursed herself, blamed herself. Devdas would not have come to such a pass if she had been there to support him. While Devdas' life was being torn to pieces, she was spending her life attending to the family of another man. She was distributing food to others every day while the person who meant everything to her was dying of self-imposed neglect and starvation. 'I have to see him again,' she resolved, 'even if it means knocking my head on the floor and dying at his feet.'

She went to his house that very morning. Devdas was sitting on the bed, serene in his sadness, when she entered the room. He raised his eyes and saw her. She closed the door and sat on the floor near him. Devdas laughed and said: 'And what if I tell the whole world about your visit to my room alone, and stain your character?' Parvati blushed, looked at him and lowered her eyes again. She was haunted by the terrible things she had said to him. She had come to unburden herself, but now she felt tongue-tied. 'O, I understand,' Devdas said. 'You are ashamed of what happened that day. But we were both mere kids at that time, Parvati. You have no reason to feel guilty. You were angry and uttered harsh words. But I too lost my self-control and put a mark on your forehead.'

Devdas said these things in a perfectly simple and natural way. He seemed strangely calm while recalling that tragic episode. But Parvati felt that her heart was about to burst through unbearable sadness. She held her breath from time to time and said in an almost inaudible voice, as if speaking to herself: 'Devda, that scar upon my face, given by you, will remain the only source of consolation to me for the rest of my life. It was your boundless affection for me which led you to write the history of our childhood through that scar. It is not a stain, it is something which makes me proud.'

'Paro!' There was infinite tenderness in his voice when he called her.

Without unveiling her face she said: 'What is it, Devda?'

Devdas was no longer calm. His throat was choking with emotion. 'Paro,' he said, 'I am truly angry with you. My father has passed away. There is so much sorrow in my heart. If you had been by my side I would not have felt any anxiety. You know the kind of person my elder brother is. And you also know how self-centred his wife is. Now in this situation what shall I do with my mother? I don't know what is going to happen to me, Parvati. If only I could have entrusted all my cares to you, I would have lived peacefully.'

Parvati started crying. He changed the subject. 'Isn't it funny, Paro,' he said with a forced smile. 'You were so little, and now you have become a big landlady. . . big mansion, large landed estates, distinguished husband, grown-up son and daughter.' Then Devdas suddenly became serious. 'Can you do me a favour, Paro?' he said, 'Find a good girl for me. I want to marry.'

Parvati was pleased. She said: 'The girl will have to be very beautiful, I know.'

'Yes, like you.'

'And she has to be gentle, meek, well-behaved?'

'No, no! She must be mischievous, headstrong . . . like you . . . so that we can have fights.'

How can I find a girl who can be as gentle with him as I would have been if I had married him? Can any girl give her the kind of love that I would have given? Such were Parvati's thoughts. But what she actually said was: 'Devda, a thousand girls like me would willingly fall at your feet and consider themselves blessed to be accepted.' Then after a good deal of hesitation, she asked: 'Devda, why did you learn to drink?'

Devdas laughed and said: 'This is not something that needs to be learned. Who told you? Dharmadas?'

'It makes no difference who told me. Is it true that you drink heavily?'

'Yes, it is true.'

'And I hear that you have given expensive jewellery to some woman. Who is she?'

'I have not given the jewellery,' Devdas said in a jocular way. 'I have merely purchased it. Would you like to take it, Parvati?'

Parvati stretched out her hand and said: 'Yes, give it to me. Don't you see that there is not a single ornament on my body?'

Devdas was surprised. 'I am sure your husband must have given you a lot of jewellery,' he said.

'Yes, but I gave away everything to his daughter.'

Devdas knew that no woman would part with her jewellery unless she was suffering intensely. This thought brought tears to his eyes. 'No, Paro,' he said. 'I do not love any other woman. Nor have I given jewellery to any one.'

They were both silent for a long time. Then Parvati asked him to promise that he would not drink again. Devdas refused to make such a promise. 'Can you promise that you will never think about me?' he asked. Parvati did not answer. Just then the sound of a conch-shell was heard, announcing the time of evening worship at the temple. 'It is getting late, Parvati,' Devdas said. 'You should go home now.' But she refused to budge unless he swore to give up liquor.

'I cannot do what you are asking,' he said.

'Why not?'

'Because there are things that a person simply cannot do. Can you elope with me tonight?'

Devdas asked her to open the door. She sat down, blocking the door firmly with her back. Devdas said: 'What is the point of forcing me to make a promise that I cannot keep? Paro, I may swear to stop drinking today, and tomorrow I may resume it. Why do you want to make a liar out of me?'

A distant clock struck nine. Devdas was worried. Parvati was a married woman. She should not be with him alone late at night. She was now lying on the floor sobbing loudly. 'Paro,' he called softly.

'I am heart-broken, Devda,' she said, still sobbing. 'My agony has now become unbearable altogether.'

'I know, Paro. I know very well.'

'My only desire in life was to serve you, care for you. Come with me, Devda. Stay in my house. There is no one here who can comfort you.'

'If I come to your house, will you nurse me, Parvati? Will you look after me?'

'That is what I have wanted to do since my childhood. O gods in heaven, fulfil this wish. Let me be of service to Devda. Then if death comes I will welcome it.'

Devdas could not restrain his tears. 'I will come to your house some day, Parvati,' he said. 'Yes, some day I will come.'

'Touch me and swear by my life that you will come,' Parvati demanded.

Devdas touched her feet and said: 'I will never forget this, Parvati. If serving me can bring you a little relief in your suffering, I will do what you are asking. I swear, Paro, that before I die I will come to your house.'

XIII

Devdas stayed at his father's house for a few months after his death. It was a trying period for him. His brother and sister-in-law became increasingly selfish. His mother was urging him to get married and settle down. Memories of Parvati made him restless. Finally, he took his mother to the holy city of Banaras, made arrangements for her stay there, and left for Calcutta.

When he reached Calcutta, Devdas looked for Chunnilal but was told that he had shifted to a different location. One evening he felt a strong urge to see Chandramukhi. He located her house and knocked at her door for a long time. At last, a woman opened the door and asked him whether his name was Devdas. 'Yes,' he said, 'can you tell me where Chandramukhi is?'

She smiled and said: 'Come upstairs. I will tell you'. He went inside and was shocked to see Chandramukhi. She was wearing a plain cotton sari, unwashed and crumpled. The two bangles on her wrist were her only ornaments. All the paintings had been removed from the walls. A small cot, covered with an old sheet, was the only furniture in the room. The wall clock was not working. There were cobwebs around it. An oil lamp was burning in a corner. It shed barely enough light for Devdas to see her.

'Why are you living in such a terrible condition, Chandra?' Devdas asked, looking around the room.

'Why do your say that this is a terrible condition?' she said with a smile. 'On the contrary, I think that fortune has smiled upon me at last.'

She told him that she had sold all her jewellery, paintings, furniture and other possessions. Devdas asked her about Chunnilal. She said Chunnilal had come with a very wealthy man who wanted to keep her and had offered a large amount of money. She was disgusted at the thought and had turned them out of the house. She had only nine hundred rupees left which she had invested in a grocer's shop. She hoped to live on the interest, which worked out to twenty rupees a month. She had decided to move to a small, inexpensive town and lead a simple life.

Devdas was puzzled. 'If you have changed your way of life altogether,' he asked, 'why are you still in Calcutta?'

Although she hesitated to express her feelings, Chandramukhi said: 'I was hoping that you would come . . . that I will see you once more before leaving. Now you have come. I will leave tomorrow.'

Devdas could hardly conceal his surprise. He said: 'You stayed on in Calcutta all these days merely in the hope of seeing me again? Why?'

'Because you hated me so much, Devdas,' she replied. 'I was fascinated by you the very first time you came to my house. Not because of your wealth. Wealthy people come to me all the time—but because I felt the beauty of your heart, the strength of your inner self.'

It was not easy for Devdas to grasp immediately the extent of Chandramukhi's transformation. 'I made a complete break with my past,' she continued, 'but you, Devdas . . . you started drinking. I hate liquor. I was always angry with any one who got drunk in my house. But with you I did not feel any anger. When I saw you in a drunken state, the only thing I experienced was pain and sorrow. But one evening, after getting intoxicated, you said something which touched me. You described my life as a living example of the humiliation and injustice to which women are subjected. Your words aroused in me my self-respect as a woman, as a human being, and I decided to give up my profession.'

Chandramukhi had chosen a small village on the outskirts of Calcutta as her future home. Devdas expressed the fear that she might again succumb to temptation if she lived close to the city. But she assured him of her firm determination to give up her degrading profession and said that no temptation would ever induce her to resume it. He was worried that she would not be able to subsist on twenty rupees a month and asked her to promise that she would let him help her in times of difficulty.

While promising to turn to him for help whenever she was in need, Chandramukhi held his hand tenderly and asked him: 'Devdas, has Parvati caused you too much pain?'

He was shaken when Parvati's name was mentioned. 'Why do you ask?' he said.

'It is important for me to know,' Chandra said in serious tone. 'I have heard you talk in your sleep many times after your drinking bouts. Devdas, I am convinced that Parvati has always been loyal to you. The notion that women are fickle and faithless is an invention of males. Men can express themselves freely. Women are unable to do so. Their voice is throttled. Moreover, women lack the boldness to declare their love openly. They carry it in their hearts and suffer silently.'

Chandra went on speaking. It was a revelation to Devdas that a woman whom he had once looked down upon as a mere plaything of desire could make such deep observations about life. 'Remember, Devdas,' she said, 'genuine love gives a person the strength to endure pain, even injustice. Alas, men rarely understand how much contentment there is in loving inwardly, silently. No, Devdas, Parvati has never deviated from her love for you. Some day you will realize this.'

XIV

Chandramukhi's words, full of truth and sincerity, moved Devdas to tears. While he was absorbing what she had said, Chandra was thinking about Parvati. 'She must be an extremely beautiful woman,' she mused, 'and yet I feel Devdas has not expressed his love for her. Parvati must have been the first to fall in love and to let Devdas know how she felt.' In this way she was speculating about Devdas and Parvati when she unwittingly allowed some words to become audible, though faintly: 'I can understand from my own feelings the extent of Parvati's love for you.'

Devdas heard those words and got up with a start. 'What!' he exclaimed. 'What was it you just said?'

'No, no, nothing,' Chandramukhi said. 'I was merely saying that Parvati's attraction for you could not have been merely physical. Devdas, underneath your sharp and dry exterior there is great inner beauty. Few can see it. But whoever does see it cannot stop being attracted to you.'

There was a note of frustration in Chandramukhi's voice when she continued, although Devdas had not responded: 'Whoever has loved you must know of your inner power to draw a person to yourself like a magnet. And I doubt if there is any woman in the world who, once drawn to you, would willingly move away. Devdas, this kind of inner beauty cannot be seen by the eyes.'

Devdas was surprised, touched, but also felt uneasy. 'What has happened to you, Chandra?' he said. 'Why are you saying all these things today?'

Chandramukhi was now calm and said with a smile: 'I can understand what a difficult situation it must be, Devdas, when a person does not love a woman but is forced to hear from her the tiresome story of her love. . . . But I am pleading Parvati's

case, not mine.' Devdas said he wanted to leave but Chandra
pressed him to stay a little longer. 'This is the first time,' she
said, 'that I have the opportunity to hold your hand and talk
to you freely. I am not trying to tempt you. Those days are
over. Now I have the same disgust and hatred for the kind of
life I led which you once expressed to me.'

She reminded him of the time when he refused to be near
her unless he was completely drunk. 'I gave up drinking after
my father's death,' he said. 'But I should be going now. Keep
me informed, wherever you may be. And don't hesitate to ask
me if you ever need my support.'

Chandramukhi bent down, touched his feet with her
fingers and then touched her head with those fingers. 'Give
me your blessings, Devdas,' she said, 'and remember me if
you ever need someone to serve you, nurse you and look
after you.'

XV

Parvati's stepson, Mahendra, was now a married man. His
wife, Jaladabala, took over the household management. Parvati
spent most of her time attending to her husband's needs, and
in religious ceremonies and charities. She supported orphanages,
homes for widows, and other institutions. Hermits, beggars,
students and other needy people came to the Chaudhari
mansion for help. Parvati was so generous that no one ever
returned empty-handed. So much money was spent in charities
that even the servants became worried about the drain on
resources. One day Jaladabala said to her husband: 'Don't you
have any voice in the management of this household? Your
father has left everything to your stepmother. She is spending
money without a thought. She has no children of her own to
worry about. But we have to think of our future. Some day we
will have to raise children.'

Mahendra had so much respect for his mother that he could
not tolerate any complaints against her. He went straight to

Parvati and said: 'Mother, your daughter-in-law has been speaking ill of you. I cannot permit this. I will not have anything to do with her from now on.' Parvati pacified him and pointed out that she was only thinking of the good of the family. Jaladabala apologized to her for complaining about her charities. Parvati promised to control her extravagance. From that day onwards she started spending more time in prayer and worship in the garden and in the solitude of her own room. She discouraged people from gathering in the compound in large numbers to attend elaborate religious functions and rituals.

Sometimes, when she held the bowl of holy water for offering to the deity, her tears dropped into it. She rarely laughed. Parvati had all the comforts that any woman could desire. But she had nothing to do, no aim to attain, no purpose to work for. Her sorrow-laden mind wandered to the village of Tal Sonapur. In her daydreams she saw the bamboo grove, the mango orchard, the pond, the open fields, the school where she had spent the carefree childhood years of her life in the company of Devdas.

The fame of her generosity and kindness had spread far beyond her husband's large estates. She was referred to as a *yogini*, as Annapurna, the Giver of Food, as Lakshmi, the Goddess of Wellbeing and Abundance. Yet Parvati remained gentle, humble, with a gracious smile and a kind word for every one. One day, a sudden change came over her. She appeared to have become hard, determined. The reason for this change was a letter from her friend, Manorama.

After the usual enquiries about Parvati's health and family, and after describing her own household, Manorama had written: 'Parvati, for a long time I have hesitated to give you news about Devdas. You will suffer deeply when you read what I am about to write. But sooner or later you will hear about Devdas anyway. Parvati, God has saved you. It would have been terrible if a self-respecting woman like you had become the wife of a man like Devdas. He came to the village a week ago to get money from his brother. His mother now lives in Banaras. His brother, Dwijdas, is very careful about his portion of the property. But Devdas is said to have squandered away most of his share on liquor and prostitutes.

'Only Yama, the God of Death, can save him. And that day is not far off. Mercifully, he has not married. I feel very sorry for him, dear Parvati. His beautiful face and golden complexion have been ruined. It is difficult to recognize him. His eyes are like two deep pits. His ribs and bones are sticking out. He wanders all day by the side of the river, shooting birds with his gun. In the evening he gets drunk and again wanders aimlessly. God knows if he ever gets any sleep.

'One day when I had gone to the river to fetch water, Devdas saw me. I was scared to death. It was God's grace that nothing happened to me. He did not misbehave in any way. He was calm and courteous when he talked to me. "'How are you, Mano?" he said. "Is everything all right with you? The sight of you and your friends gives me pleasure. May you be happy, sister." And then he slowly walked away. I ran home as fast as I could.'

On the day Manorama's letter arrived Parvati was benumbed and could do nothing. The next morning she asked Mahendra to get two palanquins ready. The porters were summoned and she set off. The same evening, after dark, she reached Tal Sonapur and went straight to Devdas' house. He had left for Calcutta only a few hours earlier. Disappointed, she went to see Manorama.

'Paro, did you come to meet Devdas?' Manorama asked.

'No, Manorama, I did not come just to meet him,' Parvati said, 'I came to take him home with me. There is no one here to look after him.'

Manorama was shocked. 'What are you saying, Paro?' she exclaimed. 'Have you no sense of shame?'

Parvati laughed and said: 'I came to take away what belongs to me. Why should I be ashamed?'

Parvati spent the night with her parents. The following morning she touched their feet, asked for their blessings, and returned to her husband's home.

XVI

Chandramukhi built a small mud hut in village Ashatjhuri. Her little dwelling was near the river. There was a milkman named Bhairav who lived in the neighbourhood. Chandramukhi helped him in many ways and he respected her. He was always ready to do little chores for her. Chandra was contented with her simple life in the village. Devdas had given her a little money which was sufficient for her needs. The village people brought her vegetables and firewood in lieu of the money she lent them from time to time without charging any interest. She had informed Devdas of her address and kept writing to him about her satisfying life in the village. In his replies Devdas always thanked her and wished her well but did not write anything about himself.

After a while, Devdas' letters stopped abruptly. Chandramukhi was worried. She sent letters by registered mail but they were returned by the Post Office. She became so anxious that one day she requested Bhairav to accompany her and set out in search of Devdas. She first went to Devdas' home in the village of Tal Sonapur. She met Devdas' sister-in-law who was now in charge of the property and who looked every inch a proud proprietress. She was laden with jewellery. Chandramukhi learnt from her that Devdas came to the village only when he needed money. 'Much of what he possessed,' she said, 'has been pawned to my husband. Only the other day he took twelve thousand rupees and transferred much of his land to us. He has some terrible disease. He is not likely to live much longer. No one knows his address in Calcutta.'

On reaching Calcutta, Chandramukhi sought out some of the friends of her courtesan days. With their help she found a small flat and decided to stay there until she could find Devdas. She started singing and dancing again as there was no other way in which she could earn enough money to live in Calcutta. She purchased inexpensive dresses, ornaments of imitation gold, drums, anklets and other accessories needed in her profession. When her friends saw her dressed once again in a courtesan's outfit, they remarked that her beauty had remained undiminished in spite of her advancing years. Having settled down, she began her search for Devdas. She went to all his likely haunts and asked people there if they had seen a man with fair complexion, somewhat curly hair, a scar on the left side of his forehead, and one who was a big spender. But no one had seen a man to fit her description. Day after day Chandramukhi continued her search and returned to her flat at night, disappointed and dejected.

After a month of search, her quest was over. One evening she saw a drunk at the door of a house on a side street, talking to himself. How could she fail to recognize that voice? She approached him, touched his shoulder and asked him who he was. He talked incoherently and started humming the first line of a song. 'Come home with me, Devdas,' she said.

'No, I am fine here,' he mumbled.

'Would you like to drink wine?' she said.

'Of course I would,' he said, trying to embrace her. 'O kind brother, you have come as a true friend . . . who are you?'

She helped him into a carriage and took him home. He kept on muttering that there was not a single coin in his pocket. 'O beautiful one!' he said. 'What do you want with me? I cannot pay you even one rupee.' On reaching her flat Chandramukhi somehow managed to put him to bed and spent the night in the other room.

When Devdas woke up he looked round at the unfamiliar surroundings. The only thing he remembered about the preceding night was that someone had helped him and very gently brought him to a place where he had slept comfortably. Chandramukhi came into the room wearing a plain cotton sari. But he saw her jewellery and was surprised. 'They are all fake . . . polished,' she said. 'I was forced to do all this because I had to stay in Calcutta to find you. But you did not even recognize me last night.'

'It is true that I did not recognize you,' Devdas said. 'But I recognized your affection, your gentle attention. I was thinking about you. Who else but my Chandra, I was telling myself, can nurse me with such tenderness.'

Chandramukhi was happy. 'Devdas,' she said, 'do you still hate me?'

'No, Chandra,' he said. 'On the contrary I now love you.' Devdas looked so ill that Chandramukhi sent for a doctor the same day. After examining him the doctor said that the liver and lungs had been affected and utmost care was required. Dharmadas was informed about Devdas' illness. He came as soon as he could. Devdas was running a high temperature. 'You came at the right time, Chandra,' he said, 'otherwise you would never have seen me again.' Chandramukhi prayed every day for his recovery.

Rest and proper nursing gradually led to an improvement in his health. After a month his temperature returned to normal. One day Devdas asked Chandra: 'What am I to you? Why are you doing all this for me?'

'Have you not understood even now, Devdas, that you are my everything?'

'It seems you are destined to suffer because of me, as Parvati is suffering.'

Chandramukhi covered her face to conceal her tears and sat at the edge of the bed.

'How different you are from Parvati,' Devdas said. 'She is proud and stubborn, you are calm and restrained. She cannot tolerate the slightest affront, you put up with everything. She is honoured and respected by every one, you are looked down upon as a fallen woman. Every one loves Parvati. No one really loves you except me. I do not know how you will be judged by the Great Arbiter of virtue and sin. But, Chandramukhi, if there is actually such a thing as meeting in another lifetime, I am certain that we will meet again.'

Two months later Devdas, feeling restless, decided to travel. He told Chandra that he wanted to travel because a change of environment would be good for his health. He had a premonition that his final wanderings were about to begin. With the ever-faithful Dharmadas by his side, he went westward to Allahabad. Before leaving Calcutta he gave two thousand rupees to Chandra. She accepted the money because she did not want to hurt his feelings. 'I beg of you,' she said, 'that if you fall ill again you must inform me immediately.' Devdas promised to respect her wishes and took leave of her.

XVII

During his stay at Allahabad, Devdas wrote a letter to Chandramukhi. He remembered her with great affection and felt grateful for the way she had helped him back to recovery. The image of Chandramukhi came into his mind alternately with that of Parvati. Sometimes the two images came together. Devdas fantasized that Parvati and Chandramukhi had become dear friends and had developed affection for each other. When the images faded away he became agitated, and restless.

From Allahabad he travelled to Lahore in Punjab. He had heard that Chunnilal had moved to Lahore. Shortly after his arrival at Lahore he somehow managed to get in touch with Chunnilal. They were happy to meet each other and talked for long talks about their days in Calcutta. But in Chunnilal's company Devdas again started drinking, and having broken his resolve not to touch liquor he was unable to exercise any control over himself. It was not long before he was ill again. Moreover, the climate of Lahore did not agree with him. Dharmadas persuaded him to leave Lahore. 'Let us inform your mother at Banaras,' he said, 'and let us go there to meet her.' But Devdas said that he was ashamed to show his face to his mother. So Dharmadas brought him back to Allahabad.

After a few days, when there was slight improvement in his health, he felt like setting off on a journey once again. He asked Dharmadas to take him to Bombay. Dharmadas was pained to see Devdas so restless. 'Devdas,' he said, 'I will now take you either to Banaras to meet your mother or to your home in the village of Tal Sonapur. There is no sense in wandering like this from place to place.' But Devdas insisted, and they went to Bombay.

After a few months Devdas became very sick and had to be admitted to a hospital. By the time he was discharged from the hospital he had become so weak that he had to lean on Dharmadas for support. Dharmadas once again urged him to meet his mother. At the mention of his mother Devdas burst into tears. During the preceding two months, memories of his mother had haunted him constantly. Lying in his hospital bed he used to ponder over his good fortune of having so many people who cared for him. 'I have my mother. I have an elder brother. I have Parvati, Chandramukhi, Dharmadas. They are all mine, but I am nobody's.' Such were his thoughts when Dharmadas asked him where he wanted to go from Bombay.

Dharmadas was weary and had aged considerably. 'Mother is still alive, Devdas,' he said in a voice broken by emotion. 'Let us go and meet her.'

'No, not yet,' Devdas said. 'The time to go to Banaras has not yet come.'

Ultimately he agreed to go back to his village home. The train passed a station close to Banaras, but at that time he was lying unconscious with high fever. When they reached Patna, Dharmadas suggested that they detrain there and seek medical aid. Devdas refused. It rained all night. Dharmadas fell asleep on his berth. When the train stopped at a small station in the district where Parvati lived, Devdas quietly opened the door of the compartment. Dharmadas did not hear anything. Devdas touched his forehead gently and went out on the station platform, closing the door behind him. Dharmadas was alone. The train started, carrying Dharmadas towards Calcutta.

Shivering, Devdas walked out of the station. There was a sole horse carriage, whose driver refused to make the thirty-five mile trip to Parvati's village on a muddy road in pouring rain. He offered to find a bullock-cart driver who might agree to take Devdas to Hathipota estate. The cart driver said that it would take two whole days to make the journey. Devdas agreed and with great difficulty climbed into the bullock-cart.

The cart moved slowly on the uneven road. Devdas sat shivering. At every jolt he felt that time was running out. He had to reach Parvati's house before the end. He had to meet Parvati before drawing his last breath. The time had come to keep his promise. But would he complete the journey in time?

His mother's kind face came before him. How tender was that face, how sacred! And Chandramukhi? She, whom he had once despised as a sinner was now on the canvas of his mind seated by the side of his mother. He would never see Chandramukhi again. There was no one to inform her of his death. 'God knows how long it would be before Chandra hears of my end,' Devdas mumbled.

The road was broken at several places. The driver had to get down and push the cart wheels with all his strength. The poor bullocks felt the impact of his stick from time to time. 'How much longer, brother,' Devdas said when they had spent more than a day and a half on the road. 'I have very little time left, my friend.' The driver said that they would reach late that night. But actually it was after midnight when the driver stopped the cart under a large tree in front of the landlord's mansion at Hathipota.

'We have reached, Sir, please come out'. There was no sound. The driver took a close look at Devdas who was trying in vain to raise his hand. Tears were trickling down his cheeks. The driver lifted him and placed him on a paved platform under the tree. With great effort Devdas brought out a hundred rupee note from his pocket and gave it to the driver. Then he sighed and lay down. Soon, he stopped breathing. It was the end of Devdas' life.

At dawn some people from the mansion came out and saw a man wearing an expensive shawl and shining shoes who had just drawn his last breath under a tree. Parvati's son, Mahendra, came to see the dead man. He was followed by his father. A police inspector was called from the village. He made an inventory of Devdas' possessions: a shawl, money, a sapphire ring and two letters. No one was willing to touch his body or perform the cremation rites. A few hours later, *chandalas* took away Devdas' body and tried to burn it. But the fire did not last long. So they left the half-burnt body and went away. Vultures soon descended and pecked at it. When they flew away, dogs and jackals fought over the remains of Devdas.

Parvati was vaguely aware of the excitement outside the mansion. But she did not pay any attention to it because she had become indifferent to what happened in the estate. In the evening she asked the maid whether she knew who had died. 'I do not know,' the maid said, 'Mahendra Babu can tell you. It seems some unfortunate person came here just to die. He must have purchased a small portion of this land in his previous life.'

Parvati asked Mahendra whether he had identified the dead man. 'He was from your village,' Mahendra said, 'some one called Devdas Mukherji.'

'What! Devda? How do you know?'

'Two letters were found in his pocket. One was from Dwijdas Mukherji.'

'Yes, his elder brother.'

'The other letter was from Harimati Devi of Banaras.'

'Yes, yes . . . his mother.'

'A sapphire ring.'

'Yes, at the time of Devda's thread ceremony his father gave him that ring.'

Suddenly, Parvati came down the steps and started running. 'Where are you going, mother?' Mahendra said anxiously.

'To meet Devdas.'

'But the *chandalas* have already taken away his body.'

Hearing these words Parvati shrieked, 'O my God, my God!'

She pushed Mahendra aside and ran towards the gate. Her husband was informed. He rushed out of the house and saw Parvati running towards the gate followed by Mahendra. 'Have you all become mad?' he shouted. 'Stop her and bring her back. She has lost her mind.' By the time Mahendra and the servants caught up with her, Parvati had fainted. They brought her inside the house and placed her on a bed.

She remained unconscious for more than a day. When she regained consciousness she opened her eyes and looked round.

She asked the maid in a faint voice: 'Did Devda come to me last night? Was he here throughout the night?' Parvati remained completely motionless. For a very long time not a word emerged from her lips.

XVIII

No one knows what happened to Parvati after that. As for Devdas, one can only have sympathy for him. Those of you who have read this account of his tragic life must have been undoubtedly touched by his sufferings. If you ever meet any wayward and unfortunate person like Devdas, please pray for him. Please pray to God that whatever else he has to endure, he should be spared the kind of death that Devdas had. Everyone has to die some day. But let him not die like Devdas, forsaken, alone. Let his forehead feel the touch of gentle and loving fingers at the time of death. Let the flame of his life be extinguished while gazing upon some affectionate face. Let him at least see one tear-drop in the eye of a caring human being. That will be happiness enough for him at the moment of final departure.

Srikanta

*T*oday, when my gypsy existence is in its concluding phase, I see a strange procession of images whenever I look back at the past. Decidedly, the world has not approved of me. Those who were close to me joined hands with strangers in condemning the tramp that has always lurked within me. But those whom God decides to post at unusual places in his creation are rarely 'good boys' intent on passing every school test creditably. Nor does God give such persons much talent for story telling. They are allotted a certain degree of intelligence, which the world interprets as cleverness, but they are not bestowed with wisdom. Their knack of getting into strange situations causes amusement for some time. Then they are forgotten and left free to carry the burden of their errors by themselves.

But enough of all this. Let me turn to the events I set out to narrate in spite of my diffidence, in spite of my extremely limited ability to recreate my experiences. To talk about something is not the same as to describe it. Whoever has two healthy legs can walk. But a man with two hands does not necessarily become a writer. I have not been blessed with a poetic imagination. I perceive only what I can see with these aching eyes of mine, nothing more than that. To me a tree is a tree, a bird is a bird and a mountain is a mountain. When I look at a lake I see only water. Since providence has denied me the gift of imagination, I will not indulge in poetic flights of fancy. All I can do is to set down the facts as I remember them, candidly and spontaneously.

From *Srikanta, Pratham Parva* (Srikanta, Part One), January, 1917.

How did I become a tramp? To explain this, I must introduce you to the person who drew me out of my sheltered existence and enabled me to taste the joy of aimless wandering. His name was Indranath. I do not know whether he is still alive. Many years ago he left his home, his dear ones, and all that he possessed. Ah, how can I ever forget the day when he left me forever and disappeared into open space with nothing but the shirt on his back?

I first met Indranath at a football field. I was watching a hotly contested match between two famous teams. Suddenly a fight broke out and somehow I became a part of the melee. I have not yet figured out why a group of students supporting one of the rival teams had singled me out and attacked me. They would have beaten me mercilessly if some one had not jumped into the fray and rescued me. He was dark-skinned and his face bore a few pock marks. His forehead was broad and his nose was long like a bamboo flute. But the extraordinary feature of his body was the length of his arms. They reached below his knees, ending in a pair of fists whose power left his adversaries dazed.

'Don't be scared,' he said as he pushed aside my attackers. 'Follow me . . . quick . . . hurry up.' The two of us slipped out of the cordon of students around me. Indranath asked me to run away, while he prepared himself for a fight.

'What about you?' I protested.

'Idiot! . . take to your heels,' he shouted impatiently.

I obeyed him. By the time I reached the main road it had become dark. There were lights in the stores, and the municipal gas lamps were also being kindled. Indranath joined me after some time. 'We are safe now,' he said. His calmness amazed me. In a casual tone he asked me what my name was. When I told him my name he said in the same nonchalant manner: 'Well, Srikanta, I gave them a good hiding.' Then he took out some dry leaves from the pocket of his kurta and gave me some while he stuffed his mouth with the rest. I asked him what it was. 'It is *bhang*,' he said. 'Chew it and gulp it down. It will give you a wonderful feeling.' When I refused he was annoyed. Snatching the leaves from my hand, he started chewing them himself.

I saw Indranath again a month later. At that time my brothers and I were staying in my aunt's house. We call her Pishima. All of us went to the same school. At home we were subjected to the rigorous rule of my aunt's son, whom every one addressed as Mejda. He imposed strict discipline upon us and made us study hard, although he had himself flunked the Entrance Examination several times. We were not allowed to leave the study room in the evening without his permission. We had to write on small slips of paper our reasons for wanting to go out. No one dared to leave without getting his slip initialled by Mejda. At the end of each day the room was littered with slips of paper with 'reasons for leaving'. Among these the common ones were 'to blow nose,' 'need a drink of water,' 'call of nature' and 'got to spit'.

One night, when we were sleeping on the roof after studying our lessons under Mejda's tyrannical supervision, we heard the distant notes of a flute. It was pitch dark. The air was hot and still. Not a leaf stirred. The melody played on the flute came through a grove of mango and jackfruit trees behind the house. It pierced the thick air and gradually faded away.

'Who is playing the flute at the dead of night?' Pishima asked.

'Who else but Indra,' Mejda said. 'God knows how many have died of snake-bite in that jungle. But Indranath is not afraid.'

'What a strange lad,' said Pishima and went back to sleep.

I envied Indranath. I wished I could play the flute like him and had a fraction of his courage. I wanted to be his friend but was not sure that he would accept my friendship. Moreover, he had left school. One day the Headmaster punished him for one of his pranks. Sometimes our Hindi teacher used to doze in the classroom. Catching him in one such blissful moment, Indranath had cut off a portion of the Pandit's pigtail. The Pandit was furious when he woke up. He complained to the Headmaster who took a very serious view of the offence. Indranath argued that he did not deserve any punishment because he had replaced the severed tuft of hair in the teacher's shirt pocket. But the Headmaster expelled him. After leaving school Indranath spent much of his time on the river, rowing his small canoe.

Indranath would sometimes vanish for weeks. Once in a way he would be seen tramping through the village playing his flute. I met him again under very strange circumstances. It was the rainy season. That day it had rained intermittently since early morning. In the evening, the sky was still heavy and overcast. We were studying by the light of an oil lamp under Mejda's watchful eye. Ramkamal Bhattacharya, an old friend of the family, sat in the verandah puffing at his hookah. Suddenly I heard a loud, rumbling sound. My younger brother, who was sitting behind me, screamed that a wild beast was about to devour him. Mejda ran in panic, upsetting the lamp and plunging the room in darkness.

There was utter confusion in the house. 'Catch him!' 'Beat up the monster.' 'Smash his head! . . .' Those who shouted like this did not have the least idea *who* was to be caught and *whose* head was to be smashed. 'It was a bear, a huge brown bear,' said Bhattacharya. Others were equally sure that it was a royal Bengal tiger. 'Bring my spear,' said one. 'Where is my gun?' said another. But very soon we all huddled together in the drawing-room. The verandah was emptied of all the brave people who had vowed to destroy the carnivore.

Was it a bear or a tiger? The argument was heating up when we saw a boyish figure approaching the house. It was Indranath, who seemed a bit confused by all the sounds he had heard. When he was told about the 'wild beast' he calmly picked up a lantern and went into the jungle looking for the intruder who had caused so much panic. We prayed for his life. Pishima started crying. Others prayed to the family deity. Within a few minutes, however, Indranath reappeared, dragging a man who wore a tiger mask. The ferocious tiger turned out to be nothing more dangerous than a poor impersonator named Srinatha, who earned his meagre livelihood by assuming the forms of different animals and men for the amusement of the village folk. Srinatha's tiger

incarnation, however, did not cause any merriment. Bhattacharya
beat him up with his slippers. Some one cut off the tail of his
tiger mask. After being abused and beaten up, Srinatha was
released. He ran away with his tail in his pocket. Indranath took
me aside and said: 'So, this is where you live.'

'Yes,' I said, 'but why did you come so late at night?'

'It is not really so late. Come, let us row on the river and
catch some fish.'

I was scared at the thought of boating on the river on such
a dark night. But Indranath urged me on. 'It is more fun in
the dark,' he said, 'and we can net more fish. Can you swim?'
I assured him that I was an excellent swimmer and followed
him without another word. While Indranath led me through
the zigzag jungle path, I kept on asking myself: 'Am I really
going to the river on a dark night, defying Mejda's strict
discipline, with an adventurous youth whom I hardly know?'
I seemed to be moving in a dream. The experience seemed
unreal. Even today, after so many years, I have not been able
to fathom the extraordinary attraction which impelled me to
go with Indranath on that dark night.

We reached the bank of the Ganga. Above us spread the
branches of an ancient *peepal* tree. Below us was the swirling,
swollen current of the river. Indranath's small boat was dimly
visible from above. He asked me to hold on to the rope with
which the boat was towed and grope my way down the steep
boulder. 'When you reach the boat,' he said, 'I will untie the
rope and jump down.' I did as I was told and waited near the
river. Nothing was heard for a while except the roar of the river
and the pounding of my heart. Suddenly, Indra emerged out of
the darkness. He laughed as he pushed the canoe into the
current and leapt into the rower's seat. The little boat whirled
sharply and then moved downstream with the speed of lightning.

II

A turbulent river in flood. A sky wrapped in a thick sheet of
darkness. A small, crudely-fashioned boat leaping forward with

a frightening speed. And two boys of tender age bent upon adventure! How can I ever forget that situation? Indranath sat silent, his hands on the oars. There was no need to row. The boat advanced with its own momentum because of the swift current. Abruptly, he asked: 'Are you scared, Srikanta?' I told him that I was not afraid, though my voice must have betrayed my fear. 'Good,' he said, 'if you know how to swim there is no reason to be frightened.' I was petrified by the very thought of swimming in that furious river at the dead of night.

But where was he taking me? My heart sank when he explained his fishing strategy. There was a place where the river had gone inland and formed a small lake. Fishermen cast their nets at that spot at night and picked up the catch in the morning. Our job was to remove from the nets all the fish that had already been trapped, load the catch in our boat, and hurry back. In plain words, we were about to *steal* fish. 'We must be very careful,' Indranath said. 'Row gently. If the fishermen get to know, they will break our heads with their sticks.'

We soon approached the nets. Indra lifted the largest of the fishes he could find in the nets and flung them into our boat. Some of them must have weighed more than fifteen kilograms each. We rowed out of the fishing area as quickly as we could. But the fishermen had spotted us. Within a few minutes we saw their boats chasing us. Indranath pretended that he was not worried, but we were clearly in grave danger. If the pursuers threw their nets over us, our fate would be the same as that of the fish. When we came close to the bank, the oars got stuck in the slush. Indranath used a bamboo as a lever and pushed the boat hard. We concealed ourselves and held our breath. We could hear the voices of the fishermen as they went past us. It was a narrow escape. After a while we heard the sound of canisters being struck with sticks. Indranath explained that the farmers were trying to drive away a wild boar—hardly a reassuring piece of information in that situation.

We were in a farm, up to our knees in mud. I heard the thud of strange objects falling from trees. They were snakes. One fell so close to me that I was terrified. The night was so dark that

I could barely see my own hands. Once again I silently questioned myself: what am I doing in a flooded river, on the edge of a dense jungle, on a dark rainy night? Who is this strange person . . . is he a human being at all? Or is he a god . . . or a demon? Is he altogether oblivious of the fact that there is an emotion called fear which people sometimes experience?

Indra pushed the boat into the main stream again, jumped in, and sat beside me. The young moon peeped out of a thick curtain of clouds. It was a relief to be able to see at least the faint outline of trees on the bank. The boat moved steadily in the river. There were no more eddies and whirlpools. We were advancing smoothly.

III

'I feel sleepy, Indra. I just cannot keep my eyes open any more.' He responded with a smile and said to me in a voice almost feminine in its gentleness: 'Yes, Srikanta, you really must be tired. I still have some work to do. Why don't you sleep?'

He did not have to press me. I slept for two hours. When I woke up, I discovered that Indra was rowing towards the other bank. But before I could ask where we were going, I sank into slumber again. Vaguely I saw the moon play hide and seek with the clouds. Dimly I heard the sound of waves. When I woke up again I saw that the boat had run into a sandy part of the bank. Were we home at last? No, we were nowhere near our home. I saw only the vast expanse of sand. I was trying to get my sensations in order when I heard the loud barking of dogs. We were near a fishermen's village on the other side of the river.

Asking me to wait there, Indranath set off. But within a few minutes he hurried back. 'I came to warn you,' he said. 'Don't part with the fish on any account. Don't be intimidated if any one tries to bully you. We must not lose the fish.' It had become a mystery to me why the fish was so important to Indranath. But curiosity was soon replaced by fear. Why was he warning me? Was he expecting someone to sneak up from behind and attack me? After an hour, which seemed like ten hours to me, he returned. He was accompanied by two men, one of whom appeared to be from a hill tribe. They talked in whispers. Then the two men took all the fish from our boat and handed Indranath something. It was too dark to see what it was, but the jingling sound told me that it was money.

I was bitterly disillusioned. So this was Indra in his true colours! He had made me risk my life, not in a spirit of fun and adventure but merely for a handful of coins. A few minutes earlier I could have embraced him with joy when I saw his dim outline emerge from the dark. Now I was angry. In my eyes stealing the fish was pure and simple theft.

Indra complimented me on my courage. 'I love you dearly, Srikanta,' he said. 'No one else would have remained alone at night in a place like this.' I kept silent. The moon emerged from the clouds again, and I saw his face. He looked so young, so completely innocent, that my displeasure and resentment melted away. I asked him whether he was afraid of ghosts and goblins. He said he had never seen them but firmly believed in their existence.

'I protect myself with the power of *Ramanama*,' he said. 'If you repeat Rama's name, you will remain unharmed. If you show fear, these supernatural beings will pounce upon you.' Meanwhile we were gliding downstream rapidly. Even the willows and reeds on the bank must have admired our courage. When the branches of banyan trees swayed in the wind, I thought they were asking us not to proceed further. A gust of breeze suddenly brought a foul smell to our nostrils. 'It must be a corpse,' Indra said. 'Hundreds are dying of cholera in these parts. Some people don't have money even to cremate their relatives. Jackals and wild dogs nibble at the bodies and leave them to decompose.'

Presently we came upon the corpse of a little boy, about seven years old. He was fair-skinned. His face looked fresh and healthy. When I looked at Indra, I saw large teardrops flowing from his eyes. 'Let us take this poor fellow with us and hide him in the willows so that the jackals may not get at him.'

With these words Indra lifted the boy's body gently and placed it in the boat.

I said: 'We don't know the boy's caste, Indra. Don't you feel any hesitation in touching him?'

'A corpse has no caste,' Indra replied. 'It has only a body. It is like our boat, which has no caste. It makes no difference whether it is made from mango wood or *jamun* wood.' The analogy may not have been logically valid, but that was Indra's way of arguing. His speech, like his mind, was wholly free from anything contrived or manipulated. He often startled me by saying things that were profound as well as childlike.

We came ashore again near a thick cluster of willows. Indra placed the corpse in a concealed place and gazed upon the face of the dead boy for a long time with infinite tenderness. When we started rowing again, he said: 'Do you know, Srikanta, that the boy is still with us? His spirit is accompanying us in the boat . . . there . . . right behind you! Let us repeat the name of Rama so that we may be safe from ghosts.' I begged him, with tears in my eyes, not to speak of such things. 'I will go mad with fear,' I told him, 'if you continue to talk about ghosts.' Fortunately, I soon fell asleep. When I opened my eyes, the morning light was cutting through the mist and haze. The boat was motionless. We were on the bank and Indranath was sitting quietly by my side.

IV

I returned home. My lips were parched and there was a frightened look in my red eyes. There was great commotion in the house. They all shouted simultaneously: 'He is back,' 'Srikanta has returned,' '*Dada* is safe and sound.' I became all the more nervous when I heard their exclamations. Mejda gave me a hard look and resumed reading his book, like a tiger who sees his prey within his power but leaves the poor creature alone for a while.

Pishima rushed into the room and said: 'Where were you all night, you wretch? Do you know how much misery you have caused? And just look at you! Your eyes are burning and your face is black. You should be tied up and thrashed. And tomorrow I am going to drive you out of the house.' But, having vented her anger, my beloved aunt drew me close and petted me. 'Come inside,' she said, 'I'll feed you and put you to bed.'

'He is not going anywhere,' Mejda roared.

I braced myself for punishment, but my aunt came to my rescue. 'Shut up, Satish,' she said. 'Leave him alone. I have been noticing that you torture these kids all the time. From tomorrow they will stay in a different room.' What a reversal of fortunes! Not only did I go scot-free, but my escapade had also resulted in the liberation of my brothers from Mejda's tyranny.

It was a long time before I saw Indranath again. As I sat on the river bank watching some fishermen, a voice behind me said: 'Have you been well, Srikanta? Come sit near me.' I felt as though I had received an electric shock. I had been hoping to meet him again all those days, and at the same time I was dreading another encounter with that strange lad. I did not know what to say to him. He asked me whether I was punished severely for our nocturnal adventure. I told him I was rebuked but not beaten. He was happy. 'I prayed to Goddess Kali for a long time,' he said, 'beseeching her to save you from being thrashed. She heard my prayer.' He folded his hands devoutly and touched his forehead in gratitude to the Goddess.

Indranath, usually so cheerful, was morose that day. We sat silently for a while. Then he asked me whether I could give him five rupees. I offered to pay the money immediately, though that was all I possessed. He said it would be quite some time before he could repay the loan. I assured him that I did not want it back at all. 'It is not for myself,' he said, 'it is for . . . for some one else . . . they are very poor.' I could feel the pain in his voice. Indranath asked me to accompany him and give the money with my own hands.

'*Didi* refuses to take money from me,' he said. 'If I offer it, she will think that I have stolen it for her from my mother's cash box.'

'So you need the money for your sister?'

'No, she is not my sister. But I call her *didi* because I look upon her as my elder sister. Come tomorrow after your morning meal. I will take you there and bring you back.' He held my hand affectionately. I could not refuse.

I spent the night with mingled feelings of fear and anticipation. Next morning, when I proceeded towards the river bank, at every step I invented excuses for backing out of my promise. But when Indranath greeted me with a delightful smile, I willingly climbed into the boat. Today I thank my lucky stars that I did not turn back. An extraordinary experience was in store for me. I do not know whether Indranath's *didi*, that pure souled woman, is still alive. And even if she is, I cannot visualise what condition she is in. She ordered me not to search for her. I have respected her wishes, though I have inwardly offered my homage to her countless times.

We left our boat near the cremation ground and entered the forest. A narrow path, winding through a wooded area, led us to a small thatched hut. Indranath loosened the rope and opened the bamboo gate. The shade of a large tamarind tree made the place look even darker than it was. As we approached, two goats started bleating. An enormous python was sleeping on the road. Indra lifted it by its belly and put it on one side of the path. 'He is perfectly harmless, Srikanta,' he said. 'His name is Rahim.'

We entered the hut. Peering into the darkened room, I was able to make out the figure of a tall, emaciated man. He was lying on a dirty, torn mat. His hair was tied up in a large braid and he was wearing many garlands and necklaces. He had a long beard and had on a ragged yellow robe. I recognized him. He was a snake-charmer whom I had often seen in the village.

The man seemed to be coughing his soul out. And yet he asked for the clay pipe in which he smoked *ganja*. Indranath filled the pipe and lit it. The old man, whom Indra addressed as Shahji, talked about something which I did not understand. But Indra must have said something which made the snake-charmer furious. The old man screamed in a shrill voice and abused Indranath in such foul language that I was amazed at my friend's patience.

Shahji fell asleep after his angry outburst. 'Are we not going to your *didi's* house, Indranath?' I asked. He replied that we were already in *didi's* house. I was bewildered. How could *didi* be in the house of a Muslim snake-charmer? Concealing his agony, Indranath said that some day he would tell me the whole story. Changing the subject, he asked whether I would like to see the snakes dancing. I tried to stop him, but he darted into the adjoining room and returned with a basket and a *been*. He started playing a tune on the *been* and lifted the lid of the basket. A large cobra came out of the basket, struck viciously at Indra's hand, and slipped away.

Indra was taken by surprise. 'This is not the snake I used to play with,' he said. 'This cobra is altogether wild.' At that very moment, he saw *didi* entering the room and warned her to stay at a distance as the snake was hiding somewhere. I turned my head and looked at her. She seemed to have emerged after years of asceticism, so pale was her face. She carried a bundle of dry firewood under her left arm and a small basket of vegetables in her right hand. She was wearing an ochre-coloured robe in the Muslim style. Putting down the bundle of firewood she asked us why we were excited. Indra told her what had happened.

'Don't worry,' she said, 'I will catch him.'

Indra blocked her way and said: 'No, *didi*, I won't let you take the risk. Let us wake up Shahji.'

She thanked Indranath for his love and concern. I could see that her eyes were moist. But she controlled her emotion and said: 'Alas, I am not so lucky. No cobra is going to bite me.' Within a few minutes, she caught the snake and put him back in the basket. Indra bent down and touched her feet. 'If only you had been my sister!' he said. *Didi* touched his chin with the fingers of her right hand and kissed those fingers. When she turned her head I knew she was hiding her face. There were tears in her eyes.

V

Didi chided Indranath for playing with a wild, poisonous snake. 'I had protected myself,' he said with a chuckle. Untying his waist cloth he brought out the dried root of a jungle shrub. He was like a child displaying a new toy. 'I am not a fool, *didi*,' he said. 'I don't mess around with snakes without protecting myself with this root which Shahji has given me. No snake will bite a person carrying this root. And even if I had been bitten, Shahji would have removed the poison with his *bezoar*, which is an unfailing antidote. Tell me, *didi*, how long does it take for the *bezoar* to become effective? Half an hour?'

Didi looked at him for a long time but did not say a word. Indranath implored her to give him a *bezoar*. 'You have two or three, I know,' he said. 'You *have* to give me one. I have asked you so many times. If you refuse again, I will go away and never return.' Indra was talking like a petulant child. He did not notice *didi's* embarrassment and sorrow. Forcing herself to smile, she said: 'Indra, do you come to visit your *didi* only to get the antidote?'

'What else?' said Indra peevishly. 'I have served Shahji faithfully. I have massaged his feet, filled his pipe, and have done so many other chores for him. But he has avoided giving me the *bezoar* on one pretext or another.' Then he turned towards me and said: 'Srikanta, you don't know what amazing things these people can do. Shahji may be a *ganja* addict, but he has supernatural powers. He can bring a corpse back to life. *Didi*, can you also revive a dead man?'

Didi laughed heartily. How sweet and melodious was that laughter! Even today, when I think of her, that laughter rings in my ears. 'I am sure Shahji has given you the secret *mantra* for reviving the dead,' Indranath persisted. *Didi* shook her head in a gesture of denial. 'Well, then he must have taught you how to throw shells,' Indra said.

Didi's face was now grave. 'No, Indra,' she said, 'I don't even know what you mean by "throwing the shells".'

Indra was annoyed. 'You simply don't wish to tell me,' he said, 'I am now convinced of that. Srikanta, have you ever seen a master snake-charmer throw shells? He recites a secret *mantra* and throws two shells in the air. No snake can escape from these shells. Even if he runs far away the shells fly in pursuit and grab his head. The snake is subdued and brought back to the master's feet.'

Didi bent her head and remained quiet for a long time. Then she looked at us and said in a slow, measured tone: 'Indra, your *didi* knows absolutely nothing about all this secret lore. I will tell you the whole truth, if you are willing to believe me. It will be a relief to unburden myself.'

I had hardly spoken to *didi* upto that moment. But now I felt impelled to speak. '*Didi*,' I said, 'I will believe every word that you utter.'

'Of course you will, Srikanta. And so will Indranath. You boys are from respectable families. Now listen carefully. All this talk about supernatural powers is pure nonsense. Our profession is based on deception. Please, Indra, don't waste your time in the hope that Shahji will give you anything unusual. Believe me, we have no *mantra*, we cannot revive the dead, and we cannot catch snakes with miraculous shells.'

I believed *didi* implicitly, although I had known her for only a couple of hours. But Indra was suspicious. 'If you have no miraculous powers, how do you catch snakes?' he said sharply.

'It is nothing but sleight of hand,' *didi* said.

Indra was furious at this revelation. 'If you have no special powers,' he said angrily, 'why did you fleece me all these days? Why did you take my money for the magical skills you were supposed to teach?'

Didi's face was white as a sheet. 'We are snake-charmers,' she said, 'and deception is an inseparable part of the way we earn our livelihood.' Indranath caught hold of my right hand and started pulling me towards the door. 'Come, Srikanta,' he said, 'even the shadow of such rascals is sinful.' I took out the money which he had asked me to bring and offered it to *didi*.

But Indra pounced upon the money. 'These people have taken a lot of money from me,' he shrieked, 'now let them starve to death.'

I pressed his hand gently and said, 'No, Indra, you must not speak to *didi* in this way. Let me give these five rupees to her.'

Meanwhile, Shahji had emerged from his stupor. Indra abused him violently and threatened to thrash him if he dared to pass through the village again. 'You cheat!,' he thundered, 'you have no secret powers. Why did you take my money?' Shahji winced and asked, 'Who told you that I have no powers?'

Indra pointed to *didi*. Shahji's eyes were burning like coal. When I looked into those eyes, I realized what a dangerous man he was. Clutching his dishevelled hair, he lunged towards *didi*. Indranath was so angry that he ignored the threat to *didi* and made for the door, dragging me with him. We had hardly gone a few paces outside the house when we heard a heart-rending shriek. Indra dashed back into the house. I would have gone with him had I not tripped and fallen into a thorny bush.

When I went inside I found *didi* lying unconscious in a corner while Indra and Shahji were at each other's throats. Shahji had a lot of strength, in spite of his frail body. But Indra knocked him down and was choking him when I intervened. Indra was bleeding. Shahji had wounded him with a spear. With my help, Indra tied his hands. 'Just look at this scoundrel,' Indra said, 'I stole money from my own parents and gave it to him. And he repays me with a spear-thrust.'

Indra sprinkled water on *didi's* face and brought her round. She untied Shahji and helped him into the other room where he fell asleep. Then she asked Indra to promise that he would never return to the hut again. 'That's justice for you!' Indra shouted. 'He almost killed me, but you don't say a word to him. I merely tied his hands and you ask me not to return. You are ungrateful wretches, both of you.' *Didi* did not utter a word. Before going out of the house I left the money at the door.

Indra was still muttering: 'A Hindu girl who runs away with a Muslim cheat, has no caste, no religion. Let her go to hell. I am not going to bother about her any more.' We reached the river. Indra started rowing. I saw him wipe his eyes from time to time. I let him weep in silence. As we passed by the cremation ground I did not even feel afraid, as I always did. Nor did I think of the punishment that awaited me at home. The night was almost over when our boat touched the ghat. 'Go home, Srikanta,' Indra said. 'You bring bad luck. Whenever I take you with me, something goes wrong. Go, and don't come to me again.' Indra pushed the boat back into the river and started rowing. I stood alone on the bank for a while, bewildered and saddened, until Indranath's boat faded out of sight.

VI

I was deeply hurt. Indra had judged me as a worthless fellow, as one who brought ill fortune. I had defied the folks at home and given of my friendship wholeheartedly. And yet he could be so harsh and leave me alone on a deserted river-bank on a dark night. For a long time I tried to forget him and avoided him when I saw him from a distance. One evening the local theatre enthusiasts were staging *Meghnad-vadh* to celebrate some festival. I watched with bated breath when Lakshmana and Meghnad performed incredible deeds of valour on the stage. Suddenly I felt a finger prodding me in the back. It was Indranath.

'Come with me, Srikanta,' he whispered. '*Didi* is calling you.'

'*Didi*! Where is she?'

'Come outside, I will tell you.'

We hardly exchanged more than a few sentences as we walked up to the river, got into the boat, and once again took the jungle path leading to Shahji's hut. By the dim light of an oil lamp we saw *didi* sitting on the mat with Shahji's head in her lap.

Didi told us about Shahji's last hours. A rich man sent for
him to catch a snake hiding in his house. Shahji succeeded and
was rewarded handsomely. He spent the money on liquor and
returned home late at night completely drunk. In that condition
he started to play with the snakes. She tried to stop him. But
he did not listen. Lifting a cobra by the tail he tried to kiss it,
when he was bitten. Shahji knew that he would not survive.
'Let's go together, my dear fellow,' he said as he crushed the
cobra's head under his heel. Within minutes he collapsed.
Having described in detail Shahji's death, she gently lifted the
cloth from his face and touched his lips which had turned dark
blue. We sat in silence for a while, all three of us.

'You are mere boys,' *didi* said after she had regained the
strength to speak, 'but I have no one else whom I can call my
own. Please do something for him. There is a small piece of
level ground which I have always regarded as my place of
eternal sleep. Take him there. He suffered in life. Now let him
get some peace.' As Shahji was a Muslim, he must be buried.
At the break of dawn, Indra went to the place described by
didi and dug a grave. When he returned, the three of them
carried Shahji's body there and laid him to rest. It was a place
one seeks for hiding something precious. The Ganga flowed
only a few yards below Shahji's grave, shaded by wild creepers.

We sat there with heavy hearts listening to the murmur of
the river and the chirping of birds. Suddenly, *didi* lamented
loudly and rolled on the grave. 'O Mother Ganga!' she cried,
'be kind to me. Give me shelter. I have nowhere else to go.'
Indranath placed *didi's* head in his lap and tried to comfort
and soothe her. 'You have to come to my house, *Didi*,' he
said. 'My mother is still alive. She will welcome you.'

Didi remained dazed for some time. Then she stood up
determinedly. We went down to the river and bathed. *Didi*
broke the bangles on her wrists, wiped off the *sindoor* from her
forehead, and returned to the hut in the garb of a Hindu
widow. For the first time she told us that Shahji was her
husband. 'I am a Brahmin,' she said, 'and so was he. When he
became a Muslim I too had to do the same. A wife is a

companion in religion as in all other things. I never gave up my caste through my own choice or preference. Nor have I ever done anything immoral.'

Indra again tried to persuade her to accompany him. *Didi* said she could not go anywhere until she had paid Shahji's debts.

'Debts to whom?,' Indranath said impatiently. 'To those who sold him liquor and marijuana? You are not responsible for such debts. Come with me. No one can stop you.'

Didi smiled. 'You are such a child, Indra,' she said. 'What is stopping me is my own *dharma*. My husband's debts are my debts. I will sell off whatever I possess and try to clear the debts.'

I told *didi* that I had a few rupees at home which I could easily bring her.

'No, Srikanta,' she said. 'That is not necessary. The other day you gave me five rupees. I will never forget your kindness. I pray that god may dwell in your heart, and that you may shed tears of compassion for the sufferings of others.' She broke down and tears streamed from her eyes.

Didi came to the main road to see us off. She held Indranath's hand tightly and said, 'I have just given my blessings to Srikanta. But I dare not bless you. You are above the blessings of mere mortals. I am leaving you to God's kindness.'

Indra knelt and took the dust from her feet. '*Didi*, I don't have the heart to leave you alone in this jungle,' he said in a choked voice. 'I do not know why I have this feeling that I will never see you again.' *Didi* started walking back to the hut. We remained there, watching her receding figure. She did not look back.

A few days later, when I went to the school in the morning, I found Indranath waiting for me outside the gate. He was covered with dust and looked haggard. I was frightened by his appearance. '*Didi* is gone,' he said, 'she has simply vanished since yesterday. She has left this letter for you.' He handed me a crumpled, yellowing sheet of paper. Indra was so grief-stricken that he walked away without speaking to me further.

I cannot remember everything that *didi* wrote in that long letter. I will write whatever I can recall:

'Srikanta, I give both of you my blessings just before I leave. Do not grieve for me. And ask Indranath not to search for me. Today you may not be able to understand everything that I am about to write. But when you grow up many things will become clear to you. I wanted to tell you my true story long ago. But I did not have the courage to do so. The weight of sins accumulated in my former life is already very heavy. I did not want to add to it by condemning my own husband. Now he has left this world. But his passing away has not made it easier for me to speak ill of him. And yet I cannot bid farewell without telling you about my unfortunate life.

Srikanta, my name is Annada. The reason for concealing my husband's name will become clear to you later. My father was a respectable, well-to-do man. I had no brother, only a sister. Shortly after her marriage, my sister became a widow. She returned to stay with my father. He selected a promising young man from a poor family as a match for me. Father wanted to educate my husband and give him a good start in life. One day my husband murdered my sister and disappeared. You can easily guess why he committed that ghastly crime. Srikanta, can you imagine my agony and my shame? My only sister had been dishonoured and killed by the man to whom I was bound by the vows of matrimony.

The anguish in my heart has burnt slowly like a flame all those years. Even then, I was loyal to him and endured my sufferings patiently. I saw him again seven years later in the snake-charmer's garb with which you are familiar. He was playing on his *been* and making snakes dance on the street right in front of my house. No one else recognized him. But my eyes were not deceived. I jumped out of the bedroom window and left my home for the sake of my husband.

My disappearance was soon the talk of the town. I have had to carry the burden of notoriety all my life. My father could never forgive the murderer of his daughter. The door of my parents' house was shut for me forever. I have repaid my

husband's debts by selling the gold earrings that I had. The
five rupees you gave me have been deposited with the grocer
whom you know. I have returned your money. But I am taking
with me your tender, loving heart.

Now I have only one request to make: do not be unhappy
because of me. Your *didi* is now beyond sorrow. She will be
all right. Sorrow no longer touches her. I do not know with
what words I should bless you. So I will say only this: if God
is really a friend of the pure-minded, let Him make the
friendship between you and Indranath unshakeable.'

VII

I went to the grocer's shop. He returned my five rupees and
told me that Annada *didi* had only half a rupee left after
paying back Shahji's debts. That lonely, helpless woman had
gone forth into the wide world with a few nickels and coppers
as her total assets. She had left no trace behind because she
wanted to save two affectionate boys the trouble of looking for
her. She deprived me of the pleasure of giving her a small
amount of money. Why was she so harsh? But then, in what
way had I earned the privilege of helping her? On calmer
reflection I realized that Indranath and I had not been fashioned
from the same metal. How could I aspire to do for Annada
didi what he had done?

I never saw her again. But in my imagination Annada *didi's*
gentle face comes before me repeatedly. When I think of her
character, and inwardly pay homage to her, I cannot help
exclaiming: 'O God! In this country, in my India which has
produced great women like Sita and Savitri, you have crowned
with glory those who sacrificed themselves for the sake of their
husbands. Why, then, was my Annada *didi* disgraced? Why did
you permit the world to stamp her as unchaste? O God! She
was deprived of her home, her religion, her self-respect. Was
that not enough? Had she not been subjected to more than
her share of suffering? Was it really necessary to burden her
with the shame of being remembered as a fallen woman?'

For a long time after Annada *didi's* disappearance, I used to
find Indranath's boat tied up whenever I was by the river
bank. We were destined to row that boat only once again. And
what an experience that was! It was a bitter cold evening. The
sky was bathed in moonlight. There had been heavy showers
a day earlier and the wind seemed to penetrate our bones. As
I stood looking at the river, Indra suddenly turned up and
asked me whether I would go with him to see a play. I was
excited at the prospect and agreed to accompany him. The
place where the play was to be performed could be reached by
train, but Indra insisted on going by boat. I was surprised by
his decision. I thought we might not reach our destination on
time as we would have to row against the current. 'Don't
worry,' Indra said, 'the wind is in our favour. My cousin has
come from Calcutta and will join us. He rows very well.'

We put up the sail, fixed the oars, and waited. The cousin
was late. And when he finally arrived, I was scared. He was a
dandy and put on a superior air. He wore silk socks, shiny
pump shoes and soft gloves. A fancy overcoat draped him from
neck to knee. There was a scarf around his neck and a tilted
cap on his head. He looked at our boat with contempt, making
it obvious that he was doing us a big favour by agreeing to set
foot in such a crude contraption.

The worthy cousin climbed into the boat leaning on Indra's
shoulder for support, while he gripped my hand firmly. When
he was comfortably seated he asked my name. When I told
him it was Srikanta he decided that it was too troublesome for
him to pronounce it. So he called me 'Kant' throughout the
journey, and ordered me around as though I were his servant.
I obeyed him out of consideration for Indranath. I even filled
his hookah. As he took the hookah from me he remarked that
my woollen wrap smelt of stale oil.

The wind had stopped. Rowing against the current was
strenuous. The great cousin from Calcutta was displeased. He
simply had to be there on time, he said, as there was no one
else who could play the harmonium. Ultimately, we had to
drag the boat with a rope. The cousin sat puffing at his hookah

while we were in knee-deep water, chilled to the bone. Indra requested him to hold the oars for a moment. He refused angrily. It was too cold to take off his gloves, he said, and the gloves were too expensive to be pressed against rough-grained wood. Never have I seen such an utterly selfish human being.

The cold air made him hungry. He sent us to the village in search of food. It was midnight when we got there. People were fast asleep; no one was willing to open their door and give us food. Returning empty-handed to the boat, we found that the cousin had vanished. Stories had been heard about man-eating tigers in that area. We looked for him in vain on the sandy bank. When we found one of his shoes in the sand, we became extremely anxious. A little later we heard the barking of dogs. Following the sound, we reached a bend in the river, and there we saw Indranath's cousin standing in neck-deep water.

On the bank, dogs were barking at him and threatening him. Our guest's teeth were chattering, more from fear than cold. We drove the dogs away and rescued him. As soon as we were on dry land he bewailed the loss of one of his shoes. We assured him that the precious commodity had already been recovered. We managed to escort him back to the boat. He had to discard his wet clothes and wrap his shivering body in my woollen shawl—the very shawl which had earlier offended his nostrils by its odour of stale oil.

VIII

I have often wondered who has put together the scattered images which I am trying to reproduce. Events have not always occurred in the order in which I am recording them. Why, then, do they not appear chaotic? Many links have dropped, and yet the chain seems unbroken. Who fills up the gaps? It is a mystery.

There is something else that amazes me. It is usually believed that small things are pushed out or crushed under the pressure of big, important things. Yet I find that apparently trifling

things have occupied most of the places of honour in the
shrine of my memory, while weighty matters have been elbowed
out and have received very little attention. I cannot explain
why this happens. Perhaps small matters and unimportant events
grow in stature, unknown to me, through a slow process of
maturation. In the narrative which follows, the reader will get
a few glimpses of this process.

Many years had passed since I lost track of Indranath. Even
the images associated with Annada *didi* were gradually becoming
faint. One day I was invited to join a hunting expedition. My
host, a class-fellow of mine from school, belonged to a princely
family. Our friendship at school was based on the fact that I
used to help him with his homework and save him from the
teacher's cane. After the pre-university examination we went
our separate ways. Those who inherit large estates have
proverbially short memories of boyhood companions coming
from poor families. But when I ran into the prince, quite by
chance, he not only recognized me but also went out of his
way to treat me very cordially. Some mutual friend had told
him that I could handle a rifle with considerable skill. So he
invited me and I agreed to join his hunting party. On the
appointed day I went by train part of the way and then
proceeded to the camp on an elephant which the prince had
provided. I was tired after the twelve-mile elephant ride.

The camp was impressive. Apart from my host's own
luxurious tent there were separate tents for the servants, for
the cooking establishment and for the hunting equipment and
the guides. At some distance there was a separate camp for
two courtesans, with a portion set aside for musicians,
drummers and various musical instruments. When I entered
the prince's tent in the evening, a music and dance recital
had been in progress for some time. The prince greeted me
with genuine affection. As soon as he saw me, he appeared
to rise as if to welcome me, but then he reclined on the silk
cushions again.

My arrival had interrupted the music. When I settled down,
the prince asked me to select the melody for the next item. I

suggested a *raga* appropriate for the hour. *Baiji*, one of the courtesans, started singing. The prince had invited *Baiji* from Patna for two weeks. I was struck by her attractive face and graceful bearing. She sang the melody selected by me with evident pleasure. She seemed happy to have in her audience some one familiar with the subtleties of classical music. Thus far she had been singing merely because she was paid for it. Now she put her heart into the song. Her expression was natural and pleasant. Her gestures were refined and evocative. She had a superb voice. And she knew how to make the best use of her rich voice in conveying subtle shades of emotion. I listened to Peyari—that was *Baiji's* name—with rapt attention. It was a banquet for my ears. When she completed her exposition of the *raga*, I applauded enthusiastically. Other members of Peyari *Baiji's* audience were either drunk or asleep.

She bent her head to acknowledge my applause and smiled. Touching her forehead with folded hands she greeted me in the traditional Hindu style instead of offering the salaam as such singers usually do. When she was about to leave I approached her and said: '*Baiji*, I am truly fortunate. I will hear your wonderful music for two whole weeks.' Her reply was so unexpected that I was taken by surprise. 'You know that I have to sing because I am paid for it,' she said. 'But you are a free man. You don't have to spend two weeks in the company of these servile courtiers. Go back home tomorrow.' I did not know what to make of her words, having just met her.

The next day was spent in hunting, if one can describe killing birds with a shotgun as a 'hunt'. I declared that I was not interested in that kind of 'sport' and returned to my tent. I had just ordered a cup of tea and lit a cigarette when a servant brought the message that *Baiji* wanted to see me. The messenger told me that he was *Baiji's khansama* and that his name was Ratan.

I followed him to Peyari's tent. She looked entirely different from the woman I had seen the previous evening. At the concert she was wearing a *peshwaz*. Now she was dressed in a sari of raw silk. With her long, wet hair spread over her back she looked like a typical Bengali girl. She was sitting on a rug with her legs crossed. The paraphernalia of betel-leaf and *hookah* were near her.

She invited me to sit on a small carpet in front of her. 'I will not smoke in your presence,' she said. 'Nor will I offer you the *hookah*, though I know you do smoke sometimes. Be comfortable. There is much to talk about.' She enquired about my family. When I told her that I had lost both my parents, she said, 'So, you must now be staying with your Pishima. Have you completed your studies? I can see that you are not married.' Her eyes were glistening. Her tone was serious, although she had been almost jovial a few moments earlier.

Concealing my embarrassment I asked, 'Who are you? I don't recall having met you. And what can you possibly gain by knowing about my personal life?'

She was not offended by my curtness. 'Is gain everything?' she asked with a smile. 'Is there no such thing as affection, love? My name is Peyari. But as you have not recognized my face, I should perhaps tell you the nickname by which I was called as a child. Even that may not mean anything to you.'

I asked the name of her village. She said nothing. I asked her father's name. She bit her tongue and said, 'He is in heaven. How can I utter his name with my polluted lips?'

'But how did you recognize me?'

'There was a time when you made me cry every day. My tears would have formed a lake if the Sun God had not dried them up. Can you believe this?'

No, I did not believe what she said. And I was a bit put off by her mocking smile.

She guessed my thoughts. 'Don't be offended,' she said, 'if I seem to laugh when I speak. It is just a mannerism. But tell me, what is an intelligent man like you doing in this company of flunkeys.'

'It is better than doing nothing,' I said, controlling my irritation. 'But I should be leaving now, people might imagine things.'

'Would it be such a calamity?' she said ironically. 'And don't forget what I told you about the tears you made me shed.'

Confused and annoyed, I returned to my tent. Who is this woman? How does she know all these details about my life? What does she want from me? Obviously, she is not after money. She knows I am not rich. Such thoughts disturbed me. During the next three or four days I excused myself from the hunt on the pretext of being unwell. I saw Peyari every evening at the music recital. She tried to catch my attention but I avoided her gaze. She made some bantering remarks aimed at me indirectly. But when she saw that I resented those remarks she become discreet. On the day of my departure, the music programme was arranged for the morning. Peyari gave a wonderful rendering of a morning *raga*.

Somehow the conversation turned to the subject of ghosts and other nocturnal beings. An old gentleman, who had been telling all kinds of weird stories, said in an offended tone: 'They learn a little English and become unbelievers. There are people in the village nearby who have seen spirits of the dead with their own eyes. Anyone who goes to the cremation ground tonight can verify the existence of ghosts.'

The old gentleman challenged me to go there at midnight, and proceeded to describe the sights that awaited me: dancing vampires, heaps of skulls and so on. 'Even Englishmen are known to have run away from that spot in terror,' he added for emphasis. They all thought I would back down or, if I actually went to the cremation ground at midnight, I'd die of fright. There were satirical comments when I said that I would carry a gun. 'Bravo!' said one, 'he does not shoot birds. He keeps his gun for ghosts.' Only one person in that group, a middle-aged man named Purushottam, offered to accompany me. 'You may take the gun if you wish,' he said, 'but actually my stick is enough. Neither ghost nor goblin will come near us as long as we have this stick to protect us.'

Brave words! But when I came out of the tent an hour before midnight, I was trembling with fear. It was pitch dark.

I remembered Indranath's words: repeat the holy name of
Rama, and no harm will come to you. Indra believed in the
existence of ghosts. I thought I didn't. But perhaps my
scepticism was not very deep, after all. These musings were
interrupted by Ratan, who said that *Baiji* wanted to see me at
once. I did not like this midnight invitation. But I checked
myself in the servant's presence and told him that I would see
her in the morning.

Ratan's manners were perfect. A servant of the old school,
he bowed respectfully and said: 'Please, Sir. She needs you
urgently. If you don't go, she will come here. Please don't
refuse.' I did not want Peyari Bai to come to my tent at that
late hour. So I followed Ratan. As soon as she saw me Peyari
said: 'What is all this talk about going to a haunted cremation
ground at midnight? Can anyone return safely from a place
like that? I will not let you go.' There were tears in her eyes.
I was taken aback. A woman I did not know was weeping at
the thought that I might be in danger. 'Will you never grow
up?' she said, wiping her tears. 'If you insist on going, I will
come with you.' And she picked up a shawl.

'Very well, let's go together,' I taunted.

'That would be just wonderful for your reputation, would
it not?' she said sharply. 'The gentleman comes to hunt wild
animals but sets out with a courtesan at midnight looking for
ghosts. Have you lost all sense of shame? You were not like
this.'

'Why talk of reputation?' I said. 'Who could have imagined
that you would become a courtesan.'

I started walking away. She blocked my way and repeated
that she would not allow me to go to the cremation ground.
I could not help laughing at the ridiculous situation. 'I have
never believed in ghosts,' I said, 'but I am beginning to wonder
if you are a ghost yourself.'

My remark startled her. 'So you have recognized me,' she
said, 'and you think that I am a ghost because I have apparently
come back from the land of the departed. But believe me, it
was not I who spread the rumour about my death.'

As soon as I heard these words, the door of my memory was suddenly flung open. I recognized her completely. Events forgotten since my school days came back to me with incredible vividness. This was Rajalakshmi, a childhood friend. She had gone with her mother on a pilgrimage. The mother returned and announced that Rajalakshmi had died of cholera. I recalled that even as a child she used to bite her lips when she was sad. Even after all these years she had retained that habit. But could Peyari Bai, the famous courtesan, really be Rajalakshmi, the little girl I knew at school? I now remembered all the details about her family.

Rajalakshmi was nine at the time. Her elder sister, Suralakshmi, was thirteen. Their father had left their mother and taken another wife. The mother found grooms for the girls. The two sisters were married on the same day. It was not long before the two husbands collected their dowries and disappeared. The mother somehow supported the two daughters, enduring the taunts of all the respectable people in the town. Two years later the elder daughter died of hepatitis. And a year after that Rajalakshmi also—so we were told—had died at Banaras. The episode was soon forgotten. The mother had returned from Banaras alone. When she announced her daughter's death, it never occurred to anyone to question her report. There was no reason to doubt her.

When Rajalakshmi was in my class I had somehow acquired a great hold upon her. She used to obey me without questioning. I often asked her to collect berries from the forest and weave them into a garland for me. If any garland was short of the required length, I would slap her. She cried. But next morning she was again in the forest collecting berries. It was not easy for her to get away from home. But she did not complain. At that time I thought that she obeyed me from fear. Now I know better.

I was thinking about those childhood days when Rajalakshmi interrupted me. She said: 'Shall I tell you what you have been thinking of during the past ten minutes?'

'What?' I asked, emerging from my reverie.

'This is what you were thinking: "Oh, now much have I tortured her in childhood! How harsh was I in making her gather berries for me, and how cruelly I used to beat her! Today she is requesting me not to go looking for ghosts. Surely I ought to respect her wishes." Tell me truly, weren't these your thoughts?'

I smiled at her cleverness. Peyari coaxed me into staying with her for a while. Ratan took off my boots. I sat on the carpet by her side. She again talked about our school days.

'You women know how to cast a spell and control a man,' I said in jest.

'Spells are cast on strangers,' she said. 'How can I hope to influence someone whose power I have felt since I was a little girl? Do you think I was afraid of you when I gathered those berries for you in the scorching heat? Rajalakshmi is not a person to fear anyone. I have treasured those berry-gathering moments all my life. And you? It has taken you such a long time even to recognize me.'

It was nearly midnight, time for me to leave for the cremation ground. She made no further attempts to stop me. . . . 'If something happens to you,' she said, 'these princes and courtiers will not help you. Perhaps you think you are being very masculine by being indifferent to me. But I have a woman's heart. I will be there in your hour of trouble.'

'There is no one whom I can call my very own,' I said, 'and it is comforting to know that there is at least a woman who will not desert me.'

'I will never abandon you. I wish I could. That would have taught you a lesson. But women are like that. Once they love some one they are committed.' She turned her face. Even in the dim light I could see that she was concealing her tears.

I was engrossed in thoughts of Peyari as I crossed the mango grove and went towards the river. I could never have suspected that the school girl who gathered berries for me was weaving a garland for my worship. Even more amazing was the revelation that she had retained this childhood crush through all these years, through all her other relationships as a song-and-dance girl. She was, after all, a courtesan. Where did she find the emotional nourishment to sustain such unwavering love?

My musings were interrupted rudely by a low, piteous cry which came from the overhanging branches. I looked up and saw hundreds of vultures perched motionless on the top branches of several silk-cotton trees. One of the baby vultures, separated from its mother, had uttered the frightened moan which had startled me. My midnight *sojourn* in that awesome land of death was full of terrifying experiences. The uncanny sense of danger never left me. I imagined that someone was pursuing me, and I could feel his breath upon my neck. It was so dark that every object I approached assumed a weird shape. I heard eerie sighs, and laughter that was agonizing in its very strangeness. But nothing shook me up as powerfully as the wail of that baby vulture.

I prayed that a tiger or a bear should appear, as it would have been a relief to see something terrestrial. Unexpectedly, a human voice was heard. Someone was calling me. 'Please do not shoot,' said the voice. 'I am Ratan, *Baiji*'s servant.' I wanted to shout with joy but words failed to come out of my throat. Anxious for my safety, Peyari had sent Ratan, along with a watchman, to find me.

They were offered a reward of three months' extra wages. When we approached the tents, Ratan urged me to visit Peyari and relieve her of her anxiety. But I said I would see her in the morning before returning home, and hurriedly went back to my tent.

IX

With these very eyes of mine I once saw Annada *didi*. How many times, on lonely nights, have I not said: 'Dear Annada *didi*, where are you? You touched me with your heart and turned into gold that which was iron in me. I wish I could share your magical power with others. If only I could get, like Devi Chaudhurani, seven jars of gold, I would build a throne for Annada *didi*. And I would clear a portion of the forest to make an open-air pavilion so that people from all over the country can come and sit around Annada *didi's* throne.' And yet today, Srikanta was stirred by the sight of another woman's tears.

Can there be any comparison between this woman and the ascetic Annada *didi*? A week ago I could not have imagined caring for another woman. But the fact is that I cannot resist the lure of shining brass, despite Annada *didi*. The reader may well exclaim: 'Enough of this circumlocution! Why don't you say plainly that Peyari's pretty face is causing your heart to throb? Once you turned her away from the doorstep of your mind. Today you are inviting her into the inner chamber of your heart.' I can only reply that I am not a hypocrite. I admit my weakness, although I cannot understand it.

The prince sent for me in the morning. Everyone was eager to hear about my nocturnal adventure. The prince and all the members of his entourage congratulated me and lauded me for my courage. When I gave them an account of my experiences, the old gentleman who had challenged me said: 'You are a pure-minded Brahmin. That is why you returned safely from that horrible place. I salute your parents. Their blessings have saved you.' After expressing his appreciation in this way, he bent down and touched my feet. Unknown to me, Peyari had come quietly and heard the old gentleman's compliments. I could see on her fair cheeks furrows caused by tears. She wiped her eyes, salaamed the prince, and left without a word.

She had given up her bantering, ironical tone and had become serious. She was also sad, but her sadness, I must confess, did not cause me pain. On the contrary, I was happy that she cared for me so much. She had not taken my indifference as an affront but as the feigned unconcern of a man whose love she had kindled. Unlike all the others in that camp, she abstained from praising me. She was sulking. She should have been the first to hear an account of my adventure. But she was actually the last. Yes, she was sulking; and for the first time in my life I realized how sweet it can be to watch someone sulk. I savoured the experience like a child tasting a new sort of candy.

Alone in my tent, I hoped that Ratan would bring a message from Peyari that night. But how was I to pass the afternoon? Not far from the camp there was an old reservoir. No one seemed to know when it was built and by whom. I walked over to that tank and sat on one of its crumbling walls. After sunset the water in that old tank looked black like ink. Two thirsty jackals came, drank their fill, and went away. I have no idea how long I sat there. It must have been after midnight when I got up and started walking. But where was I going? Where were the camp lights? I was going on and on. The narrow path seemed endless. I was advancing like one in a trance—beyond the cluster of tamarind trees, towards the dark horizon. When I stopped, I found myself on an embankment. The river was below me. And on the other side of the embankment lay the land of death. I had come back to the cremation ground.

X

As I sat on that embankment I realized that the night had its own shape and form. I discovered that the beauty of the night could be observed separately from other phenomena of nature such as mountains, forests and lakes. I saw Night as a maiden sitting in meditation with eyes closed. Beauty surged all around me. How clever must be the liar, I thought, who established the notion that only light has beauty, not darkness. How did the world swallow such blatantly false propaganda? O Darkness, you who pervade heaven and earth, the sky and the nether regions, I bow to you. You are incomparable. You are a cataract of loveliness.

All that is deep, limitless and inscrutable in the universe is enveloped in darkness. The unfathomable ocean is dark. So is the impenetrable forest. Dark, too, is that Supreme Person who is the source of all movement, life and beauty. And Krishna, whose adorable form flows out of Radha's eyes and inundates the world—he, too, is dark like a cloud. The strangest part was that I experienced this intimate feeling for the beauty of darkness sitting near the crematorium. It suddenly occurred to me that Death itself has been unjustly condemned. When it comes for me, Death may well dazzle me by its beauty. Why, then, should I hesitate to visit Death's favourite abode, the cremation ground? Why should I not step right inside it?

I got up, entered the cremation ground, and sat down there. I cannot now recollect how long I sat there and when I fell asleep. When I woke up, darkness was receding. Shukra shone in lonely splendour in a corner of the sky. Behind the silk-cotton trees some people were crossing the embankment. They carried lanterns in their hands. I walked towards them and saw two ox-carts at some distance. Someone called me. It was Ratan who had once again been sent to look for me. I approached one of the ox-carts. Drawing the curtain aside, Peyari peeped out and asked me to step inside. I said I wanted to return to the camp as soon as possible. She gripped my right hand firmly and said: 'Don't make a scene in the presence of servants. Come inside, I beseech you.'

I listened to her and climbed into the cart. 'Why did you come here again?' she asked in a sharp voice.

'I did not come of my own free will,' I said. 'Some unknown force dragged me towards the cremation ground. You may not believe me, Rajalakshmi, but I am speaking the truth. I do not have any idea why I came, or how, or when.'

She released my hand and touched my feet. 'I will not allow you to return to the prince's camp,' she said. 'Nor will I take you with me. I will buy you a train ticket and send you home.'

The cart came to a bend in the road and turned. I faced the east. The sun was rising. It seemed to me that the eastern horizon was not unlike the heart of this supposedly 'fallen' woman. In both, a resplendent ball of fire was bursting forth from a veil of darkness. Rajalakshmi removed the ring from her finger and placed it at my feet. Then she lifted up the ring, touched her forehead with it, and slipped it into my pocket.

'I will allow you to go back to the camp now,' she said, 'only if you promise not to spend the night there. Collect your things from the tent and go home.'

I promised to do as she had asked. I got out of the cart and walked quickly on the dusty road leading to my tent. I did not turn round. But I could feel two moist eyes following me. When I reached the camp, I found that Peyari's tent had been dismantled. She was also preparing to go away. I felt a strange sense of dejection.

XI

Rajalakshmi had made me promise that I would write to her as soon as possible after reaching home. I kept my promise. A few days later I received a pleasant reply to my letter. She did not write anything about her house at Patna. Nor did she invite me to visit her. But the concluding sentence of her letter moved me deeply: 'If not in times of happiness, think of me at least in moments of sorrow. This is my only prayer to you.'

It was the night of the Holi festival. I had returned home drenched with coloured water. I lay in bed, exhausted. The mellow night of the full moon filtered into the room through the branches of a large peepul tree. Suddenly, I felt suffocated. An uncontrollable impulse pushed me out of the house. I went to the railway-station, purchased a ticket and boarded the night train to Patna. On another strange impulse, I got off at a station not far from Patna. I felt my pockets and found that I had only a few coins left. With half of these I ate a meal of rice-flakes and curd at a shop outside the station. Then I wandered aimlessly until I came to a mango orchard.

A *sanyasi* had set up an ashram deep inside the orchard. I went there and saw the Babaji sitting near a fire his eyes half-closed. The ashram was full of activities. Water was being heated in a large brass pot. A hermit boy was milking a goat. A camel, two mules, a cow and a calf were tied to trees nearby. A disciple, a young man about my age, was pounding marijuana leaves with a stone pestle. I touched the holy man's feet and thanked God for guiding me to his ashram. Why bother about Peyari *Baiji* now that the doorway to liberation had been flung open for me?

Within a couple of days I won Babaji's favour. I was given an ochre robe and several bead necklaces. Dressed in my hermit's attire, I rubbed ash over my face. Then I asked for a mirror. A disciple brought an old mirror with a tin frame. When I looked at my face I was amused at my transformation. Could this be the same Srikanta who, not so long ago, lolled on silk cushions in a prince's luxurious tent and enjoyed a courtesan's erotic songs?

Babaji had decided to move to Prayag. On the way we stopped at Arrah, a small town in western Bihar. We were to stay there only for a few days. But before we could resume our journey, an epidemic of smallpox broke out. People started leaving Arrah in panic. We nursed many sick people and miraculous cures were attributed to Babaji's spiritual powers. One day I felt severe pain all over my body. Within a few hours I was down with high fever. I was staying at the house of Ram Babu, whose two sons had been cured through Babaji's blessings. Ram Babu looked after me as long as he could. But eventually he had to go away with his family. I was on the street again.

I trudged a long distance and then sought shelter in one of the bullock-carts on the highway. Seeing my condition, an old gentleman took me into his cart and dropped me near the railway station, in the shade of a tree. He introduced me to a young man from the station who agreed to help me. He carried me to an abandoned inn and offered to inform my relatives about my illness. I hesitated to let him spend money for me. But I was getting weaker every hour and finally accepted his offer. I requested him to send a telegram to Rajalakshmi at Patna. I must have fainted shortly after that.

When I regained consciousness, my first sensation was that of an ice-bag on my forehead. I opened my eyes and found myself lying on a cot. On a small table near the cot there was a lamp and a few medicine bottles. There was another improvised bed near mine on which a young man was reclining.

After some time he got up. Someone sitting behind me asked the young man to give me one of the medicines. It was Rajalakshmi's voice.

'Why don't you sleep for a little while, Mother,' the young man said. 'The doctor has assured us that it is not smallpox. You should stop worrying.'

Peyari said: 'Banku, do you think that a woman's anxiety can be allayed by a doctor's words? Change the ice-bag and go to sleep.'

I called Peyari in a voice that had become woefully faint. She wiped my forehead with her sari and bent down until her face was close to mine. I asked her where I was.

'We are still in Arrah. But tomorrow I am going to take you home to Patna.'

'Who is this lad, Rajalakshmi?'

'He is Banku, my adopted son. He stays with me at Patna and studies in a college. But you must not strain yourself by talking. I will tell you everything tomorrow.'

She placed her hand on my mouth and silenced me. I pressed her other hand with mine, turned on one side and went to sleep.

XII

The doctor's diagnosis was correct. My disease had an impressive medical name. But it was not smallpox. Next morning Peyari sent Banku to the railway station to reserve seats for Patna. I called her. She came near me, pressed my forehead with her hand, and said: 'There is no fever now. In a few days this ailment will be a thing of the past. But what about your real illness?' I asked her what she meant by my 'real illness'.

'To think one thing, say another thing, and do something else again—that has been your real illness ever since I have known you. Whatever else you may be, a hermit you are not. Then why this craze about becoming the disciple of a *sanyasi*? You were sleeping on a torn piece of sack-cloth, covered with dust from head to foot. Your head, with its knotted hair,

looked like a gnarled tree top. I writhed in agony when I saw
the state you were in.' She could hardly restrain her tears when
she said this.

We left Arrah the same evening. A doctor escorted us to
Patna. Rajalakshmi nursed me back to health in a couple of
weeks. When I was able to walk around I saw all the rooms in
her house and was by impressed by the combination of simplicity
and comfort. Houses of this type are usually cluttered up with
all kinds of showy things—chandeliers, overstuffed sofas, large
mirrors, glass cabinets and what not. But here every object
seemed to belong logically to the place it was in. Nothing had
been allowed to occupy any space unless it conformed to the
wishes, requirements and tastes of the mistress of the house.
I was also struck by the fact that although Peyari was a famous
singer-courtesan, there were no musical instruments or dance
costumes in the house.

After seeing the other rooms I came to a corner room on
the first floor. I peeped in. It was obviously her bedroom, but
how different from what one might have expected! Plain,
whitewashed walls; the floor made of polished white stone; a
wooden divan which served as a bed; a shelf with a few clothes;
and a steel almirah at one end of the room. I took off my shoes,
went in, and sat on the edge of the divan. A pleasant breeze was
blowing through the open window. Peyari came in, humming
a sweet tune. She was returning after a bath in the Ganges and
her clothes were still wet. She went straight to the shelf.

'Why don't you take some dry clothes with you when you
go bathing in the Ganga?' I asked.

She turned round in surprise and laughed. Then she went
into another room, changed into her dry clothes, and returned.
'Why did you sneak into my room?' she joked. 'There is nothing
worth stealing here.'

'Am I so ungrateful?' I said. 'Would I rob you after all that
you have done for me?' I saw that she had not liked my
remark, so I tried to soothe her by saying: 'Does one steal
one's own treasure?' But I had hurt her by referring to the way
she had helped me.

'You don't need to be so grateful,' she said in a sad voice. 'You sent for me in your hour of need. That act of kindness is sufficient for me.'

I was pained at the thought that I had unwittingly taken away the bloom from her fair face. Her smile was so enchanting that whenever it faded I felt as though I had suffered a great loss. To regain my lost treasure I said: 'Lakshmi, you know the true situation. If you had not arrived in time, I would have drawn my last breath on that rubbish-heap. No one would have bothered to send me to a hospital. You had asked me in your letter to think of you in times of adversity. I remembered your words because I was destined to live on this planet a little while longer.'

She recovered her good humour. 'In other words,' she said, 'you owe your life to me. In that case I suppose I have a claim upon it.'

'Why not?' I said in the same light-hearted manner. 'But it is worth so little that you will never be tempted to assert your claim.'

'Heaven be thanked,' she rejoined, 'that you have finally assessed yourself correctly. But enough of this joking. Tell me, when are you going home? You have now recovered from your illness.'

I was surprised by her question and said that I wanted to stay for a few more days. Peyari pointed out that her son might misinterpret the situation if I postponed my departure too long.

'Let him think what he likes,' I said. 'I am not one to give up such comforts so easily.' I could see that she did not like my remarks.

The next day I had a long chat with Banku. He was a fine lad and answered all my questions without any hesitation. It was obvious that he was deeply attached to his foster-mother who had arranged the marriages of his sisters and was spending a lot of money educating the children of his village. Banku told me that inspite of her generosity, orthodox villagers treated Peyari with contempt. They considered her to be an outcaste because she was a professional singer. Many of them refused to take water from the well which had been dug at her expense. Banku praised Peyari's kind and affectionate nature. When I told him that I would soon be leaving he said: 'But you are still so weak. Why do you wish to leave us? Have we done anything that has made you feel uncomfortable? Mother is so happy when you are here.' He blushed as he said this, got up, and went away. The boy is simple, I said to myself, but by no means unintelligent.

Pondering over my conversation with Banku, I realized that Rajalakshmi was no longer a free bird. She had imposed a bond upon herself, the bond of motherhood. I had noticed earlier that she did not like to be addressed as 'Peyari' in the presence of Banku. Rajalakshmi now appeared before me in a new light. Our mutual attraction was bringing us closer. At the same time the mother within her heart stood as a barrier between us. I decided to go away as soon as possible, without leaving behind any relic of desire which might give me an excuse to return.

I was restless throughout that day. In the evening she saw me sitting in the verandah. She was carrying an incense-burner. 'You will catch a cold here,' she said. 'Go inside the room and lie down!' She called Ratan and asked him to rub cologne on my temples. Poor Ratan got a big scolding for not thinking of it himself.

'I hear you are going home tomorrow,' she said. I confirmed that I was leaving. 'Very well, then. I will send someone to the railway station to get a copy of the time-table.' I wondered why she was so abrupt with me. Why does she want to get rid of me? She has self-control, intelligence, good judgment. I may not be very intelligent, but I can claim to have a certain measure of control over my feelings. I have not done anything to offend her. If she is upset because of something which she has herself done, why is she taking it out on me? This acerbity at the time of parting was painful to me.

Late at night I was awakened by the sound of footsteps. Rajalakshmi came into my room. She removed the oil lamp from the bedside table and placed it in a corner. She closed the window and approached my bed. Lifting one end of the mosquito-net gently, she placed her hand on my head and felt my temperature. She unbuttoned my shirt to feel my chest for fever and buttoned it up again. I blushed at her touch, but reminded myself that she must have touched my body several times when I was unconscious and she was looking after me. She pulled the coverlet over me, folded the mosquito-net under the mattress, tiptoed to the door and closed it gently behind her. I saw everything, understood everything. She had come secretly, and I allowed her to go away secretly. But she had no idea how much of herself she had left behind with me in the silence of the night.

Next morning I got up with fever. My eyes were burning, my mouth was dry and the entire body ached. But I had made up my mind to leave, as much for Rajalakshmi's sake as for my own. She had wiped off the stain which her profession had left upon her life. There was someone to whom she was a mother. There were many to whom she was a guardian and benefactress. I felt I had no right to drag her away from that house, permeated with devotion and affection.

When she asked how I felt I said I was feeling well enough to travel. She did not try to stop me. She only asked me to inform her about my health on reaching home. I promised to write to her. As I climbed into the palanquin, I saw her standing in the balcony upstairs. She silently watched me go. I thought of Annada *didi*. One day I had seen her in the same posture, serene and solemn, eyes glistening with unshed tears. I wondered if I would have found the same unspoken suffering had I been able to peer into Rajalakshmi's deep, dark eyes at that moment.

A great love does not merely draw people together. It also has the strength to push them away. An ordinary love would not have given me the courage to banish myself, for my own good, from that haven of affection and happiness. The palanquin-bearers lifted me up and carried me swiftly towards the railway station. My lips were silent, but my eyes were saying: 'Do not grieve for me, Rajalakshmi. My going away is all for the good. I know that in this lifetime I will never be able to repay your kindness. You have given me a new lease of life. I will not insult you by misusing it. This is my resolve. Rajalakshmi, take this as a promise from me.'

❖

A Summary of Parts II, III and IV of Srikanta

Srikanta is a long, rambling novel which remained incomplete when the author died. Srikanta's relationship with Rajalakshmi remains the focal point of the narrative throughout. A brief sketch of parts II, III and IV is given below.

II

Srikanta travels to Burma in search of a job. Most of the passengers get sick and are quarantined. Among them is Abhaya, a girl deserted by her husband. She is travelling to Burma in the hope of finding him, and is accompanied by Rohini Babu, an old friend of the family. Srikanta gets a good job in a timber company at Rangoon. Abhaya and her escort live in poverty in a small room and Srikanta succeeds in locating Abhaya's husband who is a drunkard and a thief. Abhaya goes to his house only to be humiliated openly and beaten up. She returns to Rohini Babu and starts living with him in spite of the censure of the entire Indian community. Srikanta writes long letters to Rajalakshmi, who has resumed her life as a professional singer. He returns to Calcutta and meets her. Srikanta falls ill and Rajalakshmi takes him for rest and convalescence to her country cottage, at a place called Gangamati.

III

Vajrananda, a young Brahmin who has renounced his home and has dedicated himself to the service of the poor, visits Gangamati. Srikanta travels with him and passes through many villages. He sees with deep sadness the poverty, disease, illiteracy and superstition of rural India. He is impressed by Vajrananda's intelligent and compassionate manner of handling the villagers' problems.

Srikanta revisits his ancestral village and meets some of his childhood friends. One of them is Satish Bharadwaj, an overseer in the Railway Engineering Service. Srikanta and Satish reminisce about their happy years at school. But their reunion ends abruptly. Satish is infected by cholera. Srikanta sits by Satish's bedside during his last hours. A few days later Srikanta is himself down with malaria. He takes shelter in the house of a poor Brahmin family until Rajalakshmi, hearing of his illness, takes him to her home. He has hardly recovered when he gets a letter from Abhaya who is in great difficulties and needs his help. Srikanta goes to Burma to deal with the situation.

IV

On his return, Srikanta meets another long-lost schoolmate, Gauhar, who lives in a small farm-house bequeathed to him by his late father. Although Gauhar is a Muslim, he writes poems about Rama, Sita and other figures from Hindu mythology. An old family servant, Navin, looks after his needs. Srikanta promises to visit his garden house. But when he goes there, he finds that Gauhar has gone to the ashram of a holy man, Baba Dwarkadas. Srikanta and Rajalakshmi go to the ashram together. Navin acts as their guide.

Rajalakshmi and Srikanta meet Baba Dwarkadas. They find peace and beauty in the atmosphere of the ashram. In the evening, when the entire ashram community gets together for worship, Rajalakshmi offers to sing a devotional song. Srikanta is deeply moved when he sees her sensitive face lit up by an intensely religious expression, so different from her light-hearted rendering of romantic songs in the drawing-rooms of princes and aristocrats. When Rajalakshmi concludes her song, Swami Dwarkadas applauds her. He takes the jasmine garland offered to the deity and places it around Rajalakshmi's neck. Srikanta looks on with joy and pride. He realizes that he is now more deeply in love with Rajalakshmi than ever before.

Anupama's Love

SEPARATION

Anupama's introduction to novels and stories was at the age of eleven. Her mind was filled with fiction. She thought that she had gathered and assimilated all the love, sweetness, beauty and thirst that could possibly exist in human hearts. She felt sure that she now understood everything about human nature, about life and character, and that there was nothing more to know or learn. She refused to believe that any one else in the world could comprehend the greatness of love and the power of devotion as she did. She regarded herself as a jasmine creeper which can bloom only when embraced by the loving branch of a tree.

And so Anupama selected in her own mind a companion, to whom she gave everything, her heart, her life, and her youth. Everyone has the right to give and receive whatever pleases the imagination. But Anupama forgot that before the jasmine climber is actually embraced, the consent of the branch is also necessary. How was she to tell him that she was the jasmine creeper waiting to blossom forth at his touch and that, if he refused to support her, the creeper would fall to the ground, the buds would wilt and it would be the end of her life?

Her 'chosen one' knew nothing of this. But that did not make any difference to Anupama. Her love became all the more intense. She knew that there is poison in nectar, pain in pleasure and parting in union. After suffering the pangs of separation for a long time Anupama whispered to herself: 'Oh my master, whether you accept me or reject me, whether you look at me or turn your eyes away, I am eternally at your

---

'Anupamar Prem' from *Kashinath O Anyanya Galpa* (Kashinath and Other Stories), September 1917

command. I can bear death, but I cannot bear losing you. We will surely meet, in some other lifetime if not in this. And then you will see how much power there is in the slender hands of a loving woman.'

Anupama's father was an affluent man. Adjoining his house there was a large garden with a lake. The moon shed its mellow light there, lotuses bloomed, nightingales sang and honey-bees hummed. Anupama found this an ideal place to revel in the sorrow of separation. She wandered in the garden with dishevelled hair, having discarded her jewellery. Sometimes she gazed upon her reflection in the lake. Sometimes she kissed rose buds. She lay under trees, weeping and sighing.

She lost her appetite, was unable to sleep, became indifferent to her looks and lost all interest in others around her. Her mother became anxious. Anupama was her only daughter. Whenever she asked Anupama what had happened to her, she muttered something unintelligible. One day Anupama's mother spoke to her husband, Jagadbandhu Babu. 'Are you not going to pay any attention to Anupama?' she asked. 'She is your only daughter, you know. And she is dying without any treatment.'

'What's the matter with her?' Jagadbandhu Babu said in surprise.

'No one knows. Doctor Saheb has examined her. He says there is nothing wrong with her. Then why is she behaving in this way?'

'How should I know?' said Anupama's father irritably.

'Then are we going to just let her die?'

'This is an amazing situation. There is no fever, no other health problem. If she insists on dying without any reason at all, how can I stop her?'

Having failed to get any support from her husband, Anupama's mother turned to her daughter-in-law. 'Why does my Anu wander in this way?' she asked.

'I don't know, mother,' the daughter-in-law said.

'Don't you and Anu talk to each other about her condition?'

'No, mother.'

'If she continues to wander like this, without sleep and nourishment, how long can she survive? I will drown myself in the lake unless people in this house do something and make Anupama return to normal life.'

The daughter-in-law thought for a while and said: 'Find a good match and marry her off. When she has to run a household, she will be cured automatically.'

The suggestion was placed before Anupama's father. He agreed readily. The family *ghatak* came the very next day. There was no dearth of prospective bridegrooms for Anupama. She was beautiful and her father was wealthy. Within a week the matchmaker selected a groom and informed Jagadbandhu Babu. Anupama came to know of these developments. A couple of days later, when her forthcoming wedding was being discussed, Anupama entered the room looking miserable, with a rose in her hand. Her mother looked at her wild hair and said: 'My darling daughter is looking like a *sanyasini* today.'

The discussion about the marriage continued. The boy was about to appear for his B. A. examination. 'A very good match,' said the daughter-in-law, 'but he had better be handsome, otherwise my sister-in-law will not like him.'

'Of course she will like him,' said Anupama's mother. 'He is very handsome.'

Anupama stood in a corner with her head bent. In her agitation she seemed to be scratching the floor with her toenails. She declared determinedly that she would not marry. Her mother at first could not understand what she had said. 'She refuses to get married,' the daughter-in-law explained. Wearing an expression of disbelief her mother left the room.

The daughter-in-law continued to question Anupama: 'Why are you refusing to marry? What reason can there be?'

'To be handed over like merchandise to some unknown man cannot be described as marriage,' Anupama replied.

'What do you mean? If parents don't arrange their matches, are girls supposed to find their own husbands?'

'Exactly. That's just what I mean.'

'So in your opinion my marriage is also a mistake. Before I was married to your brother, I didn't even know his name.'

'All women are not like you.'

The daughter-in-law burst into laughter. 'Have you found a young man after your heart, Anupama?' she said in a bantering tone.

'Are you making fun of me?' Anupama said with a solemn face. 'Is this a time for joking?'

Anupama felt as though the husband she had chosen for herself was being destroyed before her own eyes, like the husbands of some of the medieval heroines in the novels she had read. 'Can I not do what those women did?' she muttered. 'Is there any sacrifice beyond the strength of a loving wife?'

Suddenly, her eyes started glowing with an unnatural, flame-like lustre. She tied her wrist tightly with the end of her sari. She fell on her knees, clutched an empty bed, and shouted: 'Oh my Master! Oh Lord of my life! Today I am accepting you openly. Let the world see. You are mine and I am yours. I am not embracing the legs of a bed at this moment. I am embracing your feet. In the name of *dharma* I am taking you as my husband. I swear by your feet that no one else in the world can touch me. Nobody can dare to separate us while we are alive. Help me . . . Divine Mother . . . Goddess!'

The daughter-in-law rushed out of the room and told everyone about Anupama's weird behaviour. Very soon a crowd gathered. Anupama's mother, her brother Chandra Babu, her father, and many neighbours came and surrounded her. Everyone was excited and wanted to know what exactly had happened. Anupama lay unconscious near the bed. Her mother started crying. 'Sprinkle water on her face,' someone said. 'Call the doctor,' said another. 'Fan her,' said a neighbour, while another advised rubbing sandal-paste on the girl's temples.

Anupama regained consciousness after some time. 'Where am I?' she asked in a faint voice. Her mother brushed Anupama's forehead with her lips and said in gently and affectionately: 'You are in your mother's lap, dearest.'

'Oh, it is you!' Anupama said, disappointedly. 'I thought I was in the land of dreams . . . floating with him . . . my only one.' Her cheeks were wet with tears.

'Why are you crying, my child?' said her bewildered mother. 'What are you mumbling about?' Anupama heaved a deep sigh and kept silent.

At night the daughter-in-law came and sat near Anupama. 'Tell me,' she said, 'is there someone who will make you happy, someone you wish to marry?'

'Happiness and sorrow no longer matter to me. He alone is my lord.'

'Yes, yes, I understand. But who is this "he"? You have to tell us. Otherwise how can we help you?'

'Suresh . . . Suresh. . . .' Anupama said.

'Suresh? Are you talking about the son of Rakhal Majumdar?'

'Yes, he is the one . . . the only one.'

Anupama's mother learnt about this and the very next morning went to Rakhal Majumdar's house. She met Suresh's mother and said abruptly: 'Please arrange your son's marriage with my daughter.'

'It is a good idea. The proposal sounds all right to me.'

'Merely saying "all right" is not enough. You have to finalize this match.'

'I have to ask Suresh first. He is in the house. If he agrees, I am sure his father will not have any objection.'

Suresh was working hard for his university examination. Every minute was precious to him. When his mother came and said, 'Suresh, you have to get married,' he was irritated.

'I know,' he said, 'but why are you asking me just now? Such talk disturbs me in my studies.'

'No, I'm not asking you to get married right away,' his mother said. 'We will wait until your examination is over. The marriage will take place when you are free.'

'Where? And with whom?'

'In this very village. With the daughter of Jagadbandhu Babu.'

'What? With Chandra Babu's sister, whom he calls "Lalli"?'

'Her name is Anupama. "Lalli" may be her pet name.'

'Yes, yes, Anupama. Forget it. She is ugly.'

'On the contrary, she is very good-looking, Suresh'.

'Even if she is, I don't like the idea of having my in-laws in the same village as my parents. Moreover, I propose to continue my studies.'

When Suresh's rejection of the proposal was communicated to Anupama's mother, she again approached her husband and extracted from him the promise that he would somehow persuade the Majumdars to accept their daughter as their son's bride. When Suresh persisted in his refusal, and his parents said they were helpless, Anupama's father used the time-tested weapon of financial temptation. The Majumdars were offered an additional dowry of five thousand rupees. They could not resist the temptation. They called Suresh and told him that he would have to marry Anupama. All his protests were in vain. Ultimately, he agreed to go through the marriage after his examination.

The news brought joy not only to Anupama's parents but also to the servants in the household. The daughter-in-law said to Anupama: 'I hear that your bridegroom has been hooked.'

'I knew it all along,' said Anupama, blushing deeply.

'How did you know? Did you exchange letters with him?'

'Love knows everything. We used to exchange messages mentally.'

When Anupama went out of the room, the daughter-in-law said to her husband: 'It makes me angry when a young person talks big. I am a mother of three kids and now this slip of a girl wants to teach me what love is!'

THE CONSEQUENCES OF LOVE

Lalit Mohan was the only son of Durlabh Babu who had accumulated considerable wealth in his lifetime. On the death of his father, Lalit inherited all his assets. After performing the ceremonies on the thirteenth day for his departed father, he went straight to the school and asked the teacher to strike off his name from the roster. When the teacher asked what had happened, Lalit replied: 'What's the use of reading and writing? I already have that for which people work hard at school. My father studied enough. And now he has left me enough.'

'Then you have nothing to worry about,' said the teacher ironically. 'Eat, drink and be merry. Have a good time.'

A young man, and a lot of money! Lalit Mohan was soon surrounded by companions. Tobacco, liquor, marijuana and hemp were consumed freely. Dancing girls and courtesans did not lose much time in finding their way to Lalit's house. The hard-earned wealth bequeathed to him by his father began to dwindle rapidly. Lalit's mother beseeched him tearfully to mend his ways, but in vain. One day he came to his mother, his face flushed and his eyes red, demanding fifty rupees at once. The mother said she didn't have any money. Lalit Mohan went out, returned with an axe, broke open her wooden chest and took away fifty rupees.

Next morning Lalit's mother gave him a key and said: 'My son, this is the key with which you can open that steel almirah. It contains the money left by your father. Take it and spend it as you desire. My only prayer to God is that after I go away you may come to your senses.'

'Where are you going, Mother?' Lalit asked in surprise.

'I do not know, son, where one goes after committing suicide. I do know that it is a sin to put an end to one's life. But what can I do? Such is my fate.'

Lalit knew his mother's nature very well. She was not one to make idle threats. He fell at her feet and asked her forgiveness. He promised to give up his bad habits and begged her to stay.

'What about your freebooting, merry-making pals?' his mother asked. 'Where will they go?'

Lalit Mohan said that he did not care for any of them and that he would live on whatever money she gave him. His mother offered him hundred rupees each month as pocket money. He agreed. His friends disappeared one by one. He became lonely and found it difficult to pass the time. The parasites were gone, but he could not give up drinking altogether. He started going out for walks to calm himself. One of the roads on which he wandered went past Jagadbandhu Babu's house. He would often see Anupama walking alone in her garden.

There was an opening in the boundary wall through which he saw her plucking flowers, weaving garlands, wetting her feet in the lake, or sitting quietly as though in meditation. It became a daily ritual for him to visit that spot shortly after sunset. Watching Anupama soon became the most important source of joy for Lalit. It did not take very long for him to realize that he had fallen in love. And the more intense his love became, the more clearly he understood its futility. I am a drunkard, an ignoramus, I am totally unworthy of her, he told himself. And yet his resolve to stop visiting that spot was broken every evening.

One day Anupama's brother, Chandra Babu, spotted him when he was climbing over the wall. 'Catch him, take him to the police station,' Chandra Babu shouted to the watchman. The watchman was afraid of getting into a scuffle with Lalit who had the reputation of being a vagabond. Lalit slipped away, but Chandra Babu filed a complaint with the police. The police inspector came and asked Anupama to give evidence against the intruder. Although her parents wanted to take a soft line, both Anupama and her brother testified against Lalit Mohan. He was prosecuted. His mother spent a lot of money to save her son. But nothing prevailed over the strong evidence against him. He was sentenced to rigorous imprisonment for three years and sent to jail.

Meanwhile, the B. A. results were announced and Suresh Majumdar not only passed the examination but was also placed in the first division. Anupama's mother was very happy. 'My daughter has brought him good luck,' she said to Suresh's mother. 'Just wait and see how prosperous your son becomes after his marriage.' A couple of days later Rakhal Babu called his son and told him that the marriage ceremony would take place in the summer.

Suresh said he was not in the least ready to get married. 'I have been awarded the Gilchrist Scholarship,' he said. 'I have an excellent opportunity of going to England for further studies.'

His father was angry. 'Too much reading has corroded your mind,' he said. 'Never dare to talk about going to England again.' Suresh protested that a free voyage to England was too good a prospect to be thrown away, but his father terminated the conversation and dismissed him. 'These youngsters read a few English books and think that they can argue with their parents,' he muttered.

When the arrangements for the wedding were completed, Anupama's sister-in-law said to her: 'Our village is not large enough to contain your bridegroom's fame and success.'

Anupama smiled and said: 'All the doors of happiness have been opened for him because he has the complete love of his wife.'

'Wife? But the wedding has not yet taken place, Lalli.'

'We were married long ago. The world may not know it, but our hearts have already been united.'

The sister-in-law did not like this remark at all. 'I feel ashamed even to hear such things,' she said. 'You talk as if you are acting on a stage, in a theatre. If you continue to behave like this, people will think that you are mad.'

'But I am mad,' Anupama replied. 'It is the madness of love.'

MARRIAGE

The entire village was excited about Anupama's wedding. Jagadbandhu Babu's house and garden were jammed with people. The sound of musical instruments filled the air. As the auspicious moment approached, everything was ready. Only one item was missing: the bridegroom! Every corner of Rakhal Majumdar's house had been searched. Suresh was nowhere to be found.

An hour had passed after the appointed time. Jagadbandhu Babu was tearing his hair in anger and frustration. He yelled at his wife for putting him in that terrible situation. As for Anupama's mother, her misery was indescribable. And Anupama herself was fainting with grief every half an hour. The night was advancing. Ten, eleven, midnight: there was no trace of Suresh.

But Anupama had to be married immediately, otherwise the Majumdars would lose their status and the prestige of their family would be shattered. So at about three in the morning, some elderly well-wishers of the neighbourhood got hold of a man of fifty-two called Ramdulal Datta, dressed him up in the bridegroom's outfit, and brought him to the place where the ceremony had almost begun. When Anupama realized that her life was about to be destroyed, she rolled in agony at her mother's feet. 'Save me, mother,' she wailed. 'Do not slit my throat. If this marriage takes place, I will surely kill myself.' Her mother pleaded with Jagadbandhu Babu, but his mind was made up. He said: 'Get up, Anupama. The ceremony of giving the bride away has to be completed.'

Anupama begged her father to kill her instead. But his heart had turned into stone. When Anupama declared that she would swallow poison rather than go through such a terrible marriage, he said: 'You can do what you please tomorrow. Just now I have to save my status and protect the honour of my family. After that you are free to swallow poison or drown yourself.'

Anupama was appalled by her father's cruelty. But her piteous weeping did not prevent the marriage. Ramdulal Datta was a very happy man. His means were extremely limited. He had been living alone in a small house. Suddenly, he had found a young bride and a rich father-in-law. Fortune had smiled upon him. He carried Anupama to his house with servants, foodstuffs and household things provided by her father. When Anupama returned to her parents' home after a few days, she looked so pitiable that even the servants had to hide their faces to wipe their tears.

Death was the only way out for her. Late at night, when every one in the house was asleep, she went into the garden and sat on the steps leading to the lake. Tonight I must actually die, not just think about dying, she said to herself. She remembered that she had made similar attempts earlier in a state of depression. She had failed, because a man had come from behind and pulled her away from the water. Who was that man? Suddenly, his face came back to her. She realized with a shock that the man who had saved her life was none other than Lalit Mohan, who was languishing in jail because of her evidence against him. What did I gain by helping my brother in sending my saviour to prison? Is it possible that his love for me was sincere? The poor man is being forced to break stones in the prison. Perhaps he has been yoked to a grinding stone. All because of me. And the man whom I wanted to give everything is on a ship to England, thinking only of his own advancement.

She entered the lake—knee-deep, then chest-deep. Now she was up to the neck in water. She pushed her head into the lake, swallowed a lot of water, and came up again. This happened many times. She just could not drown herself. From the novels that she had read, she had gathered that the hero or heroine could live or die at will. She returned home at dawn, convinced that what she had learnt from novels was not correct. It was not easy to perish. She was doomed to live.

Meanwhile, her husband had started shifting to her father's house by stages, and finally established himself as a permanent house guest. He was treated courteously for a while and then ignored. But neither the indifference of his wife nor the contempt with which people in the house treated him made any difference to Ramdulal. He was very comfortable and enjoyed his life in that wealthy household to the fullest extent. This enjoyment, however, did not last very long. His old friends, asthma and tuberculosis, caught up with him. He was sent to Calcutta for treatment. But the tuberculosis had penetrated too far into his lungs. Within a year after his marriage, Ramdulal Datta's earthly career came to an end leaving poor Anupama in another tragic situation.

WIDOWHOOD

Anupama cried and mourned; that is what a Hindu widow is supposed to do. She discarded all her ornaments and wore only white cotton saris. Her mother said: 'My child, wear at least one bracelet. Your appearance causes me great pain.' But Anupama was determined to fulfil all the duties of a widow.

'You are still a girl,' her mother said.

'For a widow,' said Anupama, 'there is no difference between youth and old age.'

People in the village were not at all surprised to hear that Anupama had lost her husband. Her father had married her to a sick old man. What else could anyone expect?

Anupama lived on a handful of rice which she cooked for herself. She kept all the traditional fasts. Shaken by their daughter's misery, her parents suggested that she should marry again. Anupama refused. She had already lost everything in this world, she said, and by remarrying she would lose everything in the next world also. Her father tried to convince her that remarriage was not contrary to religion. But all his arguments proved futile.

'Why are you being punished this way?' he cried in sorrow. 'What have you done to deserve such agony?'

'My sufferings must be the result of past *karmas*,' she said.

'And who will look after you when I am no more? Chandra is your stepbrother, not your real brother. I have misgivings about his nature.'

'If my brother ill-treats me, I will commit suicide.'

Her father again pointed out that, after his death, she would not be able to face the ordeals of life alone, that she needed the support of a husband.

'But if you arrange my marriage a second time, you will lose your social status, father,' Anupama said.

'No, no, my child. I will not lose anything. My eyes have now been opened. Moreover, I am now approaching the end of my life.'

Anupama merely shook her head. How strange, she thought, that her father should have talked about caste status and family honour when he handed her over to a sickly old man. And now he was asking his widowed daughter to remarry, contrary to orthodox Hindu conventions. Why did he not think of the consequences at that time when he shut his eyes and ears and sacrificed her at the altar of caste and prestige?

When Jagadbandhu Babu realized that he would not be able to change Anupama's decision, he said sadly: 'Very well, my daughter, do whatever you consider best. I do not wish to arrange another marriage for you against your wishes. But I will provide for you adequately, so that you may be able to live comfortably after me. Dedicate yourself to *dharma* and do whatever makes you happy.'

CHANDRANATH BABU'S HOUSEHOLD

Lalit Mohan was released from jail after three years. But he did not go home. People said he was ashamed to show his face in the village. For two years he wandered from place to place before finally going back there. His mother embraced him joyfully. 'My son,' she said, 'now get married and settle down. What has happened cannot be undone.' Lalit promised to lead a steady life. He noticed many changes in the village, but none more drastic than those in Anupama's house.

Jagadbandhu Babu and his wife had passed away. Chandranath was now the master. Anupama thought that with the money her father had left her she could go to a holy place to spend her life in spiritual pursuits. But when her father's will was made public she was shocked. Only five hundred rupees had been left to her. No one in the village believed that a wealthy man like Jagadbandhu Babu could have made such an unfair will. It was obvious that Chandranath, in collusion with the lawyers and the local authorities, had tampered with the original bequests. Nothing could now be done. The court accepted Chandranath's version. Anupama was forced to live in her parents' house at the mercy of her stepbrother who soon revealed his true colours. He turned out to be mean, greedy and utterly heartless in his treatment of her once he got hold of the property.

Anupama was insulted, taunted and humiliated every day. He had always been jealous of her. Now her very sight became repugnant to him. He did his utmost to make her life miserable. His wife's behaviour was as petty as her husband's. Anupama was now an unfortunate widow, helpless, totally dependent on her stepbrother and his wife for a few crumbs. She was forced to do all the housework and to look after her brother's three small children. If there was the slightest complaint from any of them, she was rebuked mercilessly. She had to cook food for her brother, even when she was fasting.

Servants in the house, Anupama realized, were much better off than she was. A servant could always say: 'I cannot work here any more. Give me a month's wage and I will go away.' But she could not give any notice to quit. She was an unpaid drudge. One day, when Anupama was immersed in praying, her sister-in-law yelled at her. 'Don't earn so much merit,' she said, 'otherwise it will overflow. Are you going to pray the whole day? If so, why don't you go away to a forest? If you want to stay here, you will have to do all the housework.' Anupama quietly swallowed the insults. Enraged by her silence, the sister-in-law shouted: 'You may be fasting, but we are not. Come to the kitchen at once and start cooking.'

'I am not feeling well today,' Anupama said. 'Ask one of the servants.'

'Your brother does not like food cooked by any of the servants. You have to cook the meal. Besides, the servant who knows how to cook is ill.'

Anupama's self-respect suddenly asserted itself. 'If the servant is ill, why don't you cook the food yourself?' she said. 'And if you cannot, let everyone fast today.'

'Very well, I will go and report this to your brother at once. I know you are just pretending to be ill. You just had a bath. I am sure you will soon be ready to gobble food.'

'I am not a slave purchased by you. You cannot talk to me like this. You would not have dared to treat me in such a way if my brother himself had not been so callous.'

'Why? What has he done? You live, eat, and get clothes here. What else should he do? You can't expect him to drive *me* away and attend only to your comforts. You better control your temper.'

At this point Anupama lost her patience completely. 'He is not feeding me from his own pocket,' she said. 'My meals come out of the same money as his. It is my father's money.'

'Oh really?,' the sister-in-law taunted. 'Had that been the case your father would not have cut you out of his will and left you a beggar.'

'He has not left me a beggar. You and your husband have brought me to this condition. The whole village knows that my father could not have left me financially helpless. My brother has grabbed all the money. That is why I have to hear all your taunts.'

When Anupama's remarks were conveyed to her brother, he did not say anything at the time. He had something much more diabolical in mind. A couple of days later, Chandranath ordered a servant boy, Bhola, to come to his room at once. When Bhola came, Chandranath started to abuse and beat him. Bhola's screams brought other servants to the room. Anupama was worshipping the deities at the time. She rushed to her brother's room. The beating continued. Bhola's nose was bleeding profusely.

'What are you doing?' Anupama said. 'He will die if you beat him so cruelly.'

'Let him die,' Chandranath retorted. 'I want to kill him. And if you had not been a woman I would have killed you too. I will not tolerate such shameful goings-on in my house. I will give you the five hundred rupees left for you by my father. Take the money and clear out immediately.'

'But what has happened?' said Anupama, dumbfounded.

'You know very well what has happened. Take Bhola with you. Do what you like outside my house.'

Anupama fainted. Chandranath kicked Bhola once again and went out of the room.

THE LAST DAY

It was Anupama's last day in her parents' house. She could not stay there any longer. Happiness had eluded her all her life. When she was a mere child she had destroyed her peace of mind with romantic notions of love. The one whom she had selected as her love had rejected her. And she had driven away the one who had offered his love. Now she had no father, no mother, no place of her own. In the silence of the moonlit night, she opened the back door of the house, went into the garden and once again sat on the steps leading to the lake.

Anupama had learnt a lesson from experience. Her last attempt to commit suicide had failed because she was a good swimmer. Her swimmer's reflexes had brought her to the surface and prevented her from drowning. This time she brought a heavy pitcher with her. She would first probe the lake, see where the water was deepest, tie herself to the pitcher and take the plunge. There would be no mistake.

The world looks extremely beautiful in the moments before death. The sky, the moon and the stars, the surface of the lake, trees and creepers, leaves and flowers: everything looks lovely. Wherever the eyes turn, they see enchanting things. They all seem to be pointing at you and saying: 'Do not die. See how happy we are. Endure your pain. Some day happiness will come to you. Come to us. We will give you pleasure. Do not fling into purgatory the soul that God has given you.'

Men and women thus turn back from death's door again and again. But when they return to the world of human beings, and find it bereft of even an iota of pleasure, the urge to put an end to one's life becomes strong again. The inner voice, however, is not silenced together. It again resists the thought of death and says: 'For God's sake desist from this ghastly deed. Will suicide put an end to your sufferings? How do you know that it will not lead to even more terrible pain?' Anupama was aware of the implications. But this time she was determined to die. She *had* to die. She was convinced that there was no other way.

Memories flooded her. She remembered her father's words. She thought of her mother. And then she remembered Lalit Mohan. Those who loved me have gone away, except one person: Lalit. He is the only one among my well-wishers who is still alive, she reflected. He loved me. He came to me asking for love. He installed me in his heart as a goddess. I rejected him, insulted him and was even instrumental in sending him to jail. How many hardships must he have endured there!

Lalit Mohan must have cursed me. Perhaps my suffering is the result of my own sin—the sin of sending him to jail. They say he has given up drinking and has turned over a new leaf. Does he still remember me? And even if he does, he must have heard of my shame. Tomorrow the whole village will know that Anupama, the widow who took a servant boy as her paramour, has drowned herself. When my body floats on the surface of the lake, with what contempt and disgust will Lalit Mohan look at it!

Anupama picked up the pitcher. She was tying it to her neck with one end of her sari when someone called her name loudly from behind. She turned round and saw the dim figure of a tall man standing at a short distance. 'Anupama, do not kill yourself,' he said in an anxious voice.

'How do you know that I am about to commit suicide?'

'Why else would you tie a pitcher around your neck? . . .Do you know what one gets by committing suicide?'

'What?'

'Eternal hell.'

Anupama shivered. She slowly untied the pitcher and kept it on the ground. 'There is no place for me in this world,' she said.

'Have you forgotten?' Lalit said. 'Let me remind you. A long time ago an unfortunate soul wanted to offer you a permanent place beside him. Do you remember?'

'Yes, I remember.'

'Then you have to give up your resolve to die.'

'My name has been blackened. I am tainted. I don't wish to live.'

'Will death wipe out that stain?'

'Perhaps not. But at least I won't have to hear those terrible accusations.'

'You are mistaken, Anupama. If you kill yourself, the stain will follow you forever like a shadow.'

'But where can I go? Is there a place where I can live . . . where I can be accepted?'

'Come with me,' Lalit said eagerly.

Anupama thought: Perhaps I should fall at his feet and beg his forgiveness. Perhaps I can ask him to give me a small amount of money . . . as charity . . . so that I can go to some far-off place and hide there.

But, after a long silence, she said: 'No, I will not go with you,' and suddenly she jumped into the lake.

When Anupama regained consciousness she found herself in a pleasant room. She was lying on a bed. Lalit Mohan was sitting by her side. Anupama opened her eyes and said in a plaintive voice: 'Oh why? . . . Why did you rescue me?'

Mahesh

*K*ashipur was a small village. The *zamindar* had absolute authority over his tenants, even though his estates and assets were not particularly large. In Kashipur his word was law. No one dared to defy his wishes.

It was the birthday of the zamindar's youngest son. Tarkaratna Mahashaya, the manager, was returning home after the ceremonial worship to celebrate the birthday. The first month of summer was almost over, but there was not a cloud in the sky. The fear of drought loomed large over the village. Open fields that stretched to the horizon lay parched with hundreds of cracks. Through those cracks the earths's blood seemed to have turned into smoke. A mere look at them made one feel giddy.

On the road adjacent to one of the fields lived Ghafoor, a weaver, in a small hut. One of the mud walls of his hut had collapsed and the courtyard had merged with the road. It seemed as though the dignity of its occupant had surrendered itself to the compassion of passers-by. Tarkaratna stopped near the hut, placed his basket in the shade of a tree, and shouted, 'Ghafoor, are you at home? Come out at once.'

The weaver's ten-year-old daughter came to the door and said that her father was lying in bed with fever. 'Call the rascal immediately,' the manager thundered. 'Fever indeed! The damned hypocrite *mlechha*.'

On hearing the manager's loud voice Ghafoor came out and stood at the door shivering. Near the dilapidated wall there was an acacia tree, to which Ghafoor's bullock, Mahesh, was tethered. Tarkaratna pointed to Mahesh and said: 'Ghafoor, what are you

---

'Mahesh' from *Harilakshmi O Anyanya Galpa* (Harilakshmi and Other Stories), March, 1926.

trying to do? This is a Hindu village and the landlord is a Brahmin. Are you out of your mind?'

The pandit's face was red with heat and anger and his words were sharp. This much Ghafoor could make out. But he could not understand the precise reason for the manager's displeasure and simply stared at him without a word. 'I saw your bull tied up in the morning,' Tarkaratna Mahashaya said with mounting anger, 'and now it's afternoon and he is still tied up. If he does not graze, he will die of hunger. To kill a cow's offspring is a terrible sin. If you let him die the zamindar will bury you alive. He is no ordinary Brahmin.'

'What can I do, Maharaj?' Ghafoor said. 'I have become so helpless. I have been ill for several days. I used to lead him by the rope and take him out to graze. But I don't have the strength. I feel dizzy.'

'Just release him and let him find a place to graze,' the manager said.

'How can I do that, sir?' Ghafoor moaned. 'People have harvested the paddy, but they have not yet winnowed and stored it. And the fields are all dry. There is not a handful of grass anywhere. If I let him go there will be trouble. He may start eating grain off someone's farm. Or he may destroy the straw which people have stored for thatching their huts. I have to keep him tied up.'

'If you can't let the bull loose, you can tie him up in the shade and throw a little straw before him to chew. And you can give him the water which is left over when your daughter has finished cooking rice.'

Ghafoor did not answer. He just sighed and stared at Tarkaratna Mahashaya helplessly, indicating by his gestures that he had no straw.

'What? No straw left? I know you got your share from the landlord. What happened to it? Did you sell it all off to get money to fill your belly? Left nothing for the poor bullock. You really are a butcher.'

Ghafoor was dumbfounded by this cruel accusation. After a while, he said in a low voice: 'My share of the reeds was withheld by the master in lieu of arrears of rent. I begged and wept. I fell at his feet and implored: 'Sir, you are the Lord here. Please give me some reeds and straw. I have to thatch my roof. My daughter and I will manage somehow. We will patch the roof with palm leaves. But unless you give me straw my poor Mahesh will die of hunger.' But the master did not have pity on me.'

Tarkaratna laughed, 'Shut up!' he said. 'Mahesh! What a grandiose name you have given to your bullock. It is amusing.'

'All my pleading was in vain,' Ghafoor continued. 'The landlord gave us a little rice, barely enough for two months. He refused to give reeds or fodder. My Mahesh got nothing.' Ghafoor choked with sorrow.

Tarkaratna did not feel the slightest sympathy for him. 'What a wretched grumbler you are!' he said. 'If you are in debt, why should the landlord not withhold something from you as part payment? Do you except him to pay from his own pocket? You don't realise that you are living in *Rama Raj*. After all, you belong to a low, degraded community. That is why you go around speaking ill of such a good master.'

'I don't speak ill of him, Sir,' the weaver said. 'But tell me, how could I pay the landlord's dues? There was drought for two years. The paddy I planted in my small piece of land dried up. The two of us barely get two meals a day. Just look at my house. When it rains, I take my daughter Ameena in my lap and sit in a corner for the entire night. There is no space even to stretch our legs, I cannot bear to look at Mahesh. He has become skin and bones. His ribs are sticking out. Have pity, *Maharaj*. Give me a little fodder. Give it as a loan. I will return it. If only I could feed my unfortunate Mahesh for a couple of days. . . . Please, Sir.'

With these words Ghafoor dropped on the ground and sat at the Brahmin's feet. Tarkaratna stepped back in horror. 'Keep away, inauspicious one,' he yelled. 'Do you want to pollute me with your touch?'

'How could I dare to touch you, *Maharaj*? Please, Sir, give me a little fodder this year. There are four huge stacks of fodder in your yard. I saw them yesterday. If you give me a little, it will not make any difference to you. Mahesh is a simple, harmless creature. He does not say anything. He just looks at me with his big eyes and sheds tears.'

'So, you want a loan. And how do you propose to repay it?'

Ghafoor thought there was a ray of hope. 'Somehow I will repay you, *Maharaj*,' he said. 'I will not deceive you. I will return your fodder.'

Tarkaratna twisted his lips, imitated Ghafoor's choked voice, and mimicked his words: 'I won't deceive. . . somehow I will return . . . what an actor! Out, out of my way. I have to go home. I am getting late.'

As he turned to go, he saw the bullock shaking his horns. Tarkaratna was furious. 'Look at the beast,' he said. 'He is getting ready to attack me.'

Ghafoor pointed to the basket in which the Pandit was carrying fruits and cooked rice. 'Mahesh has smelt food,' he said. 'He is starved. He shook his horns merely to beg for food.'

'He is only asking for food,' Tarkaratna mimicked again. 'The bullock is like his owner. No manners at all. He can't get even fodder, and he is asking for bananas and rice. Take him away at once and tie him at a distance from the road.' The manager crossed over to the other side of the road and went away.

Ghafoor stood there for a long time, staring at Mahesh, looking into his deep, dark eyes steeped in the agony of hunger.

'He did not give you even a handful of food, Mahesh,' he said in a quivering voice. 'They have so much. Yet they don't give anything to others. Very well, let them not.'

Tears flowed from Ghafoor's eyes as he rubbed Mahesh's neck and back gently with his hands. 'Mahesh,' he said, 'you are like my son. For eight years you have toiled to provide food for us. Now you are getting old, but I cannot even feed you properly. But you know how much I love you.'

Mahesh responded by raising his head and shutting his eyes. Ghafoor wiped his tears on Mahesh's back and said: 'The landlord has snatched the morsels from your mouth. You once grazed in the small field near the cremation ground. Even that has been rented out by the greedy landlord. This is a time of famine and drought. Tell me, how should I keep you alive? If I let you go, hunger will drive you into someone's barn. Or you will trample upon banana plants and eat the leaves. Oh Mahesh! What can I do to save you? The village people do not like you. They say you should be sold.' Ghafoor's eyes were full of tears as he spoke to Mahesh.

Ghafoor searched every corner of his hut for something which Mahesh could eat. Finally, he pulled down a piece of thatch from the broken-down roof and placed it before Mahesh. 'Eat it up quickly,' he said. His daughter, Ameena, called him from inside and asked him to come for his meal. As he did not respond, she came out and stood at the door. She saw what Ghafoor had done.

'You are again feeding Mahesh with a portion of the roof, father,' she said resentfully.

'It was rotting and falling down anyway,' Ghafoor said.

'No, father. I heard the sound when you pulled down the thatch. If you weaken the roof, the wall will also crumble.'

Ghafoor knew that she was right. He kept quiet and went inside to eat rice. 'Ameena, give me the water from the cooking pot,' he said. 'Let Mahesh have it.' Ameena told him that all the water had been absorbed in the rice. She served a little rice with a small portion of cooked lentils in a brass dish and handed it to her father. Then she sat down on the floor with a little rice for herself.

After much hesitation, Ghafoor said: 'Ameena, it seems my fever is rising again. I feel cold. I don't think I should eat rice in this condition.'

'Eat, father,' Ameena protested. 'Only a little while ago you said that you were very hungry.'

'Perhaps I did not have fever when I said that.'

'All right. Let me keep the rice. You can eat it later in the evening.'

'But cold rice will not be good for me, Ameena.'

'Then tell me what I should do.'

'Give this rice to Mahesh, my daughter. Can you not cook some rice again for me at night?'

'Yes, father, I can,' said Ameena with resignation.

No one knew about Ghafoor's play-acting for getting a few morsels of food for his bullock without hurting his daughter. No one saw what happened between these two simple, unfortunate souls, father and daughter. Or perhaps there was one witness, high up in his heavenly realm.

II

A few days later, Ghafoor sat at the doorstep with an anxious face. Mahesh was nowhere to be seen. Ghafoor was too ill to venture out. Ameena had gone away in the morning looking for Mahesh. She came back in the evening with the news that a man called Manik Babu had sent Mahesh to the cattle pound because plants in his kitchen garden had been trampled upon. Ghafoor was stunned. He did not expect this from a neighbour like Manik Ghosh whose respect for cows and their calves was known to the entire village.

Late that evening Ameena said: 'Father, are you not going to bring Mahesh back from the cattle pound?'

'No,' said Ghafoor.

'But Manik Babu's servant was telling me that if the bullock was not claimed within three days he would be auctioned in the cattle market.'

'Let him be sold.'

Ameena remembered that her father used to flinch at the very mention of the market, where butchers purchased unclaimed cattle. Today he quietly listened to the news that Mahesh could be sold. Next morning Ghafoor went to the shop of Banshi, the pawnbroker. He had brought with him the brass dish in which Ameena always served his rice. 'You have to give me one rupee, Banshi,' Ghafoor said. Banshi knew the weight and the price of that dish very well. It had been pawned and redeemed four times in the past. So he paid the money. Ghafoor paid the fine at the cattle pound and Mahesh was back at his old place. The same acacia tree, the same branch, the same empty trough, the same hungry, dark eyes.

An old Muslim butcher with calculating eyes kept looking at Mahesh. Ghafoor was sitting nearby, his knees crossed. The old man untied a soiled ten-rupee note from his wrap and straightened it. 'I won't bargain with you,' he said.' Keep this note. I won't ask for any change.'

Ghafoor took the note without a word. But as soon as the buyer touched the rope Ghafoor got up suddenly and said: 'Don't you dare touch my bull. I am warning you.'

'Why?' the old man asked in surprise.

'It is my property, that's why. I am not selling.'

'But you were paid the deposit yesterday.'

Ghafoor flung the money at the butcher, took out a rupee and said: 'Here is your deposit.'

The prospective buyer did not want a quarrel. 'All right,' he said patiently.

'I will give you two extra rupees as pocket money for your daughter.'

Ghafoor was adamant. 'You won't get a pice more for this bull, I'm telling you,' the butcher said. Ghafoor shook his head with a jerk and refused the money.

The old man was angry. 'You know very well that I won't be able to sell anything except the hide,' he said. 'There is nothing else left in this wretched creature.'

'Oh Allah! Oh my Allah!,' said Ghafoor, recoiling in horror. He heaped abuses upon the butcher and asked him to get out of the village at once. Otherwise, he threatened, the *zamindar's* men would be called in to drive him away with a shoe-beating. By this time a small crowd had gathered around Ghafoor's hut. The news of the incident reached the landlord. Presently a messenger came and asked Ghafoor to appear before the Master immediately. All kinds of people were sitting in the zamindar's office when Ghafoor reached there.

'Ghafoor,' the landlord said haughtily, 'I have not yet been able to decide how you should be punished for trying to sell your bullock to a man from the slaughter-house. Don't you know whose estate you are living in?'

Ghafoor folded his hands in humility and said: 'I know,

Master. My daughter and I are dying of hunger, Sir. Otherwise
I would have paid whatever fine you may impose upon me for
my crime.'

People in the office were surprised, because they considered
Ghafoor to be rude and obstinate.

'I will never do such a thing again, Sir,' Ghafoor continued.
Then he held his ears with his hands, bent down, and crawled
rubbing his nose on the ground.

'All right, that's enough,' the landlord said. 'You can go
now. Never make such a mistake again.'

Every one in the room praised the *zamindar* for his
compassion. No one had the slightest doubt that the village had
been saved from the heinous sin of killing a cow's offspring only
because of the master's *karma* and his wise and generous
governance. Pandit Tarkaratna was present too. He gave a learned
explanation of the etymology of 'go', the Sanskrit word for cow.
In the same breath he told the villagers of the folly of allowing
ignorant, irreligious *mlechchas* to settle in their neighbourhood.

Ghafoor listened to everything quietly. He accepted the
insults and contempt heaped upon him as if he deserved
them. He returned home contented, obtained some rice
water from a neighbour's house, and gave it to Mahesh.
He passed his hand lovingly over Mahesh's body, head and
horns. He remained there for a long time muttering to
himself inaudibly.

III

The June sky was dominated by the Sun-God's terror. The
great deity showed no compassion. His power was fierce.
Looking at the blazing sky, no one dared hope to see rain-
bearing clouds on the horizon. There seemed to be no end to
the fire that was being hurled upon the earth.

One such day, Ghafoor returned home in the afternoon.
He had always avoided working for some one else on a daily
wage. He had barely shaken off his fever, and he felt weak and
exhausted. Despite walking in the sun for a long time he had

returned without finding any work. Hunger, thirst and fatigue made him giddy. Everything looked dark. He stood in the yard and said: 'Ameena, is the rice ready?' Ameena came out and stood at the door without answering him. Ghafoor raised his voice and again asked whether the rice had been cooked.

'There is no rice, father,' Ameena said, lowering her eyes.

'Why didn't you tell me in the morning.'

'I told you last night, father.'

'How can I remember what you tell me at night?' said Ghafoor angrily. 'There is no rice, she says! The sick father may go hungry, but the brat needs rice five time a day. Now I am going to keep the rice under lock and key. Go, bring me a mug of water. I am so thirsty that my chest is pounding . . . or are you going to tell me that there is no water either?' Ghafoor had lost his balance completely.

Ameena stood with her eyes fixed on the ground. When he realized that there was not a drop of water in the house, he lost his temper completely. He rushed at his daughter and slapped her hard on both cheeks. 'Worthless black-faced girl!' he thundered, 'what do you do all the day? So many people die every day. Why don't you die?' Ameena quietly picked up her pitcher and went out wiping her tears.

She was hardly out of sight when Ghafoor was overwhelmed by the agony of shame and repentance. He alone knew how difficult it had been to raise this motherless girl. She was quiet, worked hard, and she loved him dearly! It was not her fault that there was no rice or water in the house. The unfortunate girl rarely got two meals a day. Sometimes she had to subsist on rice-water. How false, how cruel it was to say that she ate up a lot of rice.

Ghafoor also knew how difficult it was to get sufficient drinking water. The two ponds in the village were dry. A small amount of water could be obtained at another pond at some distance. There was always a crowd there. Sometimes there were angry exchanges, even scuffles over water. Being a Muslim, Ameena was not permitted to touch the water. She had to wait at a distance and beg for a pitcherful of water. If someone poured water in her pitcher out of compassion, she carried it home. Otherwise she had to return empty-handed.

When he thought of all these difficulties which Ameena had to face every day, Ghafoor again shed tears of repentance for having scolded and beaten her.

His sad thoughts were interrupted by a man sent by the landlord. Like a messenger of the God of Death, the landlord's servant stood in the yard and called Ghafoor. 'The Master wants you to go to his mansion immediately,' said the arrogant lackey. Ghafoor said he had not eaten and would come later. The servant could not tolerate such impudence. He abused Ghafoor profusely: 'The Master has ordered that you should be dragged and presented before him and that you should be beaten with shoes on the way.'

Ghafoor forgot himself once again. 'There are no slaves here,' he said. 'I don't live here free of charge. The Master collects rent from me. I refuse to go.'

What happened after that need not be detailed. When Ghafoor returned from the landlord's house his mouth and eyes were swollen and there were bruises all over his body. His punishment was the result of what Mahesh had done. He had somehow broken loose, entered the landlord's garden and destroyed almost all the flowering shrubs. Before escaping from the garden, he had knocked down the landlord's youngest daughter.

Such incidents had occurred in the past. Ghafoor had been punished for them and later forgiven. But this time the insolent manner in which he talked to the landlord's servant resulted in very severe chastisement. Ghafoor took the beating and the insult quietly, came back home, and lay down. He ignored his own hunger and thirst, though his chest was burning and he was barely conscious. Suddenly, he heard his daughter's piercing scream and rushed outside. Ameena was lying in the courtyard. Her clay pitcher had cracked and water was trickling from it. Mahesh was lapping up that water, every drop of it.

Within a moment Ghafoor was overcome by rage. A couple of days earlier he had detached his ploughshare from its handle.

intending to get it repaired. He picked up the ploughshare, gripped it firmly with both hands and mustering up all his strength, hit Mahesh on the forehead.

Once, only once, Mahesh made a feeble attempt to raise his head. Then his hungry, thirsty, emaciated body fell on the ground. A few tears flowed from his eyes, a few drops of blood oozed from one of his ears. Then he shivered violently a couple of times, his legs stiffened, and he drew his last breath.

Ameena started weeping. 'What have you done, father!' she cried. 'Our Mahesh is dead.' Ghafoor did not move, did not utter a word. Then he stood up and, kept staring at Mahesh's dark, deep eyes.

Within hours cobblers and tanners came, strapped Mahesh's body to a bamboo frame and took him from the village. Ghafoor saw their sharp, glistening knives and shut his eyes. Neighbours came and informed him that the landlord had asked Pandit Tarkaratna to arrange for the *prayashchitta* ceremony to atone for the sin that had been committed in the village. One of the neighbours said: 'Your house will be sold to meet the expenses of the *prayashchitta* ceremony.' Ghafoor sat on the ground silently, his knees drawn together.

Late that night Ghafoor woke up his daughter and said: 'Ameena, let us go away from here.'

Ameena was sleeping in the yard. She woke up, rubbed her eyes, and asked: 'Where are we going, father?'

Ghafoor said he would try to find work at the jute mill in the city. Ameena was surprised. In the past her father had refused to work in the jute mill even when he was in desperate need of money. He used to say that in the jute mill women's honour was not safe.

'Hurry up, Ameena,' Ghafoor said. 'It is a long walk.'

Ameena wanted to take the water bowl and the brass dish, but Ghafoor stopped her. 'Let these things remain,' he said. 'Let the landlord sell them and use the money for the *prayashchitta*.'

Ghafoor held his daughter's hand and stepped out into the dark night. He did not have any relatives in the village. There was no need to tarry for farewells. When he saw the acacia tree where he used to tie Mahesh, he stood transfixed. A few moments later he started weeping loudly. Tears flowed from his eyes. He raised his head, gazed at the star-studded sky and said: 'Oh Allah! Punish me as you think fit. But remember, my Mahesh died of thirst. No one gave him a place to graze. No one offered him a drop of water. I beseech you, Allah! Do not forgive those who deprived Mahesh of the grass and water which is yours, which you created for living beings.'

The Devoted Wife

*H*arish was a successful and highly respected lawyer of Pabna, a city in Bengal. He was held in esteem not only as a competent advocate but also as a good human being. He was associated with several humanitarian and social movements and institutions. Hardly any important social work was undertaken in Pabna without his advice and active help.

The Society for the Suppression of Corruption had convened a special meeting that morning. Harish was a member of the Executive Committee of the Society. After attending the meeting he rushed back home as he had to go to the district court a couple of hours later. His younger sister, Uma, a young widow, was serving him breakfast. She sat beside him, supervising the meal and instructing the servant. Harish's wife, Nirmala, came into the room and approached him slowly. 'There is a report in yesterday's newspaper,' she said, 'that Lavanya Prabha has been posted here as Inspectress of the Girls' Schools.'

This might have sounded like an ordinary remark, but it had far-reaching implications, as will become clear as our story unfolds. Uma was surprised. 'Really?' she said. 'How did Lavanya manage to get such a good job here?'

Nirmala said: 'She has managed it somehow. Let us ask your brother.'

Harish raised his head and said in a sharp tone: 'How should I know? Does the Government consult me while making appointments in the Education Department?'

Nirmala said calmly: 'Oh, there is no reason to get angry.

'Sati' from *Anuradha, Sati O Paresh* (Anuradha, Sati and Paresh), March, 1934

I did not intend to annoy you. If someone can benefit by your influence and recommendation, we should all be happy about it.' And she went out of the room in the same slow, measured pace as she had entered.

Harish got up abruptly. His sister implored him to finish his meal, but he was too upset to continue eating. 'No, I cannot swallow a morsel here peacefully,' he said. 'The only way is to end my life.'

As he hurried out of the room he heard his wife muttering: 'What sad reason do *you* have for ending your life. Some day someone in this house will indeed commit suicide. And then the world will see the truth.'

To understand the context in which these bitter remarks were being exchanged that day it is necessary to go back to the time when Harish was very young. Harish was a student at the time. His father, Ram Mohan, was Sub-Judge at Barisal. Harish had come home to prepare for the Master's degree examination. His father's next-door neighbour, Harkumar Majumdar, was an Inspector of Schools. A fine scholar and administrator, Harkumar was known for his humility. Sometimes, after work, he used to visit Ram Mohan, whose house had become a meeting place for people of varied vocations and persuasions.

Almost every evening, Ram Mohan's drawing-room was the venue for lively conversations and discussions. A bald magistrate or a clean-shaven Deputy Collector, a prosperous attorney or a distinguished leader—all were welcome. The host himself was a zealous Hindu and the discussion often focused on religious issues. And, as often happens at such gatherings, profound metaphysical and spiritual questions were ultimately left undecided in the din of loud voices, name-calling and insinuations.

One day, in the middle of one such verbal battle, Harkumar Babu walked in slowly, with a cane in hand. He had always kept aloof from wordy disputes. As a follower of the Brahmo Samaj, and being a quiet, patient person, he preferred to listen rather than to express his own opinions. But that day he could not remain silent. The balding magistrate, one of the prominent participants in a hot discussion, persuaded Harkumar Babu to become the arbiter. During his recent visit to Calcutta he had heard many friends praising Harkumar Majumdar's knowledge of Indian philosophy. On the magistrate's insistence, Harkumar agreed. It soon became apparent to all that Harkumar was not the man to be impressed by stray quotations from Bengali translations of the scriptures. His standards of serious debate were much higher.

Harish sat in a corner listening to the discussion. He was impressed by Harkumar Majumdar. A man of few words, his maturity and sound knowledge became obvious whenever he spoke. A couple of days later Harish went to his house and requested him to help him to prepare for the examination. Harkumar agreed, and Harish became a frequent visitor to his house. There he met Harkumar's daughter, Lavanya Prabha.

Lavanya was a few years younger to him, and was studying for the pre-university examination. She had also come away from the noise and hectic life of Calcutta. Harish started helping her with her textbooks. Together, they got a better understanding not only of books and maps but also of something else, far more complex and important. That 'something else' need not be elaborated at this point. Anyway, as the examination approached, Harish went to Calcutta and passed creditably.

But Lavanya failed the test. When Harish met her again, he offered his sympathies. 'What has happened is behind us,' he said. 'Next time you should prepare well.'

'No matter how well I prepare, I will fail again,' she said. 'It is beyond me'.

She showed absolutely no sign of being ashamed of her failure. Harish was surprised at her nonchalance.

'Why should it be beyond you?' he asked.

'For no particular reason,' she said in the same casual manner and went away barely able to suppress her laughter.

Harish's mother came to know of his friendship with Lavanya. She told her husband about it. Ram Mohan Babu was at that time busy writing a particularly harsh judgment for the losing party in a case. He was furious when he heard about his son's philandering. 'What! . . . How dare he. . . .' His anger rose to such a pitch that he could not complete the sentence. He decided to get Harish married as soon as possible.

Many years earlier, when he was posted at Dinajpur, Ram Mohan had developed a friendship with an old lawyer. There was much in common between them. Both were orthodox Hindus and shared their admiration for the teachings of the *Bhagavad Gita*. He thought of his old friend and went to Dinajpur. There he made a firm commitment to marry his son with Nirmala, the youngest daughter of his lawyer friend, Maitra Moshay. The girl was pretty. Harish's mother had seen her several times when her husband was posted at Dinajpur. Nevertheless, when Ram Mohan Babu returned home and told her what he had done, she was worried.

'You gave your word so hastily,' she said. 'You know how boys are these days. They want . . .'

He cut her short. 'I am not a modern father,' he said. 'I can mould my children in conformity with time-honoured traditions and rules.'

She knew her husband too well to say anything further. But Ram Mohan continued to justify his decision. 'Girls of good families are not like birds without wings,' he said. 'If Nirmala comes to our house with her mother's ideal of conjugal devotion and her father's faith in Hindu values, Harish should consider himself very lucky to get such a wife.'

The news spread quickly. When Harish learnt of what his father had done, his first impulse was to run away to Calcutta and earn his living by giving tuitions. His next thought was to become a *sadhu* and break all worldly bonds. Ultimately, however, he reconciled himself to his fate, remembering the ancient *mantra*: 'The Father is heaven, the Father is *Dharma*, the Father is everything'. The girls's father, Maitra Moshay, came to Ram Mohan's house with great fanfare to perform the engagement ceremony. A large number of distinguished people had been invited. Lavanya's father, Harkumar Majumdar, also attended the function. He knew nothing about the circumstances in which Harish's marriage had been arranged so hurriedly.

Ram Mohan Babu went out of his way to praise his son's future father-in-law in the presence of the respected guests. He denounced English education and described all its shortcomings in detail. He lamented the fact that changing times had made it necessary to impart English education to boys. But some people brought this alien knowledge and alien civilization into their inner apartments, and exposed even their daughters to evil influences. Such fools, he asserted, were doomed in this world and also doomed in the next. Harkumar Majumdar was the only person in the room who did not understand that these insinuations were directed against him.

Before the engagement ceremony was over, the date of the wedding was agreed upon. The marriage was performed at the auspicious hour selected by the family astrologer. Before sending Nirmala to her husband's house, her mother explained to her the fundamentals for a bride's success. 'Listen carefully, my daughter,' she said. 'Your husband can slip out of your hands unless you keep an eye upon him constantly. Not for a moment must you stop being vigilant. Whatever else you may forget in running your household, never forget this.' Nirmala's mother had herself been a strict adherent of this policy. Her husband, Maitra Moshay, had given her many anxious moments before he had immersed himself in studying religion and rituals. She had made up her mind not to loosen her grip until the very last moment of her husband's life.

Twenty years had passed since Nirmala took charge of her household. Many changes had taken place during this long period. Her father, Maitra Moshay, and her father-in-law, Ram Mohan Babu, had both passed away. Harkumar Majumdar's daughter, Lavanya, had been married. Harish had risen from Junior Advocate to Senior Advocate. He was no longer young.

But his wife had not deviated for a moment from the *mantra*, the formula for marital success, which her mother had given her on the day of her wedding. Nirmala had kept an eye on Harish all the time.

Nirmala had, in fact, found it necessary to follow her mother's advice right from the start. One evening Harish had gone to a colleague's house to attend a religious ceremony. A famous *bhajan* singer from Calcutta had been invited for the occasion. She was young and beautiful, besides being a fine singer. Many friends had wanted to hear her for a long time. The recital of religious songs continued late into the night. When Harish came home, he saw his wife standing in the upstairs verandah looking at the road. As soon as her husband came upstairs she asked him whether he liked the music.

'She sings very well indeed,' Harish said.

'Is she beautiful?' Nirmala asked pointedly.

'Not bad. Actually she is rather pretty.'

'Well, then why didn't you stay there for the entire night?'

Harish was pained by her comment. He did not expect such petty suspiciousness from his wife. All he could say was, 'What do you mean?'

'I am not a child,' Nirmala said angrily. 'I know everything. I understand everything. Do you think you can throw dust into my eyes?'

Harish's sister, Uma, came running from the adjoining room. 'What are you saying, sister-in-law?' she asked in a frightened voice. 'If mother hears . . .'

'What if she hears!' Nirmala said. 'I am not revealing any secret.'

Uma did not know how she should respond to this remark. She was afraid that her old mother, who was sleeping, might be disturbed if voices were raised. She suppressed her anger somehow, folded her hands, and pleaded: 'Please forgive me, sister-in-law. Don't add to your shameful behaviour by shouting so loudly at this hour of night.'

This infuriated Nirmala even more. Instead of lowering her voice, she doubled the volume. 'In what way is my conduct shameful?' she almost shrieked. 'Your situation is different. Your are incapable of understanding the kind of fire that is in my heart.' Taunting Uma for her widowhood, she went back to her room and bolted the door from inside.

Harish went downstairs like a puppet and spent the rest of the night on a wooden bench placed in a corner for his clients. There was no conversation between Harish and his wife for ten days after that incident. Harish rarely went out to meet his friends. And when he did, the miserable expression on his face made him an object of ridicule. His friends resented his aloofness. One of them said ironically: 'Harish, it seems that the older you get the more infatuated you become with your wife. You have to be with her all the time. Isn't that so?'

On most occasions he kept quiet, refusing to retort to such comments. But sometimes he would blurt out: 'If you have such contempt for me, why don't you leave me alone? That would be better for me and better for all of you.' His friends began to feel that it was futile talking to him. They were convinced that Harish was doomed to waste his life within the four walls of his house.

★

An epidemic of jaundice had broken out in the city. There had been a large number of casualties. Harish caught the infection and became very ill. The doctor who examined him declared gravely that the patient's condition was very serious and his chances of recovery were remote. Harish's father was no longer alive. His old mother fainted when she heard the doctor's diagnosis.

Nirmala came out of the house and said in a firm, determined voice: 'I am a devoted wife. My mother was a devoted wife. Let us see who has the power to wipe the *sindoor* from my forehead. Look after him, all of you. I am going to the temple to pray.' When she reached the temple, she stood before the image of the goddess and said: 'If he survives, I will go home. If not, I will go with him.'

For seven days and nights, she remained in the temple, subsisting on the water with which she washed the goddess' feet. On the eighth day the doctor came with the news that Harish had been cured. A large crowd followed her when she returned home. Some took the dust of her feet. Others smeared extra layers of *sindoor* on her forehead. 'She is not a human being at all', some said, 'she is obviously a goddess.' An old man said: 'Is the legend of Savitri false? There is still some *dharma* left, even in this *kaliyuga*. She has brought her husband back from the jaws of death.'

Harish's friends discussed the episode in the Club Library. The sum and substance of their comments was: when a man comes under his wife's spell and submits to her power, there has to be a deeper reason than mere infatuation. We are all married, but none of us has a wife like Nirmala. Now it is easy to understand why Harish remains at home in the evening. One of the lawyers, who had recently gone to Banaras and obtained a secret *mantra* from a hermit, thumped the table loudly and said: 'I knew all the time that Harish would not die. The spiritual power of a wife's devotion is invincible.'

When Harish went to the court for the first time after his convalescence, he was congratulated by hundreds of people. Friends surrounded him. One of them, Brajendra Babu, said: 'Friend Harish, we teased you and called you hen-pecked. Please forgive us. Not in a thousand, perhaps not in a million, is as fortunate as you are. Indeed, you are blessed by the Divine.'

Another said: 'Our country has produced great women. Nirmala is among them. All this talk about self-rule is futile. Nothing can do any good unless our women return to those ancient ideals. I think we should establish in our city of Pabna a Womens' Education Society. And now we have an ideal woman who should become the President of that Society.'

Brajendra Babu said: 'Harish, you had a flair for writing when you were a student. You should write an article on your illness and recovery and publish it in the *Ananda Bazar Patrika*.'

Harish did not respond to any of these comments and suggestions. He merely expressed his gratitude.

★

When Gosain Charan, a prosperous landlord, passed away, there was a dispute between his sons and his widowed daughter-in-law regarding the estate he had left behind. The dispute ultimately led to litigation. Harish agreed to take up the case on behalf of the widow who was the aggrieved party. She wanted to avoid being seen by agents of the opponent's party, and had therefore come to Harish's chamber for consultation quietly, without an appointment. Harish welcomed her and asked her some questions regarding the case. They talked in whispers so as not to be overheard by the clerical staff in the adjoining room. The widow said something which revealed her complete ignorance of legal matters. Harish was amused and could not help laughing at her naivete.

Suddenly a sharp, loud voice was heard: 'I am hearing everything.' The widow was startled and Harish felt very anxious. Nirmala drew the curtain aside and came into the room looking like Chandi, the ferocious image of Goddess Durga. Shaking all over, she said: 'You can never deceive me, no matter how softly you whisper. Well, you certainly don't laugh like this when you talk to me.'

The widow was frightened. 'What's all this disturbance, Harish Babu,' she said in an agitated tone.

Harish simply said, 'Crazy!'

'So I am crazy, am I?' Nirmala yelled. 'And what can you do about it?'

She approached Harish's client, weeping loudly, fell on her knees and started banging her head on the floor. The Head Clerk rushed into the room. A junior advocate stood near the door, bewildered. She looked at them and banging her head shouted, 'I know everything. I understand everything. But I am a devoted wife. I am the daughter of a devoted wife. I have not looked at another man. I have never let another man come into my thoughts. . . .' She went on incoherently.

The widow broke down. 'What kind of a drama is this,

Harish Babu?' she said. 'Why is my reputation being assailed?'
His only thought at that moment was: 'Oh Mother Earth,
why don't you open up and swallow me?' Angry and ashamed,
he confined himself to his room for hours. There was no
question of going to the court. Late in the afternoon his sister
pleaded with him to eat a little food. In the evening the family
priest came as usual and placed some water at his feet in a
silver bowl. His devoted wife had insisted on sipping, everyday,
water touched by his feet. Harish had a strong impulse to kick
that bowl away. But he controlled himself and quitely dipped
his feet in the bowl.

At night, as he lay alone in the spare room, Harish was
thinking: When will my miserable life end? How long must I
suffer? Such thoughts had come to him many times. But he
had found no way of freeing himself from the tight bond of
his wife's unwavering devotion and loyalty. The devoted wife's
absolute dedication held him in its grip like a python around
his neck.

Two years had passed. Nirmala made enquiries and found that
Lavanya Prabha had indeed been posted as Inspectress of Girls'
Schools at Pabna, though for the time being she was still in
Calcutta. One day Harish returned from the court earlier than
usual and told Uma that he had to leave for Calcutta for
some urgent work. He said he would return in four days and
asked her to call a servant and get his bedroll and suitcase
ready.

Harish and Nirmala had not been on speaking terms for a
fortnight. The railway station was far away and he had to leave
home at eight. He was selecting his legal papers and putting
them in his brief-case when Nirmala entered the room and
asked him why he was going to Calcutta. He told her that he
was going there to represent his client at a hearing in the
Calcutta High Court. She said that she wanted to go with
him.

'You want to accompany me? And may I know where in Calcutta you expect to find a place to stay?' Harish was irritated.

But Nirmala was not to be silenced so easily. 'I can stay anywhere,' she said. 'If I am with you, I will not feel ashamed even to spend a night under a tree.'

A sweet statement, made by a devoted wife. But Harish felt as though poisonous ivy had been rubbed all over his body. 'You may not be ashamed, but I would be,' he said. 'This time I have decided not to sleep under trees but to stay at a friend's house instead.'

'That is even better,' she answered calmly. 'I am sure your friend must be a man with wife and children. I will feel very comfortable with his family.'

Harish rejected her suggestion and said it would be awkward for him to take his wife to anyone's house uninvited.

'I know,' said Nirmala satirically. 'After all, how can you take me with you when you are going to stay with Lavanya?'

Harish was angry. 'You are despicable,' he said. 'You are incredibly mean. Lavanya is a widow. She is a respectable woman. Why would I go and stay at her house? And why would she invite me? Besides, I won't have the time to go anywhere. I am going for my client's work. I will be extremely busy.'

Nirmala went out of the room, but not before taunting: 'Don't worry, you will find the time for her all right.'

When Harish returned from Calcutta three days later, Nirmala asked why he had cut short his trip. He said it was because his work had been finished.

Nirmala laughed loudly and said: 'It seems you were not able to meet Lavanya after all.'

'No, I didn't meet her.'

'Since you were in Calcutta anyway, you could have at least enquired about her health.'

'I did not have the time.'

'Well, since you were so near her, you should have found the time.' It was not difficult for Harish to gauge the sarcastic undertone of Nirmala's remarks.

A month later, when Harish was about to go to the court, he called Uma and informed her that he might return late that night. Uma asked him the reason. Although his sister was standing nearby, Harish deliberately raised his voice so that Nirmala might hear him. He said he had a legal consultation with Yogin Babu.

Harish returned after midnight, got out of the car and entered the outer chamber. As he was changing his clothes, he heard his wife's voice. She called the chauffeur from the window of her room upstairs. 'Abdul, are you coming from Yogin Babu's house,' she asked.

'No, ma,' the chauffeur said, 'we had gone to the railway station.'

'From the station? Why? Did your Saheb go to receive someone?'

'Yes. Saheb had gone to receive a lady who came from Calcutta. She has come with a child.'

'From Calcutta? Did Saheb take the lady to her home after receiving her?'

'Yes,' said Abdul and took the car into the garage.

Harish overheard the conversation. The possibility of being exposed in this way had occurred to him. But he just could not ask a servant to lie for him. There was a big row in the bedroom that night. Next morning Lavanya visited Harish's house with her son. 'I have not yet met your wife,' she said. 'Please introduce me to her.' Harish felt extremely uncomfortable. For a moment he thought of excusing himself saying he was very busy. But he decided against this course and was forced to introduce Lavanya to his wife.

Nirmala welcomed Lavanya and her ten-year-old son. She gave him some sweets and invited Lavanya to sit comfortably on a cushion. 'It is my good fortune,' Lavanya said, 'to have this opportunity of seeing you. I have heard from Harish Babu about your fasts. Even now you don't look too well.'

'This is undeserved praise,' Nirmala said. 'But when did my husband tell you about my religious observances?'

Harish was standing near them. He went pale. Lavanya said: 'He told me only recently, in Calcutta. Right through dinner he kept talking about you. He was staying with Kushal Babu, whose house is very close to mine. One can easily converse across the terrace, though one has to speak a bit loudly.'

'How convenient!'

'Yes, but I found it awkward, and I sent my son over to call him to my house.'

'Oh, really?'

'Yes, but he is so orthodox that he does not eat food cooked by Brahmans. I prepared the meal and served it myself.'

Then she looked at Harish and said affectionately: 'This is nothing to be shy about, Harish Babu.'

Harish was trembling. His lies had been exposed. But to his great surprise Nirmala heard all this quietly without throwing a tantrum. Perhaps, Harish thought, she had been stunned by the sudden confirmation of her suspicions.

Helpless and defeated, Harish sat there for a long time. Several times it had crossed his mind that Lavanya should be cautioned about his wife's suspicious nature. But his self-respect, and the lurking sense of guilt for his deception, prevented him from saying anything to that educated, straightforward and sophisticated woman.

As soon as Lavanya left, Nirmala swept into the room like a thunderstorm. 'Shame on you!' she cried, 'you are a liar. How many lies have you concocted?'

Harish glared at her, his eyes bloodshot, and said, 'I will do what I please.'

Nirmala stared at her husband's face for a few moments and burst into tears. 'Go on, tell as many lies as you want to. Deceive me to your heart's content. But if there is such a thing as *dharma*, if I have been physically and mentally loyal to you, if I am a devoted wife and daughter of a devoted wife, then some day you will have to weep for me.' With these words she stormed out of the room.

All communication between Harish and his wife ended. He slept alone and ate alone. Attending to his work at the court, he went straight back home, and confined himself to the outer chamber. He used to go to the club once in a while in the evening. Now these visits had also stopped because Lavanya's house was in the same part of the town as the club.

The eyes of the devoted wife, who was the daughter of a devoted wife, had multiplied into a dozen probing eyes, observing his every movement. They never paused, never rested. Whenever Harish looked into the mirror after his bath, he felt that his skin, veins and flesh were being consumed by the fire of his saintly, devoted wife's total love and dedication. He wondered if it was a harbinger of a speedy leap to the higher world.

Now and again, just to fill his time, he would take a copy of the *Mahabharata* from his bookshelf and savour the legends about famous devoted wives of antiquity. How heroic they were! And then they and their husbands lived together in heavenly bliss for an entire *kalpa*. Harish did not know the exact duration of a *kalpa*, but his impression was that it lasted for millions of earthly years. The very thought of being together with Nirmala for a *kalpa* made him shiver, the more so when he remembered his teacher's admonition never to doubt the words of sages and saints.

Failing to find any consolation for his lot in the celestial world, his thoughts turned again to his life on earth. No hope of redemption! Had he been an Englishman, a separation could have been arranged by legal methods. Had he been a Muslim he would have secured *talaq* and freed himself. But for a simple, helpless Bengali Hindu, there was no way out. Through the influence of English-educated reformers, polygamy had been made unlawful. And to abandon a woman like Nirmala, whose entire life was focused on her husband, and whose spotless reputation made her immune from all blame—that was unthinkable. How could he show his face if he even contemplated such a step? His community would hound him and destroy him.

As he thought about what lay ahead, he felt his eyes

and ears burning. He got up from his bed, sprinkled cold water on his face and head, and spent the rest of the night sitting in a chair. For a month, Harish continued to be miserable. Then one day the moment of crisis arrived. He was getting ready to go to the District Court, when the maidservant brought him a letter. She said the messenger who had brought the letter was waiting for a reply. The envelope was open. Lavanya had written her name in a corner of the envelope.

'Who opened my letter?' Harish demanded.

'It was opened by *ma*,' the maid answered.

Harish read the letter. This is what Lavanya had written: 'You know that I have been ill. How is it you never enquired whether I am still alive? In this city, away from home, there is no one except you whom I can regard as my own. Anyway, I am alive and my illness is behind me. This is not a letter of complaint. Today is my son's birthday and I would like you to stop over at my house on your way back from the District Court to bless the boy.' There was a postscript to the letter. Lavanya wished Harish to stay on for dinner, after which a music programme had been arranged.

The letter made Harish sad. When he looked up, he saw the maid trying to conceal her laughter. So now even the household servants poked fun at him. Was there no limit to what Nirmala was capable of doing? His blood boiled. The more I endure her ways, he thought, the more she torments me.

'Who brought this letter?' he asked

'A servant girl from the other house,' the maid said.

'Tell her that I will come over after finishing my work at the court.'

Harish got into the car and went to the District Court. He returned from Lavanya's house after midnight. When he was coming out of the car he saw Nirmala standing near the bedroom window upstairs. She looked like one devoid of life, like a stone statue.

★

A team of doctors was just leaving. Gyan Babu, the family
physician had certified that Nirmala was now out of danger,
the opium having been expelled by the emetic administered.
The old physician ignored what Harish was mumbling. 'It is
no use brooding over what has happened,' he said. 'Now be
with her constantly and be very careful. There won't be any
further complications.'

That day Harish's friends at the Bar Association Library
condemned him in the harshest possible words.

Birendra Babu said: 'My guru always says that no one can
be trusted, human nature being what it is. Do you remember
the gossip about the widow who went to his chamber alone
for legal advice? You all said at the time that Harish could not
have had an affair with her. Now what has happened. Praised
be my guru! I know many things you cannot dream of.'

'How cunning is Harish!' said Brajendra Babu. 'His wife is
the personification of devotion and chastity. Yet he wants to
enjoy extra-marital pleasure. Such wonderful wives invariably
fall to the lot of rogues.'

Yogin Babu cut in: 'Just see, what a noble example our
School Inspectress is setting for our girls! I think we should
take up this matter of Lavanya Prabha's conduct with the
government.

'Yes, indeed,' said Birendra Babu. 'It is absolutely necessary
to draw the attention of the authorities to such behaviour.'

Before the day was out, everyone knew how despicable a
character was Harish, the fortunate husband of a pure, devoted,
and saintly wife. And through the courtesy of his friends all
the gossip was promptly communicated to Harish himself. His
sister Uma came, wiping her eyes, and said: 'Brother, you should
now take another wife.'

'Don't be silly, Uma.'

'I am not being silly. There was a time when polygamy was
permitted in our country.'

'At that time we were uncivilised barbarians.'

'There is nothing barbaric about polygamy. No one understands your suffering. I am the only one who knows the real situation. Are you going to let your entire life be wasted like this?'

'What is the way out, sister?' Harish said. 'I know it is possible for a *man* to leave his wife and marry again. But in our society a *woman* cannot do the same. I would have accepted your suggestion if Nirmala were to tread the same path.'

'I cannot understand what you are talking about, brother,' Uma said and left the room very displeased.

Harish sat there silently. Only one feeling pervaded his dark, despairing heart: there was no way out, none at all. Misery was his destiny. The evening had advanced and the room was now almost dark. Suddenly, the sound of devotional music reached his ears. Some Vaishnava mendicants were singing outside the neighbouring house.

It was a sad song in which a *duti* or messenger girl was describing the sorrow of the *gopis* when Krishna went away from Vrindavan. Particularly unbearable was the suffering which Radha had to endure when she was separated from her beloved Krishna. The composer of the song, and the musicians who were singing it, were obviously on the side of the girls who had been left behind. Krishna emerged from the song as cruel and heartless. The mendicant singers conveyed the pathos vividly.

Harish's sympathies, however, lay with Krishna. He became Krishna's advocate. The lawyer within him said: 'O Messenger-girl, it is all very well to praise a woman's unwavering devotion. Indeed, there is nothing in the world comparable to her dedication. But there is something which needs to be pointed out, something which you will probably not be able to appreciate. I know what scared Krishna and why he escaped from Vrindavan. He must have found Radha's absolute devotion unbearably oppressive. Her unshakeable, ever-watchful devotion must have become so overwhelming that Krishna felt imprisoned and sought a release.'

Harish paused thinking for a while. He re-examined the

dilemma and muttered to himself: Krishna's situation was different. He had a convenient place in Mathura where he could hide. But I am in real trouble. No way of escape, no place to hide! Now only Krishna can save me. May the Lord call me to his heavenly abode and give me a place at his feet. That is my only hope.

The Picture

This story goes back to a period when Burma had not yet become a British colony. The Burmese had their own monarchy, their own military commanders, their own allies. They were sovereign. Mandalay was the capital. But many members of the royal family had settled down in other cities. One of them had migrated, a long time ago, to Imedin, a village about ten miles south of the city of Pegu. Wealthy, and possessing considerable land, he lived in a large mansion with an extensive garden.

When the master of this estate thought he was being called from above, he sent for his dearest friend and said to him: 'Ba Ko, it was my desire to see my daughter married to your son in my lifetime. But that was not to be. My time has come. I am leaving Ma-Shoye behind. Please look after her.'

The dying man did not consider it necessary to say anything else. Ba Ko was his childhood friend. There was a time when Ba Ko, too, had been a very wealthy man. But he had spent all his wealth on charities and on the construction of temples. Not only had he lost all his assets but he was also heavily in debt. And yet his friend had not hesitated to entrust him with his daughter and all his property. At that moment Ba Ko realized the true meaning of friendship. But he did not have to carry the burden of his responsibility too long. He, too, was called away, without having experienced the joys and sorrows of old age.

Such was the love and devotion of the village folk towards this pious person, who had remained poor by choice, that his funerary rites were performed on a lavish scale. Ba Ko's body was decorated with garlands and sandal-paste. It was then placed on a raised

'Chhabi' from *Chhabi O Anyanya Galpa* (Chhabi and Other Stories), January 1920

pyre to the accompaniment of music and dance. Food was distributed. It seemed as though the celebration would never cease. Escaping for a moment from this blend of mourning and celebration, Ba Ko's son, Ba Thin, was sitting under a tree in a secluded place. He was weeping silently. Suddenly he heard a sound. When he turned his head, he saw Ma-Shoye standing behind him. She wiped her eyes with the end of her shawl and sat by his side. Holding his right hand in hers, she said slowly: 'Father is dead, but your Ma-Shoye is still alive.'

II

Ba Thin was a painter. His last painting had been sent to the royal court through an art dealer. The king was pleased with it and rewarded Ba Thin with a precious ring. Ma-Shoye's eyes glistened with joy. Coming close she said in a gentle voice: 'Ba Thin, you will become the greatest painter in the world.' Ba Thin replied with a laugh. 'Perhaps by selling my paintings I will be able to repay my father's debts.' Ma-Shoye always blushed when he referred to the money he owed her. 'If you talk like that about me being your creditor, I will never come to you again,' she said. Ba Thin kept silent. But he knew that his father's soul would not be emancipated unless the debts were repaid. He felt deeply agitated when he remembered this obligation.

For his next painting Ba Thin had selected a story from the *Jatakas*. He hardly raised his head from the canvas throughout the day. As usual, Ma-Shoye would come to his house. She used to tidy up and decorate his bedroom, drawing-room and studio with her own hands, not wanting to leave these chores to the servants.

She saw Ba Thin's reflection in a large mirror. For a long time she looked at it and said: 'Ba Thin, if you had been a woman you would have become the Chief Queen of our country by now.'

Ba Thin raised his head and said with a smile: 'Tell me, how would this have happened?'

'The King would have married you,' Ma-Shoye said, 'and placed you on the throne. He has many other queens, but does any of them have such hair, such a glowing complexion, such a lovely face?'

Ba Thin heard these compliments and resumed working on the painting. He recalled hearing such remarks when he was an art student in Mandalay. Turning to Ma-Shoye he said light-heartedly: 'But you would have found a way to steal my beauty, Ma-Shoye. Then you would have pushed me aside and sat next to the King.'

Ma-Shoye did not respond to this repartee. She was engrossed in her own thoughts. 'O Ba Thin,' she muttered, 'you are tender like a woman. Indeed you have a feminine charm. There is no limit to your beauty.'

Ba Thin was so attractive in her eyes that she often felt inferior in his presence.

III

It was the first day of spring. Many outsiders visited the village of Imedin to witness the celebrations of the Festival of Spring. Horse-racing was one of the items. Ma-Shoye came to Ba Thin's studio and stood behind him. He was painting with intense concentration and did not hear her footsteps. 'Turn round and look at me,' Ma-Shoye said.

Ba Thin was surprised to see her dressed in glamorous clothes, with make-up, and hair beautifully arranged.

'Why this sudden sprucing-up?' he asked.

'Don't you know about the horse race today? Its winner will garland me.'

'No, I had not heard anything about it.'

Ba Thin was about to lift his brush again when Ma-Shoye embraced him and said: 'Let's go. It is getting late.'

They were about the same age. Possibly, Ba Thin was a few months older. For all their nineteen years they had played together, argued, quarrelled, even come to blows. And they had always loved each other.

Ba Thin pointed to the reflections of their faces in the mirror, like two roses blooming: 'Just look at us!' he said.

Ma-Shoye looked at the two faces in the mirror with thirsty eyes. She suddenly realized that she, too, was extremely beautiful, like Ba Thin. She shut her eyes and said: 'I am like the stain on the moon.'

'No, Ma-Shoye,' he said, 'you are not a stain on the moon. You are moonlight. Just look at yourself once again.' Ma-Shoye felt shy. She did not open her eyes.

They would have continued talking like that had not a crowd of merry-makers passed by. They were on the way to the festival. 'Come, it is time to go,' Ma-Shoye said. Ba Thin said that he could not possibly go with her as he had to complete the picture within five days.

'And what if you don't finish it in five days?'

'The customer will go away to Mandalay and I won't get any money.'

The mention of money always hurt Ma-Shoye. 'But I can't let you work so hard,' she said, sounding offended. 'I can't allow you to risk your health just for money.' Ba Thin did not say anything. The thought of his late father's unpaid debt made him sad.

Ma-Shoye saw that he was worried. 'Sell your painting to me,' she said. 'I will pay double the price.'

Ba Thin knew that she could easily afford that. 'But what will you do with my painting?' he asked.

Pointing to the expensive necklace she was wearing, Ma-Shoye said: 'I will hang it on the wall in my bedroom where I can look at it all night.'

'And after that?'

'After that a big moon will rise and send its light into the room through the open window, and illumine your sleeping face.'

'And what will happen after that, Ma-Shoye?'

'After that I will gently wake you up and . . .' but she could not finish what she was about to say. Her ox-cart was waiting outside the door and the driver was calling her.

'I will hear the rest of the story later,' Ba Thin said. 'Go quickly. You are getting late.'

But Ma-Shoye showed no signs of moving. She settled down

comfortably in her chair and said that she was not feeling well enough to go.

'But you have promised to be there. Every one will be waiting for you.'

'Let them wait. I am not ashamed of breaking such a promise. I will not go.'

When Ba Thin again asked her to get up, she said she would go only if he agreed to accompany her. 'I would have certainly come,' Ba Thin said, 'if I could spare the time. But I won't allow you to break your word on my account. Don't delay any more. Get up and go to the festival.'

When she heard his firm voice and saw his serious face, Ma-Shoye stood up abruptly. 'You are pushing me away for your own convenience,' she said. 'I will never come to see you again.' Her face darkened with wounded pride. Ba Thin's dedication to his work was overshadowed by his deep affection for her. 'Don't make such a terrible resolve, Ma-Shoye,' he said with a smile, pulling her towards himself.

But she was not pacified. 'You know very well that I cannot bear to leave you,' she said. 'You need me all the time. You cannot take care of your food, clothes, anything. You know I will come back. That is why you are sending me away.' With these angry words she hurried out of the room.

IV

Ma-Shoye arrived at the festival ground in her bullock-cart which was adorned with peacock plumes and plated with silver. A large crowd greeted her enthusiastically. The most important place of honour was kept for her. She was to present flower garlands to the contestants of the race and other events. And the victor in the race was to have the privilege of garlanding her. The entire gathering would envy him for his good fortune. The horses had been decorated beautifully. The riders, wearing red robes, had already mounted them and were trying to control their excitement and impatience. Nothing in the world seemed impossible for them at that moment.

The contestants formed a line, awaiting the moment when their fortune and their valour would be tested. At last the signal was given with the ringing of a bell. The race started. The riders entered the fray, throwing all caution to the winds. This was a display of courage. It was like a war. Ma-Shoye's ancestors had all been warriors. Although she was a woman, their blood flowed through her veins. She admired their courage. She was ready to welcome the victor with all her heart. So when a young man from another village, a man unknown to her, approached her with quivering lips and garlanded her with perspiring hands, she was thrilled. Some respectable women in the audience did not approve of her eagerness.

While returning from the festival ground, she made the victor sit by her side in the cart. In Ma-Shoye's mind there was no comparison between this strong, athletic hero and the slim, gentle, scholarly painter. The young man's name was Po Thin. During their conversation, Ma-Shoye learnt that Po Thin also came from a wealthy, aristocratic family and that they were distantly related. She asked him to join her for dinner that night. She had already asked several other people. A large crowd, still in a festive mood, was following her cart. The sky resounded with their singing. When the crowd passed before Ba Thin's house, he left his work for a few moments and stood by the window watching the procession.

V

The next evening, at dinner, Ma-Shoye said to Ba Thin: 'I had a pleasant time yesterday. Many people were kind enough to come to my house for dinner. I did not invite you because I know how busy you are these days.'

Ba Thin's entire attention was focused on his canvas. Without raising his head he said, 'You did well,' and resumed his work. Ma-Shoye was shocked by his indifference. There were so many experiences she wanted to share with him. As Ba Thin had not been able to visit the festival, she ardently wanted to chat with him for a long time. Now she felt let down and frustrated.

Ma-Shoye did not have the strength to fling open the door which Ba Thin's indifference and silence had closed on her. She did not feel like doing the little chores which she always used to do at his house. For a long time she remained silent. Not once did Ba Thin raise his head, not once did he ask her about the previous evening, nor did he show the slightest curiosity. It seemed as though his work had left him barely enough time to breathe. For a long time, Ma-Shoye waited and then, feeling snubbed and slighted, told him that she was leaving. 'All right,' he said, still looking at his painting. What was really going on in his heart? For a moment, she thought that she would confront him and clear up the matter. But she could not open her lips.

When she reached home she found Po Thin waiting for her. He had come to thank her for the evening party. Ma-Shoye welcomed her guest and asked him to be comfortable. Po Thin talked about Ma-Shoye's wealth, and about her distinguished ancestry. He referred to her father's fine reputation and the esteem in which he was held by the royal family and the court. He went on talking for a long time. Some of the things he said registered on her. Others failed to catch her attention.

Besides being strong and brave, Po Thin was also very clever. He started the conversation by talking about the royal family at Mandalay. But soon he was paying Ma-Shoye compliments on her beauty and charm. He spoke with an artificial air of simplicity. Ma-Shoye blushed when he praised her beauty and youthfulness. But she also experienced an undercurrent of pleasure and vanity. Before he took leave, Po Thin managed to secure another invitation for dinner at her house.

But after Po Thin's departure, as she recalled what he had said, she felt small. She repented having invited him for dinner again. To avoid being alone with him, she immediately sent her servants with invitations to several other friends and acquaintances. They came for another evening of dinner, music, dance and light conversation punctuated by laughter. The party continued late into the night. Ma-Shoye was tired when she went to bed. But sleep eluded her. Surprisingly, she gave no thought to the person for whose sake she had been forced to throw such a big party. On the contrary she was thinking all the time about that other man who was alone in his secluded house, untouched by the noise and the boisterous conversation of her guests.

VI

Through sheer force of habit, Ma-Shoye went to Ba Thin's house again early next morning. Once again he said, 'Come in,' and resumed working on the painting.

Ma-Shoye sat close to him as usual. But she felt, as she had never felt before, that he had become very distant. For some time, she was unable to decide how to start the conversation. Then she asked him how much work remained to complete the painting. He replied he would still have to put in a lot of work.

'What have you done these past two days?' she asked. Ignoring her question, he handed her a box of cheroots with the remark that he could not bear the smell of liquor.

Ma-Shoye was stung by his words. Pushing the box aside, she said: 'I do not smoke cheroots in the morning. Nor do I try to conceal the smell of wine by smoking tobacco.'

'I am not inventing the smell of liquor,' Ba Thin said calmly. 'Perhaps your clothes somehow came in contact with it.'

Ma-Shoye stood up like lightning. 'You are jealous just as you are mean,' she said. 'That is why you have insulted me without any reason. Very well, then. I am taking away all my clothes from your house for ever.' And she made for the door.

In his usual calm, restrained manner Ba Thin said: 'No one has ever called me envious or mean. I warned you only because I see you going on the downward path.'

Ma-Shoye turned back from the door and faced him. 'And how am I taking the downward path?' she asked.

'That is what I see. That is what I think.'

'You can think what you please. But your views certainly do not correspond to those of our departed parents who gave us their blessings.'

She went away. Ba Thin remained there, motionless. He

could never have imagined that any one could hurt him so cruelly, that love could turn into poison in just a single day.

When Ma-Shoye reached home, she found Po Thin sitting in her drawing-room. He stood up and gave her a sweet smile. On seeing him smile, Ma-Shoye knit her brows and asked if there was any particular reason for his visit.

'There is nothing particular,' he said, 'But I thought . . .'

'In that case I won't have the time today,' she said and went towards the staircase leading to the upper storey. Recalling the hospitality he had received from her the previous evening, Po Thin was confused. He tipped the servant one rupee and went out of the door whistling.

VII

Two human beings who had never been separated from each other since their childhood now failed to see each other for more than a month. Ma-Shoye tried to console herself with the thought that what had happened was probably for the best. She was no longer held in bondage by a web of attachment. The proud daughter of a wealthy father, she had in the past desisted from many of the things she wanted to do because she was afraid of offending the calm, self-possessed, and restrained Ba Thin.

Now she was free. She was no longer accountable to any one for her actions. Such were the thoughts in her mind. She did not open the door leading to the inner chamber of her heart. Had she done so, she would have realized that she was deceiving herself. In that secret, silent chamber she would have seen two persons sitting, facing each other night and day—not loving, not quarrelling, simply looking at each other and shedding tears.

This pathetic image of her life was invisible to her mind's eye then. That is why the shame of defeat did not devastate her. That is why she staged the futile drama of parties and celebrations at her house. Every year, on her birthday, there used to be a dinner, accompanied by merry-making and charities. But this time, the birthday celebration at Ma-Shoye's house had been arranged on an unusually lavish scale. All the servants of the household were

busy. All the neighbours had joined in. All were enjoying
themselves. The only person who was unhappy and restless
was Ma-Shoye.

She felt that everything was purposeless. It was all a mere
show. All these years she had assumed that Ba Thin, like all
other men, was capable of feeling jealous, that he, too, had
human weaknesses. But now she wondered whether the sounds
of all the festivities being held at her house were able to penetrate
his secluded room, whether his work was being disturbed in the
slightest degree. Possibly, he might put down his brush for a
few moments, or might pace about his house unsteadily. He
might even be passing sleepless nights, tossing in bed.

Ma-Shoye used to derive a peculiar kind of pleasure in
fantasizing and day-dreaming. But today it gave her no such
pleasure. Her speculation had no basis. Nothing was happening
to Ba Thin. Nothing at all. He would not interrupt his work, she
told herself. It is false, all this talk of eternal love. It's nothing but
self-deception. He neither wants to hold any one, nor to be held
by any one. His spare, delicate body has become hard like a rock.
No storm can shake it. She kept musing. Meanwhile, the birthday
festivities were in full swing. Po Thin took part in everything. He
seemed to be everywhere. Acquaintances whispered that some
day Po Thin would be the master of Ma-Shoye's house, and
some even ventured to say that the day was not far off.

The entire village thronged to Ma-Shoye's house to
congratulate her. Everywhere there was rejoicing. But the person
who was the centre of attention, she for whom all this was
happening, was restless. The shadow of sadness darkened her
face. Except for the household servants, no one noticed it.
They understood that it was a mere travesty of a birthday
celebration. Where was that person who was always the first to
greet and bless her on her birthday and put a garland around
her neck? He was not there. The garland was not there. His
blessings and greetings were not there.

An old man from her father's time approached Ma-Shoye and
said: 'I don't see Ba Thin anywhere, little daughter. Where is he?'

The old man had retired from service and was living in

another village. He knew nothing about the misunderstanding between the two young people. He had heard vaguely from servants that there was some friction.

Ma-Shoye said to him in a sharp voice: 'If you need to see him, you should go to his house. Why have you come here?'

'Very well, I will go there,' he said, and went away, muttering to himself: 'It is no use seeing Ba Thin alone. I want to see the two of them together. Otherwise the long walk from my village will have been in vain.'

Ma-Shoye guessed the old servant's thoughts. She somehow tried to busy herself with the numerous small chores involved in entertaining guests. Suddenly, she heard a faint sound, turned her head, and saw Ba Thin. A shock went through her. Composing herself quickly, she walked away without a word.

'Little daughter,' the old man said, 'whatever may have happened, he is your guest after all. Are you not going to talk to him?'

'But I never asked you to call him here,' she protested.

'It was wrong of me to have done so,' the servant said. 'I plead guilty.'

'Moreover,' Ma-Shoye said, 'there are so many other people here who can talk to him.'

'There are, indeed. But it is no longer necessary. He has gone away.'

'O my stars! You could have at least asked him have food before he left.'

'No, I still have some self-respect left,' said the old man angrily and walked out.

VIII

The insulting treatment he had received at Ma-Shoye's house brought tears to Ba Thin's eyes. But he did not blame anyone for what had happened. 'It was shameless of me to have gone there,' he thought, 'and I deserved what I got.' He did not know at that time how he would be insulted a couple of days later, and which would be much more humiliating.

This story began with a picture that Ba Thin was painting. After more than a month of unremitting toil that picture, based on an episode from the sacred *Jatakas*, was completed. Ba Thin was happy and contented that morning. The prospective buyer was informed that the picture was ready and that he should go to the royal court where Ba Thin would give him the painting. They met, but when the cloth which covered the painting was removed the man was taken aback. He looked at it for a long time. Then sadly and much disappointed he said: 'I cannot possibly give this painting to His Majesty the King.'

With a mixture of amazement and fear, Ba Thin asked him the reason for rejecting his painting.

The purchaser, who was an art connoisseur with a perceptive eye said: 'The reason is that I recognize the face in your picture. To give a human face to a divine being is to insult the gods. The King will be furious with me if I show him this painting.'

Ba Thin was crestfallen. The purchaser looked him straight in the eye and said with an ironical smile: 'Look at it carefully. You will easily recognize the person whom the face in your picture resembles. No, this painting will not do at all.'

Ba Thin continued to stare at his own work for a long time after his client had left. Layer by layer, the mist lifted from his eyes. His pent-up feelings overflowed in a profusion of tears. He understood clearly that the beauty and sweetness that he had drawn out of his heart, and transformed into an image of perfection, did not belong to the divine being he had laboured so hard to portray. That form had not emerged from a sacred source. He had been deluding himself. What he had created was not a celestial being but his own Ma-Shoye. He closed his eyes and wailed: 'O God! Why have you punished me so cruelly? What was my crime?'

IX

Emboldened by the way Ba Thin was treated, Po Thin tried to get closer to Ma-Shoye. He approached her and said: 'Even the gods desire you, Ma-Shoye. I am a mere human being.'

Ma-Shoye, who was feeling confused, said: 'But he who does not desire me is perhaps greater than any god.' She did not wish to hear him speak about himself and his feelings. So she changed the subject of conversation and said: 'I hear that you have a lot of influence at the court. Will you do something for me . . . and quickly?'

Po Thin asked eagerly in what way he could help her. 'There is someone from whom I have to get back my money,' Ma-Shoye said, 'but I cannot recover it myself. I don't have anything in writing. Can you find a way out?' Po Thin assured her that it would be done. He reminded her that he was himself an officer appointed by the King. Ma-Shoye urged him to move in the matter without delay, if possible that very day.

All these years the debt she now wanted to recover had been totally insignificant, even laughable, in her eyes. But now, forgetting everything else, she said: 'I will not relinquish anything. Not a penny. I will suck the money out of him as a leech sucks blood. Can't we do something today, right now?'

Po Thin did not need any permission. What had happened was beyond his fondest dreams. Somehow concealing his joy he said: 'According to the rules, a notice of seven days has to be given. After that you can suck as much blood as you wish. I will not object.'

'Good,' she said. 'Now you can go.'

Po Thin swallowed the discourtesy. He thought that his designs on that foolish, thoughtless girl would soon be realized. He was happy when he returned home. 'It won't take too long now,' he chuckled. He did not know that a surprise was in store for him.

X

Ba Thin received the court summons regarding his debt. For a long time he sat quietly, the legal documents in his hand. Something had to be done as soon as possible in order to meet the deadline. He remembered that one day Ma-Shoye had expressed displeasure at his father's extravagance. He had never entirely forgiven her for that. He did not want to invite further indignity by asking her for more time. But he was not sure whether his father's debts could be completely paid off even after selling all his possessions.

Next day he went to the house of a rich money-lender whom he knew. He told the money-lender about his assets. It turned out that what he owned was more than sufficient to cover all the debts. He took the money and came home. The extent and severity of the damage done to his body and his mind by Ma-Shoye's needless cruelty suddenly became clear to him. He fell down unconscious with high fever. How he passed the days and nights, he did not know. When he regained consciousness fully, he discovered that it was the last day for making the payment.

For the sake of her own vanity, Ma-Shoye had hurt Ba Thin's pride to an unimaginable degree. Her expectation was that she would soon have him at her mercy. When the servant approached and informed her that Ba Thin was waiting downstairs, she laughed and said: 'I know. This is what I was waiting for.' Ma-Shoye climbed down the stairs. Ba Thin stood up and faced her. The pain of repentance shot through Ma-Shoye like a dagger.

What a terrible thing she had done! She did not really want to get back her money. She did not attach the slightest importance to wealth. And yet, in the name of money, she had inflicted such a cruel blow upon one so dear to her.

Ba Thin broke the silence. 'Today is the last of the seven days you had allowed me,' he said. 'Here is your money.'

Alas! How strange is human nature. Vanity clings to a person even in the face of death, let alone lesser calamities. 'I will not accept part payment,' Ma-Shoye said. 'In the court notice you were asked to repay the entire debt.'

Ba Thin's agonized lips parted in a dry smile. 'I know,' he said. 'I have brought the entire amount I owe you.'

'The entire amount?' she asked incredulously. 'Where did you get so much money?'

'You will find out tomorrow. The money is in that box. You can ask someone to count it.'

Meanwhile, the cart-driver was getting impatient. He came to the door and asked Ba Thin to hurry up. 'We should be on the road now,' he said. 'It will be difficult to find a lodging at Pegu if we reach there late at night.'

Ma-Shoye looked out of the window. She saw boxes, bedding and other pieces of luggage piled in the cart. The driver stood near it. Ma-Shoye was frightened. She hurled questions at Ba Thin in rapid succession. 'Who is going to Pegu? Whose cart is this? How did you secure so much money? Speak up! Why are you silent ? . . . Your eyes are so dry and crinkled. What has happened?. . . And why must I wait till tomorrow to find out? You have to tell me right now.'

She was speaking like one in a trance. After a few moments she came close to him, held his hand, and said anxiously: 'My God! You have high fever. No wonder your face is so pale.'

Ba Thin withdrew his hand. In his usual calm, gentle voice he asked her to sit by him. 'I am going to Mandalay,' he said. 'Now listen to me. I am going to make a last request. Find a nice young man and get married soon. It is not good for you to remain single any longer. And one more thing . . .'

Ba Thin remained silent for a while. Then, in a voice even gentler and softer than before, he continued: 'Yes, one more thing. You should keep in mind what I am about to say now. Ma-Shoye, never forget that both pride and shyness are like ornaments for a woman. But only in moderation. If vanity becomes excessive . . .'

Ma-Shoye cut him short. 'I will listen to all this some other time. First tell me how you got the money.'

'Why do you ask? Is there anything about me which is hidden from you?'

'Tell me at once. Where did you find so much money?'

'I am repaying my father's debts by selling his property. You know very well that nothing else is mine.'

'What about the flower garden?'

'The garden, too, was my father's.'

'And your valuable collection of books?'

'The library was also built by my father.'

Ma-Shoye sighed. 'All right,' she said. 'Now go upstairs and sleep.' Ba Thin said that he simply had to go to Pegu and then to Mandalay. Ma-Shoye flared up and said: 'What? In this condition? Do you actually believe that I will let you travel when you are running temperature?' She held his hand again.

Ba Thin looked at her face. He was amazed to see the complete transformation that had taken place. Her expression was totally free from pride, annoyance, displeasure or disappointment. All he saw was immeasurable love and intense, genuine anxiety. Ma-Shoye's face held him spellbound. Silently, with slow steps, he followed her upstairs and entered her bedroom.

She made him lie down on the bed and sat close to him. Gazing upon his pale face with her bubbling eyes, she said: 'Do you imagine that you have repaid the debt with a handful of coins? Mandalay is far away. I will not allow you even to step outside the house. If you dare to take one step without my permission, I will jump off the roof and kill myself. Believe me. I am warning you. Have you any idea how much sorrow you have caused me? I won't bear it any more.'

Ba Thin did not answer. He pulled a sheet over himself and heaved a deep sigh of relief. Then he turned on his side and fell asleep.

The Temple

$\mathcal{A}$ community of potters lived in a small village on the river bank. They made dolls and images out of the soft, moist clay collected from the bank. When the images were ready, the potters took them to the bazaar. Day after day they made these images. That was their only source of livelihood. The clay images provided them food and clothing. The womenfolk fetched water from the river and cooked for their husbands and children. When the fire was extinguished they took the images out of the embers and ashes and gave them to the potters. Then the images were painted.

Shaktinath, a young man from a Brahmin family, turned up quite unexpectedly one day and joined the potters. Emaciated and sickly, he had given up his friends and relatives, his studies and sports to devote all his energy to pottery. He would help the potters by sharpening the reeds and scraping off the specks of dust and mud sticking to the images. Soon, he became almost a part of them. The potters welcomed him and addressed him respectfully as Bamun Thakur or Thakur Dada. Shaktinath was, however, unhappy when he saw the clumsy manner in which the potters painted the images. They drew the eyes, brows, lips and other features with lamp-black and ink without the slightest regard for accuracy. Sometimes one of the eyebrows became thicker than the other. Sometimes black stains were left under the lips.

One day Shaktinath became impatient and pointed out the defects to the seniormost potter who was known as Sarkar Dada. 'Why do you paint these dolls so carelessly, Sarkar Dada?'

'Mandir' from *Kashinath O Anyanya Galpa* (Kashinath and Other Stories), September 1917

he asked. The craftsman looked at him gently and said: 'It would be very expensive to spend more time on details, Thakur Dada. The price would go up. Who will pay four pice for an image which sells for just one pice?'

★

Shaktinath was not satisfied by this simple explanation. A one-pice image had to be sold for only one pice, he was told. It didn't matter if it only had half an eyebrow, if its facial features were devoid of symmetry. It was a one-pice doll. Why put in the extra effort? Some child would buy it, caress it, hug it, put it to sleep. Then it would get broken and be thrown away. That was all there was to it. But Shaktinath was not convinced.

In the morning Shaktinath had made a small bundle of some rice-flakes. Now he munched what remained of the flakes, slowly and without relish. Then he returned to his dilapidated home and stood in the courtyard. There was no one in the house. His old father, Madhusudan Bhattacharya, had gone to the landlord's mansion to perform the ceremonial worship of Lord Krishna. He would bring back a portion of the food offered to the deity—soaked rice, a couple of bananas and radishes. Father and son subsisted on that meagre fare.

Their small garden was in a state of utter neglect. There were a few flowering shrubs such as oleanders, cannas and jasmines. But the garden was full of weeds. There was no lady in the house, no one to supervise or introduce any order. The poor old priest somehow passed his miserable days. And Shaktinath walked in the garden mechanically, plucking a few flowers and pruning a few branches at random.

Almost every morning, Shaktinath walked over to the potters' hut. Of late he had been occupied in colouring the images. Sarkar Dada selected some of the best ones for Shaktinath to paint. Although he knew that its price would still be one pice, Shaktinath spent a lot of time over each doll. Sometimes, however, Sarkar Dada was able to get a higher price for dolls painted by Shaktinath. This made the young man happy.

The landlord of the village was a Kayastha, not a Brahmin. Deeply devoted to Krishna and Radha, he had erected a fine temple to them. There was a beautifully, sculpted image of the family deity, Madan Mohan. Behind it, on a silver throne raised on a pedestal, there was an image of Radha plated with gold. Pictures depicting Krishna sporting with the *gopis* in Vrindavan adorned the temple walls. From a velvet lotus on the ceiling hung an enormous candelabrum. All the ingredients and silver utensils used in worship were kept aside on a marble platform. The fragrance of sandalwood powder and fresh flowers filled the temple. It seemed as though the flowers and fragrances had been offered keeping in mind the beauty and joy of heaven. The breeze gently wafted the fragrance to every corner.

Long ago, when the landlord, Raj Narain Babu, reached middle age and realized that the shadows cast by his life were becoming longer and fainter, when it dawned upon him that he was not destined to enjoy the luxuries of his estate much longer, he stood in a corner of the temple and shed tears of sorrow. His daughter, Aparna, was only five years old at this time. She stood near her father and watched the priest, Madhusudan Bhattacharya, anointing the black image of Krishna with sandal-paste and circumambulating Radha's throne with flower offerings in his hand. She felt the fragrance of flowers touching her like a blessing. From that day on, Aparna accompanied her father every day to the temple for the ceremonial worship. She felt strangely elated and amazed by all that she saw and heard.

With every passing year Aparna became increasingly attached to the temple. Like other Hindu girls she understood more and more vividly the idea of Divinity. She showed by all her actions, that the temple which meant so much to her father had become extremely dear to her heart too. She would spend the entire day in or near the temple. She kept the temple floor meticulously clean. She could not tolerate the sight of a single wilted flower or dry blade of grass. If she saw a wet spot on the floor she immediately wiped it off with the end of her garment. Raj Narain Babu's religious fervour was known to everyone. But Aparna's devotion surpassed even her father's.

So many flowers were now offered that a larger vase had to be purchased. The vessel containing sandal powder was also replaced by a new, larger one. The amount of food offered to the deities and distributed among the devotees also increased considerably. The worship became so elaborate that the old priest found it difficult to cope with the work. When Raj Narain Babu saw the transformation that had taken place in the temple he remarked that God himself had sent Aparna to his house for his own worship. He cautioned all his friends not to say a word to Aparna about her excessive zeal.

In due course Aparna was married. The thought of leaving the temple and going away to another village made her serious. The smile faded from her face. An auspicious day was selected for her journey to her father-in-law's house. As a massive rain-cloud conceals the lightning within its body and remains suspended in the sky, so did Aparna remain stunned and immobile when the day of her departure actually arrived. She approached her father and said: 'I have made all the arrangements for the service of the deities. Please see to it that the worship continues undisturbed.' Her old father burst into tears. 'I assure you, my child,' he said, 'that nothing will be disturbed.'

Aparna was silent. Her eyes were dry. She was trying in vain to console her father. Just as a warrior suppresses his own agony and with a hollow laugh mounts his horse to go into battle, leaving behind his home and family, so also Aparna climbed into the palanquin and left her village, carrying upon her head new burdens and unknown responsibilities. When tears came to her eyes, she reflected that there was no one to wipe her father's tears. Sounds from temple bells pierced her heart like arrows. Whenever she heard those familiar sounds during her journey she felt homesick. She drew aside the curtain of the palanquin and gazed into the dark sky, feeling lost, thinking of the temple she had left behind. One of the maids from her father-in-law's house, who had been instructed to walk behind the palanquin, tried to soothe Aparna. 'Why are you crying, daughter-in-law?' she said. 'This is not the way to go to your new house.' Aparna covered her face with both hands and checked her tears. Then she quickly closed the palanquin window.

While Aparna was proceeding sadly towards her new home, her father stood quietly in the temple. Radha's image appeared dimly through his tears and through the smoke of the incense. But he could see in the matchless beauty of Radha the lovely face of his own daughter.

Aparna was now in her father-in-law's house. When she spoke with her husband, she felt that conversation was being forced upon her. There was no emotion, no liveliness. Neither the coyness of intimacy nor the excitement of her first conjugal experience could restore the former lustre to her dull eyes. From the very outset of their married life, both husband and wife had a strange sense of guilt which overwhelmed them like a river in flood.

Once, late at night, her husband Amarnath asked: 'Aparna, are you not happy in my house?'

'No,' she said.

'Would you like to return to your father's house?'

'Yes, I would.'

'Would you like to go tomorrow?'

'Yes, I would like that very much.'

Amarnath was shocked by her reply. After a little while he said: 'And what if you are unable to go?'

'In that case,' Aparna said, 'I will simply remain as I am.'

'Don't you need me at all, Aparna?'

Aparna covered herself properly with a bedsheet and said: 'Please don't say such things. Such talk can only lead to conflicts.'

'How do you know that there will be a conflict?'

'I know. I have seen the quarrels between my elder brother and his wife. I find any kind of conflict extremely unpleasant.'

Amarnath was pained and annoyed. He had suddenly found the truth for which he had thus far groped in darkness. 'Come, Aparna,' he said, 'let's have a quarrel. It is better to have a conflict than to remain as we are now.'

'Why quarrel?' Aparna said calmly. 'You should get some sleep.'

Amarnath could not sleep for the rest of the night. And he was unable to guess whether his wife was awake or asleep.

The following morning Aparna decided to occupy herself in household chores. She also started spending a lot of time in prayer and worship, and refused to participate in any of the activities that were going on in the house. She ignored the taunts of her sister-in-law who referred to her husband as a hermit. She felt that day after day of her life was passing by without any meaning or purpose. A strong desire to return to her father's temple shook her, as the ocean is shaken by its attraction for the full moon. She was unable to overcome her longing either through her household work or through the amusements and diversions that were available. She brooded all the time. Her melancholy heart found no cheer in the fondness of her husband or in the respectful attention of the servants.

★

Amarnath wondered whether he had failed to appreciate what his wife wanted. So he decided to bring her some gifts. At about ten one morning, when Aparna had finished her bath and was about to begin her worship, Amarnath said to her in a sweet voice: 'Aparna, I have brought some gifts for you. Will you please accept them?' Aparna smiled and said that she would gladly accept what he had brought. Amarnath was happy. He unwrapped a fancy handkerchief and took out a small box on which Aparna's name had been engraved in gold letters.

But when he raised his head and looked at her, hoping to see a joyful face, he found that she was staring at him blankly with glassy eyes. In a moment his enthusiasm was shattered to bits. He tried to hide behind an unnatural laugh, for he had been cruelly rebuffed. Although he felt ashamed, he opened the lid of the box and started taking out small bottles of perfume and other gifts.

Aparna stopped him 'Have you brought all these gifts for me?'

'Yes.'

'Is the box also for me?'

'Yes, of course.'

'Then it is not necessary to take out these gifts. Let them remain in the box?'

'All right. I will leave them there. But will you use them?'

Aparna knit her brows. All these days she had submitted to her lot and reconciled herself to defeat. But now she was rebellious. Even her husband's gesture of affection was seen by her in a distorted way. 'Keep all these gifts,' she said harshly. 'There are others besides me who will find some use for them.' And without waiting for his answer she moved away to the *puja* room.

Wounded, Amarnath sat down helplessly, the gift box in his hands. He cursed himself for his simplicity and sighing deeply said: 'Aparna is really stone-hearted!' Tears streamed from his eyes. He wiped them off. If Aparna had openly hurt or defied him, it would have been a different matter. But she had hit him hard without actually insulting him in so many words.

How should he respond to her behaviour? Should he drag her out of the *puja* room and trample upon the gifts that she had scorned? Such ideas of vengeance assailed his mind. He even thought of calling all the people in the house to his room and declaring that he would never see his wife's face again. He contemplated wandering away aimlessly and becoming an ascetic. Then he fantasized about rescuing Aparna from a terrible calamity some day. Humiliated, he turned over all kinds of alternatives possible and impossible in his mind, weighing the pros and cons of each of them. For quite a while he sat there, weeping silently and vaguely contemplating his future actions.

★

For two days and nights after that incident Amarnath did not enter the bedroom. His mother tried to reason with him, and rebuked Aparna for hurting him. On the third night Aparna approached her husband, apologized, and said: 'Please forgive me if I have hurt you.' Amarnath did not know what to say. He sat on the edge of the bed and started straightening the sheet nervously.

'Won't you pardon me, please?' Aparna said again.

'Forgiveness?' he said without looking at her. 'For what? And do I have the right even to forgive?'

Aparna held her husband's hands. 'Don't talk like that,' she said. 'You are my lord. Where would I be if you don't forgive me? How can I live here if you are angry? Please tell me why you are angry?'

'I am not angry,' he said sadly.

'Really?' she asked. 'You are not offended?'

'No. It is all right.'

Aparna dreaded conflict or unpleasantness of any kind. She forced herself to believe him. 'That's good,' she said. 'I am relieved.' Then she lay down on one side of the bed and went to sleep.

Amarnath was astounded. He turned his head away from her and muttered to himself: 'How can she possibly believe that I am not angry? I have not entered her room for two days. I have ignored her. And yet when I say that I am not angry, she smugly takes me at my word! How can she forget so quickly the magnitude of what occurred that night? Lost in his thoughts, he glanced at Aparna and realized that she was sound asleep, without a care in the world. He got up abruptly and said determinedly: 'Aparna, it seems you have fallen asleep. Get up.'

She woke up and said: 'Did you call me?'

'Yes. I have decided to go to Calcutta tomorrow.'

'Why? I had no idea that you were intending to go to Calcutta. Can't you stay here a couple of days longer?'

'No, I cannot postpone my departure.'

Aparna thought for a few moments and said: 'Are you going away because you are annoyed with me?'

Even now Amarnath was unable to assert that he was indeed angry. He simply could not understand her calmness, her insensitivity. In the few months after their marriage, his authority as the husband had been steadily drained away by Aparna's conduct. He no longer dared even to express his irritation.

'Please don't go away annoyed,' she said. 'That will be very painful for me.'

Amarnath agreed to postpone his departure. He spent two more days in the house, conscious all the time that he had swallowed his pride.

Heavy rain has its advantages. It clears the sky. A light, persistent drizzle, on the other hand, does not scatter the clouds. It only makes the road muddy and produces a depressing atmosphere. Amarnath had, in a way, waded through mud in his village home before coming to Calcutta. He found nothing in that vast metropolis that could wash away the mud. And he was ashamed to expose his muddy feet to his friends who could have made him happy. He could not concentrate on his studies, nor did he gain satisfaction from the entertainment which

Calcutta offered. Restless in Calcutta, he felt no desire to return home. His heart was weighed down by unbearable agony. He tried to shake it off but failed miserably.

Inwardly tormented, Amarnath fell ill. His parents rushed to Calcutta as soon as they got the news. They did not bring Aparna with them. Amarnath had not expected that they would leave her behind. But he did not say a word. His condition deteriorated day by day. Naturally, there were moments when he wished to see Aparna. But he kept quiet and his parents could not understand what he wanted. He was fed up with the doctors and their constant medication. It was not long before death liberated him from his ordeal.

Aparna was stunned by her sudden widowhood. Her entire body shivered with the terrible thought that what happened might have been the result of an unconscious desire within her. Perhaps this was the freedom she had secretly wished for, a wish that providence had granted. Submerged in these frightening thoughts, she heard her father's voice. He was sobbing loudly. Was this a dream? When did he come? Aparna opened the windows and looked out. It was indeed her father, Rajnarain Babu. Griefstricken, he was rolling on the floor, like a child. Seeing him, her tears too began to flow freely. She returned to her room. Soon the floor was wet with her tears.

'O father!' she said, sobbing. Rajnarain Babu clasped his daughter in his arms and cried: 'Aparna, my child! Your Madan Mohan is calling you back to the temple.'

'Let us go, father.'

'A lot of work awaits you in the temple, Aparna.'

'Yes, father. Let us return home.'

'Come, child,' he said and kissed her forehead affectionately. He held her tightly in his arms, as though he were squeezing out all her pain. The following morning they reached home.

Her father led Aparna to the temple. 'Here is your beloved shrine, Aparna,' he said. 'And there is your Madan Mohan.'

Bereft of all jewellery, dressed in a widow's garb, Aparna

looked at the image of Krishna in a new light. She felt that God liked her more as she stood before him in her simple, white clothes, and ungroomed hair. She firmly believed, like her father, that the divine Madan Mohan had summoned her to the temple. The deity had the same smile, and the temple was steeped in fragrance as before. Aparna felt that she had somehow been elevated. Her husband had, through his own death, raised her to a new height. With folded hands she expressed her gratitude to her departed husband and prayed that he might dwell happily in heaven.

Shaktinath was totally immersed in making images of deities. He was more interested in fashioning images than in worshipping them. Carefully, he depicted each feature of the god's face and form—eyes, ears, nose, lips, and complexion. He cared little about the details of ritual or the right way of reciting *mantras*. In relation to the deity, he had promoted himself from the level of a servant to that of a guardian.

One day his father said to him: 'Shaktinath, I don't feel well today. Go to the landlord's mansion to perform the daily worship.'

'But I am busy making images,' Shaktinath said.

His ailing father got angry. 'Enough of this playing with toys,' he said. 'There is work to be done. Do as I tell you.'

Shaktinath was not at all interested in chanting *mantras*. But he had to get up and go. As instructed by his father, he had a bath, flung a cotton shawl over his shoulder, and set out. There had been a few occasions in the past when he had come to the landlord's house for worship. But what he saw in the temple this time was very different from anything he had seen before. Such a profusion of fragrant flowers, so many kinds of incense, such abundance of food and other offerings! He was even more surprised when he saw Aparna. Who was this girl? Where had she come from, and where was she all these days?

'Are you the son of Bhattacharya Moshay?' Aparna asked him.

'Yes, I am,' he said.

'Then wash your feet and sit down for worship.'

But when Shaktinath sat down facing the deity he could not remember a single *mantra*. Nor could he recall the order in which the offerings were to be made. His attention flagged and he lost his self-confidence. He was thinking only about the girl: Who was she and for whom was she performing this ceremony? Shaktinath made one mistake after another. He forgot the sequence in which he was supposed to strike the bell, place flowers on the image, or sprinkle holy water on the offerings.

Aparna sat behind him like a stern examiner critically appraising a student's performance. She understood at once that the young priest was a novice who was making a mockery of the ceremony. She had so much experience of religious ritual that she detected every mistake he made. When the ceremony was over, she turned to Shaktinath and said in a harsh tone: 'You are a Brahmin's son. Don't you know how images of gods should be worshipped?'

'But I do know,' he protested.

'No, you don't know anything,' she retorted.

Shaktinath felt devastated. He looked at Aparna just once and prepared to leave. Aparna called him back and said: 'Take all this food. But don't come here tomorrow. When your father feels better, let him come over.' She collected the food-offerings, wrapped them in his shawl, and bid him good-bye. When he stepped out of the temple, Shaktinath was trembling from head to foot.

Aparna made preparations for the ceremony all over again. Then she sent for another Brahmin to conduct the ritual worship correctly.

A month passed. Acharya Jadunath, an old Brahmin gentleman who was a close friend of the family, said to the landlord: 'You know the situation, Rajnarain Babu. Bhattacharya's son simply cannot cope with the elaborate ritual worship which needs to be performed in your temple.'

'That is what Aparna told me several days ago,' the landlord replied.

'She was right,' Acharya Jadunath said solemnly. 'Your daughter is Goddess Lakshmi in human form. She comprehends everything. It makes no difference whether the worship is offered by me or by some one else. The point is to perform the ceremony competently. As long as Madhu Bhattacharya was alive, everything was all right. It would have been appropriate for his son to take his place as the priest. But he is immature. He is good at making images and painting them. But he is ignorant about the rituals of worship.'

'I agree with you,' Rajnarain Babu said. 'I would like you to take charge. But we have to ask Aparna first.'

Aparna, however, did not approve of the proposal. 'Shaktinath is a Brahmin's son,' she said. 'He is a helpless orphan. How can we dismiss him? Let him do the best he can. I am sure Madan Mohan will be satisfied.'

Rajnarain Babu appreciated her feelings. 'I had not considered this aspect,' he said. 'The temple is yours, my child. The ceremony is yours. Do whatever you wish and entrust the worship to anyone you like. The deity will be pleased with your choice.'

Aparna sent for Shaktinath. He had not visited the temple since she had scolded him. Meanwhile his father had died and he was himself in poor health. Aparna was moved to pity when she saw his face scarred by pain and sorrow. Gently, she said to him: 'Perform the worship to the best of your ability. God will be satisfied.'

Encouraged by her kind and affectionate words, Shaktinath started offering worship at the temple. He was careful about all the details of the ritual. When the ceremony was over, Aparna prepared a packet of food for him. 'You have done well today,' she said. 'Tell me, Bamun Thakur, do you cook your own food?'

'Sometimes I do,' he said, 'but when I have fever I don't have the strength to cook.'

'Is there no one to look after you?'

'No.'

Aparna bowed before the image of Madan Mohan with folded hands and prayed: 'O God, please accept the worship offered by him. He is still a boy. Please excuse him for his mistakes.'

The next day Aparna asked her maid to find out about Shaktinath's work, his health and diet. She felt great sympathy for the Brahmin boy and supported him in every way. The two of them together now worshipped at the temple. Shaktinath performed the ritual while Aparna showed him the correct procedure. Shaktinath recited the sacred hymns and Aparna repeated them mentally. While he held the flowers and incense, she pointed out where they should be placed and how Radha's throne should be decorated with them. The complex rituals of that large temple were conducted in this manner.

Acharya Jadunath saw all this and commented that the two children were playing happily. Rajanarain Babu added: 'The main thing is that my daughter should be able to overcome her grief. If all this helps her to find peace of mind, I welcome it.'

On a stage, scenes of mountains, forests and storms can be replaced by city streets and palaces. By manipulating the background, an audience can be transported from scenes of suffering to those of pleasure and affluence. A similar change had come over Shaktinath's life. He could not understand whether he had woken up from a bad dream and found himself in a happy world or whether he was enjoying a wonderful dream which would break any moment, landing him into a painfully real world. The worship of God without any personal responsibility had become a golden chain which shackled him. He could hear its clanking. The sound reminded him of his lost freedom. He missed his clay idols, he missed his father. At such moments of nostalgia he felt he had been sold, that Aparna had purchased him. Her affection had become a bond of attraction.

One day Shaktinath's maternal cousin turned up unexpectedly. His sister was getting married. His uncle, who lived in Calcutta and was doing very well, remembered Shaktinath and had sent his son to invite him for the wedding. Shaktinath had to accept. He had to accede to his uncle's wishes. Moreover, he was excited at the prospect of spending a few days in Calcutta. All night long he chatted with his cousin and heard with wonder his cousin's descriptions of the sights and sounds, the magnificence and the opulence of the great city. He did not feel like going to the temple the next morning. When the hour of worship approached, Aparna sent for him. Shaktinath went to the landlord's mansion and told her, with much embarrassment, that he was going to Calcutta.

Aparna was silent for some time. Then she asked him how long he would be away. Shaktinath replied that he would return as soon as permitted by his uncle. Aparna did not say anything further. She informed Acharya Jadunath of what had happened, and he took charge of the ceremony. From that day on she observed the rituals silently, wearing a serious expression.

Shaktinath spent many days enjoying the wonders of Calcutta. Then he began to miss his home and the temple. The idle life in his uncle's house grew very tiresome. One night he dreamt that Aparna was beckoning him and that she had become angry when he did not respond. Next morning he told his uncle that he wanted to go back to the village. His uncle tried to detain him. 'Why do you wish to return to that barren place?' he said. 'Stay here and resume your studies. I will see that you get a job.' But when Shaktinath fell silent, with bent head, his uncle agreed.

His aunt called him and said: 'I hear you are going home tomorrow.'

'Yes, I have to leave,' he said.

'Aparna is very much in your mind, isn't she?'

'Yes.'

'Does she care for you a lot?'

'Yes, she takes good care of me.'

Shaktinath's aunt started laughing. She had heard a good deal about Aparna from him. 'I wish to send some gifts for her,' she said.

'Give them to her. She will love you even more.' With these words she brought out two bottles of perfume and handed them to Shaktinath. The fragrance thrilled him. Next day he returned home.

Shaktinath went to the temple and performed the worship. He wanted to give Aparna the perfume which he had wrapped in a piece of cloth, but hesitated to do so. He felt that within the few days of his absence she had become very distant. He longed to say: 'I have brought these perfume bottles for you from Calcutta. The deity will be pleased with the fragrance and you will also be happy.' But he did not have the courage to utter these words. For an entire week, every day he tried to give them to her. If she had talked to him as before, or if she had asked about his visit to Calcutta, he would have felt strong enough to present her the gifts. But such an occasion did not arise.

For two days Shaktinath had gone to the temple with high fever. Somehow he performed the rituals. A strange sense of anxiety gripped him. Aparna was informed that he had not eaten anything for two days. She called him and said: 'Bamun Thakur, I hear you have not eaten for several days.'

'I am running high temperature every night,' he said.

'You have high fever? Then why have you been bathing and

performing the ritual worship at the temple? Why did you not inform me about you illness?'

There were tears in Shaktinath's eyes. On an impulse he unwrapped the piece of cloth and took out the bottles of perfume. 'I have brought these bottles for you,' he said.

'For me?' she asked in surprise.

'Yes. I know that you are fond of fragrance.'

Seeing those small perfume bottles, which had tragic associations for her, Aparna burst into a rage. It was like hot milk which sizzles and steams when it comes into contact with fire.

'Give them to me,' she said in a frighteningly solemn voice.

She took the bottles and flung them outside the temple on a heap of wilted petals. Shaktinath's blood froze in his veins.

'Bamun Thakur,' she said with utmost harshness, 'so that's what your mind harbours! Never come before me again. And never let your shadow fall upon this temple.' Pointing to the door, she asked him to get out.

Three days passed. Acharya Jadunath was performing the worship while Aparna watched with melancholy eyes. As he collected his offerings at the end, he signed: 'Poor boy! He died because he could not get any medical treatment.'

Aparna stared at Acharya and exclaimed: 'What did you say? Who died?'

'It seems you have not heard. Madhu Bhattacharya's son was very sick for a few days. He died this morning.'

She continued to stare at him. As he was about to leave, Acharya Jadunath remarked: 'Sinners are punished by such death. Playing with sacred ritual in God's temple is a serious matter.'

When Acharya Jadunath had gone away, Aparna closed the door, threw herself down and started weeping loudly while knocking her head on the floor. 'For whose sin, O God?,' she shouted. 'For whose sin ?'

After a long time she got up, wiped her eyes and went out. She searched for the perfume bottles in the heap of petals.

When she found them she came inside the temple and fell at the feet of the deity. 'O God!' she said, 'I could not accept these gifts. Now you please accept them. I have never worshipped you with my own hands. I am doing so today. Please accept my offerings and be satisfied. I have no other desire.'

Light Out of Darkness

*W*hen Satyendra Chaudhuri returned home from Calcutta after passing his B.A. examination, his mother called him and said: 'The girl is like the image of Goddess Lakshmi. Listen to me, my son. Go and see her.'

Satyendra wanted to continue his studies at Calcutta for the Master's degree. He said: 'No, mother. I cannot agree to get married at this time. My studies will be disturbed.'

She assured him that after the marriage his wife would stay with her and he would be free to continue his education at Calcutta. But Satyendra said he did not even have the time to think of marriage at that point. He was just leaving when his mother stopped him and said: 'But I have given my word to the girl's mother.'

'Why did you do that without asking me?' he asked angrily.

'It was wrong of me,' she said, 'but now you have to honour my commitment. Please agree, Satyen. The girl is unhappy. Her mother is a widow.'

Satyendra went away saying that he would think about it and tell her later. His mother was sad. She wanted Satyen to marry as early as possible. Her husband had died seven years ago. She was looking forward to the day when Satyendra, her only child, would become a lawyer and take charge of the property.

One day Satyen's mother arranged a religious ceremony at her house. Among the guests was a widow who came with her daughter. As soon as she saw the girl, Satyendra's mother thought that she would make a very good daughter-in-law. When Satyendra came home that day, he found that a girl dressed in jewels was

'Andhare Alo' from *Mejdidi O Anyanya Galpa* (Mejdidi and Other Stories), December 1915.

standing just where he usually sat down for his meal. She looked like a goddess indeed.

'Sit down and eat,' his mother said.

'Not here, mother. Please serve my meal in some other room.' Satyendra felt as if he had been awakened from a dream.

His mother smiled and said: 'Why, what's the matter? Are you feeling shy because of this little girl?'

Satyendra protested that he did not feel shy in any one's presence. He sat down, ate a little food, and than joined his friends who were playing cards and chess.

Satyendra was not in a mood for such diversions. He sat there out of politeness. As soon as his visitors left, he went to his room. His mother wondered whether he was about to sleep. 'No, mother,' he said, 'I have to study. Postgraduate studies demand a lot of effort. I cannot afford to waste any time.' But when he sat at his desk, he just stared at the ceiling while an open book lay in front of him.

Suddenly, he heard the sound of bangles and anklets . . . *jham . . . jham chhum . . . . chhum . . . .* He raised his head and saw the same beautiful, goddess-like girl, decked in gold and pearl ornaments from head to foot. She came into the room, stood near him, and in a very sweet, low voice said: 'Mother wants to know your opinion.'

He was at a loss for words. 'Mother? Whose mother?' he said.

'My mother,' the girl said and turned to go. On an impulse, Satyendra asked her name.

'My name is Radharani,' she said sweetly, and went away.

II

Satyendra came to Calcutta and became busy with his studies. He vowed not to marry before taking all the degrees he had always aspired for. But the face of Radharani came before his eyes again and again. He simply could not stop thinking about her. The face of every woman he saw seemed to be transformed into goddess Lakshmi and reminded him of Radharani. He had never been a girl-watcher. In fact, he used to turn his eyes away from girls. But now he started staring at every girl on the road. Sometimes he stared so long that he felt ashamed of himself and slipped away into a side street.

His house in Calcutta was not far from the river. Satyendra enjoyed bathing and swimming in the Ganges, particularly at Jagannath Ghat where well-paved steps led from the road to the edge of the river. That day the river front was more crowded than usual because of a festival. A group of five or six persons stood there gazing in one particular direction. Coming closer, he saw that they were all looking at a young woman of extraordinary beauty.

She seemed to be eighteen or nineteen. Dressed in a simple cotton sari, she kneeled while a priest applied sandal-paste on her forehead. She was not wearing any jewellery. Satyendra knew the priest who was waiting on her. The priest used to keep his dry clothes when he entered the river. While Satyendra was handing over the clothes, he came face to face with the beautiful woman. Their eyes met. Satyendra had a quick bath and hastened back, but by that time the woman had gone away.

Satyendra passed the rest of the day in a state of excitement. Early next morning he went to the river bank and saw that the beautiful woman—let us call her that until her name is revealed—had just finished her bath and the priest was drawing lines of sandal-paste on her forehead. Their eyes met again. He was again stunned by her extraordinary loveliness. Satyendra felt   a strange kind of elation such as he had never experienced before.

III

Satyendra realized that he had never met her before because she used to come for her bath very early, while he went to the river much later. Now he started getting up before dawn to go for his bath when he was sure to find her. During the seven or eight days that followed, they looked at each other every morning but not a word was exchanged. Perhaps words were superfluous and the language of the eyes was enough. And through that language it became obvious to Satyendra that the unknown beauty had captured his heart.

One day, when he was returning from the river after the usual silent encounter, he heard a voice behind him. He looked round and saw the beautiful woman. She stood near the railway track, with a small brass pitcher under one arm and a bundle of wet clothes in the other hand. She beckoned to him and said: 'My maid has not come today. Will you kindly escort me for some distance?'

Satyendra hesitated but could not refuse. Was it proper to walk alone with that woman, a complete stranger? She guessed his thoughts and smiled. How enchanting was that smile! Nothing in the world is unattainable for a woman who can smile like that. He agreed to go with her and they walked together. 'The maid is ill,' she said, 'and I am accustomed to bathing in the Ganga every morning. Moreover, I have now become accustomed to looking at you. A bad habit, perhaps.' Satyendra did not respond to the familiarity. He simply said that he also came to the river every morning.

After they had covered about a quarter of a mile she said: 'I live in Jorasanko. You can accompany me up to the cross road. Then I can go on my own.' When they reached the crossing she said: 'My house is not far from here. I can easily go there alone. *Namaskar*.' And she gave him the same charming smile. Satyendra also said '*namaskar*' and turned in the direction of his own house.

His heart's condition at that time can be understood only by those who have been wounded by Cupid's flowery arrows. He felt a kind of intoxication in which the air, the sky, the river, everything acquired a new colour and the consciousness of the material world became faint. A face was drawing him like a magnet. When Satyendra woke up next morning the sun was already up. His entire body ached with disappointment. He thought that the day was ruined. The poor servant got a big scolding for not waking him. Dejected, Satya stepped out of his house, thinking that she must have gone home after her bath. He hired a carriage and scanned both sides of the road while the carriage sped towards the river.

But when he reached his destination, all his frustration melted away. He felt like one who had lost a precious gem and found it on the road unexpectedly. As soon as he got down from the carriage, she greeted him with her unique smile and said: 'Why so late today? I have been waiting for you for more than half an hour. My maid has again been unable to come with me. Have your bath quickly, please.' Satyendra entered the river hurriedly. He skipped the swimming, dived a couple of times, and came up. It was a quick bath indeed.

He was surprised to see that his carriage was not there. She said that she had paid the driver and sent him away. Satya tried to protest, but she said it was a small matter. The same enchanting smile again! What is happening, Satyen wondered. Is it just simplicity, innocence, or something else?

As they started walking, she said: 'What is the name of the locality where you stay? You told me the other day. I am trying to remember. Is it Chor Bagan?'

'Yes, that's the name.'

Chor Bagan, one of the old localities in Calcutta, literally means 'Thieves' Garden'. She asked jocularly: 'Do only thieves live there?'

Satyendra was surprised. 'What makes you think so?' he said.

'Because you seem to be the king of thieves,' she said, glancing at him through the corner of her eye, and continued to move gracefully like a swan. She was carrying a pitcherful of Ganga water. The bubbling sound of the water seemed to be telling Satyendra (if he could only have heard it) : 'Be on your guard, deluded young man. All this is a game, a deception, nothing more.'

On reaching the corner where they were to go their respective ways, Satyendra again offered to pay the carriage fare.

'But you have already paid it,' she said

Satyendra was confused, and could only say 'How? . . . When?'

'Well, I certainly could not have paid it. I have nothing. The only thing that was mine has been stolen by you.' And she turned her head to suppress her laughter.

Satyendra failed to see through her acting. Her glance had penetrated his heart and destroyed whatever doubt or suspicion he might have had. Such was his infatuation that for a moment he had the urge to bend down and clasp her painted feet. But he was overcome by shyness. Without even looking at his beloved, and with his head lowered, he turned home-wards.

When he was out of sight, the maid who had been instructed to wait on the footpath, met her mistress. 'Why are you making that young man dance?' she asked. 'Is he worth anything? Can you extract some money?'

The beautiful woman laughed. 'I don't know about money,' she said, 'but I enjoy putting a string through a fool's nosering and make him go round at my will.'

'Only you can do that, mistress,' the maid said. 'But he is so handsome. Looks like a prince. What eyes, what a face and what a beautiful complexion! Believe me, when I saw him standing close to you, I was reminded of two lovely roses blooming together.'

'Enough of this. If you liked him so much, why don't you keep him for yourself?'

The maid was not to be outdone. 'No, that can never happen,' she said. 'You will never part with such a precious commodity throughout your life.'

IV

Wise men have said that if something seems impossible, no attempt should be made to describe it. Even if one has seen it for oneself, ignorant people will never believe it. When Satya came home, he read Tennyson's poems, and tried his hand at translating Don Juan into Bengali. And yet this mature, scholarly person was completely beguiled. He never pondered, even for a moment, whether there was any future in such love for a strange woman whom he met by chance by the river-front. Nor did he pause to think whether he could remain unharmed by a love that was sweeping over him like a tidal wave.

Two days later, he again met the beautiful woman as she was returning from the river. She said: 'I went to the theatre last night. My heart bleeds for poor Sarla. It is difficult to see her agony. What do you think?'

Satyendra had not seen the play on the stage. But he had read the book on which the play was based. 'Yes, indeed,' he said, 'poor Sarla suffered till the very end of her life.'

She heaved a deep sigh, as though she were in great pain, and continued to talk about the play. She talked of love, of human nature, of the main characters, and the twists and turns in the plot. She recalled Pramada, an evil character, and her anger welled up. She said, 'What a demoness she was! Had I been there I would have throttled her to death.'

Seeing her so involved emotionally, Satyendra reminded her that Pramada was not a real person but a fictional character, playing a part on the stage.

'But why has such a character been created at all?' she exclaimed. 'We are told that God dwells in the heart of every human being. But after seeing Pramada's behaviour it is difficult to accept that God was in her heart. So many famous authors have written books. Has anyone become a better person by reading them? On the contrary, there are many books from which human beings have learnt to hate one another. No, I cannot believe that God dwells within each person.'

Satyendra was impressed. 'Do you read a lot of books?' he asked in amazement.

'I have not studied English,' the beautiful woman said, 'but whenever a new book is published in Bengali I try to get it. Sometimes I spend the entire night reading. But here we are. My house is only a short distance from here. Come, you must visit my house. I will show you all my books.'

Satyendra suddenly felt scared. 'No, no,' he said, 'that won't be proper.'

'There is nothing improper in this. Come with me.'

Satyendra felt strangely tired. His face became pale. 'No,

not today, some other time,' he said, as he hurried away, his legs shaking. His heart was full of admiration and respect for this mysterious woman about whom he knew nothing but who had become the object of his love.

V

Satyendra was returning from the river after his bath. He moved with slow steps. His eyes were weary and sad. For four days his unknown beloved had not come to the river. He missed her and was very anxious. All kinds of inauspicious thoughts came to his mind: Perhaps there has been an accident: she may be on her death bed; who knows, she may no longer be alive. He knew only the road on which her house was located. But he did not have any other details. He did not remember any landmarks on the way to her house and did not know the name of the landlord. He now repented having refused to go with her when she was inviting him so cordially. He was convinced that she was in love him, and that it was a pure, deep love, without a trace of selfishness.

While he was engrossed in these thoughts, someone called from behind: '*Babu, Babu.*' It was her maid. Satyendra was frightened by her expression. 'What is the matter?' he asked anxiously. 'How is she?'

'*Didimani* is very ill,' she said, 'and wants to see you.' The maid was on very intimate terms with her mistress and often addressed her as '*Didi*' or '*Didimani*' (Elder Sister).

Satyendra wiped his eyes and followed her. 'What has happened to her?,' he asked. 'Is it a serious illness?'

'No, it is not serious. She has high fever.'

Satyendra prayed for her silently as he followed the maid. They came to a large house. A watchman stood outside the gate. Satyendra said: 'If I come to visit your *didi*, will her father be offended? I am a stranger to him.'

'*Didi* has lost her father,' the maid said. 'Her mother is here and she is also eager to meet you.'

Satyendra did not ask any more questions. He entered the

house, climbed the stairs and reached a balcony on the second floor. He passed three rooms, and caught a glimpse of the lavish furniture and decorations inside. As he approached a corner, he heard loud laughter. He also heard sounds of drums and ankle-bells. The maid guided him there, drew aside the curtain and ushered him in. Then she said to her mistress: '*Didi*, here comes your elegant lover.'

Her announcement was greeted by noisy remarks and hilarity. Satyendra became so nervous and confused that he thought he was going to faint. With great difficulty he managed to compose himself and sat down at the edge of a divan in a corner. At the other end of the room three men dressed in jaunty clothes sat on thick mattresses and cushions. One of them had a harmonium in front of him. Another had his hands on the table. The third man was concentrating on the liquor glass in his hand.

And the woman he had come to visit? She had just stopped dancing. Bells tinkled on both her ankles. From head to foot, she was decked in glamorous jewellery. Her eyes, red with intoxication, moved restlessly in all directions. As soon as she saw Satyendra, she approached him and held both his hands, laughing heartily. 'Why are you crouching like that?' she said. 'Are you epileptic? Get up. Don't scare me.' At her touch Satyendra began to tremble with fear. He felt that his mind had stopped functioning.

'My name is Bijli,' she said. 'What is yours? Just Babu? Or is it Habu? Or Gabu, perhaps?'

The room was again filled with loud and vulgar laughter. The maid was so amused that she jumped on one of the tables and stretched herself, convulsed with laughter. 'O *Didimani*,' she said. 'You bring us so much fun.'

Bijli dragged Satyendra to another small divan and made him sit there. Then she folded her hands and started singing a song composed by Chandidas, beginning with the stanza:

I am so fortunate tonight,
I have seen the moonlike face of my Beloved.
My life has been fulfilled, my youth has triumphed.
My joy spreads out in all directions.

The man who was drinking fell at Satyendra's feet and said: 'O holy man, O pandit, I am a great sinner. Give me a little bit of the sacred dust of your feet.' The man with the harmonium said in a tone of sympathy: 'Why are we making a clown out of the poor fellow?'

Still laughing, Bijli said: 'This is not clowning. This is a real performance. Now tell me, crazy Babu, what did you take me for? I bathe in the Ganges every morning. So I am obviously not a Christian or Muslim. A grown woman from a Hindu family, I could be a widow. Or I could be a married lady. What was your intention in coming to me as a lover? Did you want to marry me, or did you simply want to whisk me away somewhere?' In the midst of all those taunts, all that ridicule and derisive mirth, Satyendra remained silent, with his head bowed.

Bijli got up abruptly and said: 'How thoughtless of me not to have offered our guest some refreshments.' She asked the maid to bring food. When a dish containing sweets and other snacks was brought, Bijli took it herself, crouched near Satyendra, and said, 'Raise your head and eat.' Her ironical, unkind expression suddenly changed into one of affection. Her voice was gentle and natural.

Satyendra raised his head and said: 'No, I will not eat.'

'Why? Are you afraid of losing your caste? I am not a cobbler woman or a toilet cleaner, you know.'

Satyendra's voice was again calm and self-controlled when he said: 'If you had been any of those, I would have gladly eaten from your hands.'

Bijli giggled. 'Oh!' she said, 'so our Habu Babu knows how to give dagger thrusts too.'

'My name is Satyendra, not Habu Babu. I have not learnt how to wield daggers. But I have learnt how to realize my mistakes and rectify them.'

Bijli turned on him harshly again: 'You refuse to accept food from my hands? Mark my words. You will eat in this house. If not today, a few days later. But you will come back and eat here.'

Satyendra shook his head and said: 'Look, all human beings are fallible. I know now what a terrible mistake I have made.

But you are also mistaken. Not today, not tomorrow, not in this lifetime, not in any future lifetime—never, never shall I eat food touched by you. Let me go now. Your breath is drying up my blood.'

The shadow of disgust on his face was so apparent that even the man with the liquor bottle said: 'Let him go, Bijli *Bai*, let him go. He is only spoiling the fun.'

Bijli was stunned by Satyendra's response. She could never have imagined that a simple, shy person like him could speak out in such a clear and determined manner. In a flash the enormity of her guilt became obvious to her.

Satya moved towards the door. Bijli said very gently: 'Please stay for a little while longer.' He went out of the room. She followed him, blocked his way, and said: 'I confess with folded hands that I have committed a grave sin.' He looked the other way and remained silent.

'This adjoining room is my library,' she said. 'Please come and see it. I beg you to forgive me.'

Satyendra ignored her and proceeded towards the staircase. 'Will I never see you again?' she asked. 'No, never,' he answered curtly. He was surprised to see that her eyes were full of tears, her throat was choking with emotion and her voice broke.

'I cannot believe that we will never meet again,' she said. 'But even if this is true, will you believe that I . . . that I . . .'

This bit of acting, Satyendra thought, was easy compared to the performance he had seen for an entire fortnight. The marks of absolute distrust which Bijli saw on his face devastated her. But what could she do? She herself had destroyed and thrown away every conceivable possibility of regaining his trust.

So when Satyendra asked, 'What should I believe?' she could not utter a word. Her lips moved, but no sound emerged from them. She raised her eyes, heavy with tears, and lowered them again. Satya saw them, but he knew that even tears could be faked. He waited for an answer to his question, 'What should I believe?' but she simply did not have the strength to say that she loved him. Her love was so strong that, to earn his affection, she could have gladly given away her extraordinary beauty as though it was a worthless rag. But she could not express her feelings.

Indeed, who could have believed her? Her guilt had been established. Standing before a judge with a million marks of guilt stamped on her, how could she plead that deception was not an inherent part of her profession? The more she delayed giving an answer, the more clearly she realized that the judge had reached a verdict and was about to pronounce the severest possible sentence.

Satyendra became impatient and said he would not remain there any longer. Bijli was still unable to raise her head and face him. 'All right, go,' she said. 'But, guilty though I am, you would also be making a mistake by disbelieving me. Perhaps God does dwell in the body of every human being. There may be temples in which the worship of God is neglected. But God is there all the same. You may refuse to offer your homage to Him, but you cannot ignore Him either.' She heard the sound of footsteps, raised her head, and saw Satyendra walking away slowly.

Bijli was a dancer, a courtesan. But she was also a woman. When she returned to her room, her despised, half-dead femininity was suddenly aroused, as though touched by the elixir of immortality. Even the drunken man in that room could see the change that had come over her. 'Why, Bijli,' he exclaimed, 'it seems you have been crying. What an obstinate young man he was. He didn't even touch the delicacies you offered. Now pass that dish to me.' Not waiting for anyone to give him the dish, he grabbed it and started eating. Bijli did not hear a word of what he said. She untied the ankle-bells and flung them aside as though they were scorpions which had bitten her.

'Why have you thrown away your anklets?' someone asked. She smiled and said that she would never wear them again.

'What do you mean?'

'I mean that I am giving up the dancing profession. No more ankle-bells. Your *Baiji*, the courtesan who sang and danced for you, is dead.'

'Really?' the drunkard asked. 'What was the disease which killed our *Baiji*?'

Bijli *Bai* laughed. 'The same disease,' she said, 'which kills darkness when a lamp is lit. The same disease which kills the night at sunrise. Yes, friends, the courtesan in me was struck down by the same disease. She is dead.'

VI

Five years had passed. Satyendra and Radharani were married and had a son. His birthday was being celebrated with great enthusiasm. The feast was over. Now an entertainment programme of music and dance was about to begin in a spacious courtyard outside the main house. Dancers and singers had been invited from outside Calcutta. Radharani stood in the upstairs balcony watching the preparations.

Satyendra came from behind and said: 'What are you looking at with such keen interest?'

Radharani looked at her husband and said with a smile: 'I was admiring the dress and jewellery which the *Baiji* is wearing.'

Satyendra asked her which of the women performers she liked best. She pointed to a woman sitting behind the others, dressed in very ordinary clothes.

'But she looks so sickly.'

'Yes, she does look pale. But she is certainly the most beautiful. She seems to be poor. There are no ornaments on her body.'

Satyendra said: 'Can you guess how much these women are charging?'

'I have no idea.'

'The three women in the front will be paid thirty rupees each. But the one you have described as poor gets two hundred rupees.'

'Two hundred? Why such a large fee? Does she sing exceptionally well?'

'She was a renowned singer five years ago. I don't know whether she still kept up that quality.'

Radharani was still puzzled and asked him why he was paying her such a large amount.

'Because she would not come for less than that,' he said. 'Even for such a large fee she was refusing to come. The messenger had to flatter and cajole her before she accepted the invitation.'

'When you had offered such a generous fee, why did the messenger have to flatter her?'

Satyendra moved his chair close to hers and said in a low voice: 'In the first place, she has given up her profession. And secondly I have a strong personal reason for inducing her to come to our house.'

Radharani found it difficult to believe that her husband could have a personal need to invite any courtesan, even if she had retired from her 'business'. She was eager to hear his explanation.

'Her name is Bijli. One day . . . but wait, this is not a good place to talk about her. It is a long story. We need privacy. Let us go inside.'

They went into an inner room. Satyendra told her everything, without omitting a single detail. Radharani was sitting near her husband's feet. By the time he had finished describing that strange chapter in his life, she was in tears. She wiped her eyes and said: 'So you now want to have your revenge by insulting her? That is not like you. How could you think of doing such a thing?'

Satyendra, too, was unhappy with his own decision. His voice and eyes showed how disturbed he was. 'It is necessary to insult her,' he said. 'But it will not be a public humiliation. Only the three of us will know—she, you and I. No one else will have the slightest inkling of what has happened.'

The guests had arrived. The courtyard was filled with visitors. The noisy conversation of women could be heard even in the upstairs room where Radharani and Satyendra were talking.

While the other dancers were ready to begin their performance, Bijli was still sitting motionless with her head down. Tears flowed from her eyes. Her savings had dwindled after she had given up her source of income. Poverty had compelled her to accept the invitation, but she was finding it extremely difficult to stand up and raise her head. She felt as though her body had been paralysed by the lustful ogling of strangers. Her knees were doubling up. A couple of hours earlier she could not have imagined the magnitude of the suffering she was to endure by accepting Satyendra's invitation.

Bijli heard someone calling her. She looked up and saw a boy of twelve or thirteen. He pointed to the upstairs balcony and said: 'Mother is calling you.' She asked him who he was. He said he was a servant sent by the lady of the house to call her.

'You must be mistaken,' she said. 'She is perhaps calling someone else. Go and ask her again.'

The boy went back into the house and returned after a few minutes. 'If your name is Bijli, Mother wants to speak with you,' he said. Bijli removed her anklets and accompanied the boy. She thought that the lady of the house probably wanted to make a special request for a particular song.

Radharani was standing outside the bedroom door with her baby in her arms. Bijli approached with hesitant steps and stood near her with a sad, dejected expression. Radharani held her hand affectionately, almost dragged her inside the room, and made her sit down on a comfortable divan. 'Do you recognize me, *didi*?' she said with a smile.

Bijli was too bewildered to say anything. 'I don't mind if you fail to recognize me,' Radharani said, 'although I am like your younger sister. But I will really pick a quarrel if you   don't recognize the face of my child.' And she again smiled sweetly.

Slowly the cloud of darkness receded from Bijli's vision. She turned her eyes from the glowing beauty of the young mother to the child's face, fresh like a rose that had just bloomed. She kept on gazing at the child's face while Radharani watched her. Then suddenly she got up, extended her arms, took the child from the mother's lap and clasped him in a tight embrace.

Radharani said: '*didi*, you churned the ocean and drank the poison. And you gave the nectar to me, your younger sister. I would not have got my husband if he had not first been in love with you.'

Bijli picked up a photograph of Satyendra from a table and looked at it for a long time. 'O my sister,' she said, 'the nectar of immortality is hidden in the poison itself. I do not feel deprived. What you call poison has saved a miserable sinner like me.'

Radharani heard her quietly with admiration. '*Didi*, would you like to meet him?' she asked. Bijli closed her eyes and thought deeply for a few moments. Then she said in a determind voice: 'No, sister. Five years ago, when he looked at me as though I were an untouchable, and turned away from me in disgust, I said proudly that sooner or later he would come to me again. But he did not come and my pride was shattered. He who is the Great Destroyer of arrogance humbled me and freed me from my vanity.'

Bijli wiped her eyes with the end of her sari. 'In moments of unbearable pain,' she said, 'I have often blamed God. But now I realize the infinite kindness with which God has saved a sinner. That day if I had prevailed upon him to return to my house, my life would have been reduced to ashes. I would never have gained him, and I would have lost myself.'

Radharani was unable to say anything. Her eyes were heavy with unshed tears. Bijli was about to go away. 'It was my hope,' she said, 'that if I ever meet him again I would clasp his feet and make one more attempt to persuade him to forgive me. But that is no longer necessary. Now my only request is that I should be permitted to keep this photograph. Sister, I am going now.'

'When will I see you again, *didi*?' Radharani said.

'We will not meet again, sister. I own a small house. I will sell it as soon as possible and go away. But tell me, why did he suddenly remember me after all these years?'

Radharani reddened with shame. She kept quiet.

'I think I understand. He wanted to get his revenge by insulting me. Am I right? I can think of no other reason why he should go through the trouble of sending a messenger to invite me.'

Radharani bowed her head in shame. 'Why should you feel ashamed, sister?' Bijli said, trying to soothe her. 'But I do want to say this. He is making a mistake. Tell him that in my mind I have prostrated myself at his feet a thousand times. Tell him also that he is attempting the impossible. He cannot insult me because there is nothing left in me to insult. Everything that made me what I was when I met him has ceased to exist. So if he insults me now, all the sin will fall upon him. I will remain untouched.'

'Good bye, *didi*,' Radharani said in a voice choked with emotion.

'Good bye, sister. Although I have forfeited the right to give you my blessings, I will pray with all my heart for your long and happy married life.'

Glossary And Notes

Ananda: Joy, bliss. The term is used to indicate a higher quality of pleasure.

Ananda Bazar Patrika: A popular Bengali nationalist daily published from Calcutta.

Anna: A nickel coin, no longer in circulation, worth a sixteenth part of a rupee.

Baba, Babaji: An elderly person. The term usually refers to a holy man.

Babu: See Moshay

Bai, Baiji: A courtesan. A professional singer or dancer.

Bankim Chandra Chatterji: A famous Bengali novelist of the nineteenth century, regarded as a pioneer in the field of modern Indian historical and social fiction.

Bauls: Wandering, mystical singers of rural Bengal.

Been: A string instrument suitable for playing folk-tunes.

Bhajan: A devotional song, usually in praise of a deity, or rendered as a prayer or for supplication.

Bhang: A narcotic or intoxicant made from the leaves of the hemp plant.

Brahma: The creator God, one of the trinity consisting of Brahma, Vishnu and Shiva. (Brahma is to be distinguished from Brahman, a philosophical term for the Absolute Reality).

Brahmo Samaj: 'Society of God', a movement for religious and social reform founded by Raja Ram Mohan Roy in 1832, viewed with disapproval by orthodox Hindus. The Brahmo Samaj, whose members were known as *Brahmos*, became the platform

platform for enlightened, progressive thinkers and writers who rejected external rituals and concentrated on the inner spirit of religion.

Champa: A tree of the magnolia family bearing fragrant flowers which are used in religious worship or for garlands.

Chandalas: Members of the untouchable caste, who often disposed of unclaimed dead bodies.

Chandi: A form of Devi or the Goddess in one of her terrifying, war-like aspects.

Dada, Da: An elder brother. The term indicates not only respect but also a certain degree of familiarity.

Devi: (1) A goddess, or the Goddess, the feminine aspect of the Divine. (2) A suffix added to a woman's name as a mark of courtesy or respect. e.g. Shanti Devi, Kamala Devi.

Didi, Di: These are the feminine counterparts of *Dada* and *Da*. *Didi* may mean elder sister or simply an older woman. (see *Dada*).

Devi Chaudhurani: A famous novel by Bankim Chandra Chatterji based on a folk-legend.

Dharma: Though often translated simply as 'religion', the word *dharma* suggests a wide spectrum of meanings—duty, obligation, a set of values. In the concept of *dharma*, religious, ethical and social perspectives overlap.

Durga: The most popular goddess, worshipped in Bengal, combining the aspects of compassion and power. Durga is often identified with Parvati.

Eden Gardens: A large open area in Calcutta where cricket and football matches are played.

Entrance Examination: What is now known as Matriculation or High School was at one time called Entrance Examination.

Ganja: Marijuana (*cannabis sativa*).

Ghat: Paved area on the bank of a river, with steps leading to the water.

Ghatak: A matchmaker. A marriage-broker.

Gopis: The milkmaids of Vrindavan who were under the spell of Krishna's beauty and listened with rapture when he played his flute.

Holi: The festival of colour celebrated on the day following the night of the full moon in the month of *phalgun*, corresponding to March-April.

I.C.S.: Indian Civil Service, which was regarded as the foundation of British administration in India.

Jamun: A large tree bearing deep purple berries.

Kali: Usually identified with Durga in her aspect of power. In Bengal, there are more temples dedicated to *Kali* than to any other deity.

Kaliyuga: The Dark Age when religion and morality decline to their lowest point, leading to the dissolution of the universe followed by a new Golden Age.

Kalpa: A day of Brahma, said to be the equivalent to several thousand earth years.

Krittivasa: A medieval poet who was the first to translate the epic *Ramayana* from Sanskrit to Bengali.

Mahashaya: Usually shortened to Moshay. Babu, Mahashaya and Moshay are suffixes added to the name of a person addressed formally. Usually, Babu is placed after the first name and Moshay or Mahashay after the surname or family name. e.g. if a person's name is Harish Mukherji, he may be addressed as Harish Babu or Mukherji Moshay.

Meghnad Vadh Kavya: Title of a famous long poem by Michael Madhusudan Dutt about an episode in the *Ramayana*. It is about the *vadh* (slaying) of Meghnad, the son of Ravana.

Mejda: Middle elder brother.

Mlechha: An alien. A term of contempt used to designate a person of another creed. The term is sometimes used by Hindus to refer to a Muslim.

Moksha: Liberation from the cycle of births and deaths; the ultimate objective of life according to Hinduism. *Moksha* and *Mukti* are very similar to the concept of Nirvana in Buddhism.

Mukti: Same as Moksha.

Narayana: The popular name of Vishnu.

Nataraja: 'Lord of the Dance'. Shiva as the Cosmic Dancer.

Ocean-churning: According to a famous myth, the gods and the demons together churned the primeval ocean of milk to obtain the nectar of immortality. Many precious things emerged in the process including the moon and the wish-fulfilling (*kalpa*) tree. A jar of deadly poison emerged, just before the nectar. Shiva swallowed the poison and assimilated it. The implication is that pain and suffering have to be digested if we are to experience joy.

Parampara: Tradition, consisting of social and religious rules and conventions.

Pishima: Aunt (father's sister).

Peshwaz: Costume worn by courtesans, especially dancing girls.

Prana: Breath. The vital principle.

Prakriti: Nature. Often identified with Shakti, the aspect of energy and power in the universe.

Prayag: Ancient name of the city of Allahabad situated at the confluence of the sacred rivers, Ganga and Yamuna.

Prayashchitta: A religious ceremony performed as atonement for some sin or violation of religious rules.

Sati: Shiva's wife who sacrificed her life to protect the honour of her husband. The term is now used in a general sense, to refer to any woman who is committed to the ideal of conjugal devotion.

Savitri: A princess who wanted to reclaim her dead husband from the God of Death. Through her determination she compelled the God of Death to restore her husband, Satyavan, to life. Sati-Savitri are often mentioned together as supreme examples of conjugal virtue.

Shakti: Energy, power. The Goddess (Devi) in the aspect of cosmic energy.

Shiva: One of the most important gods in the Hindu pantheon, Shiva is depicted as an ascetic meditating on the peak of Mount Kailash in the Himalayas. The word Shiva also means 'the good' or 'the auspicious'.

Shudra(s): People who belong to the lowest caste in the Hindu social hierarchy.

Shukra: The planet Venus.

Sindoor: Vermillion powder applied by married women on their forehead. When a woman becomes a widow she is expected to wipe off the *sindoor* from her forehead.

Talaq: Divorce. According to one interpretation of Islamic law, a Muslim may divorce his wife simply by repeating the word *talaq* thrice.

Tapasya: Penance. Self-imposed austerity as a means to spiritual perfection.

Vaishnava: (Feminine form: *Vaishnavi*) A worshipper of Vishnu or his incarnations, Rama and Krishna. *Vaishnavas* adhere to a religion in which God is regarded as a Supreme Personal Being who can be realized through devotion and love, rather than philosophical knowledge.

Vrindavan: Popularly pronounced as Brindaban. A village on the bank of the Yamuna river where Krishna spent his childhood and youth.

Yama: The God of Death.

Zamindar: A landlord.